RC CP. Sub
AOS   4

A Man's Heart

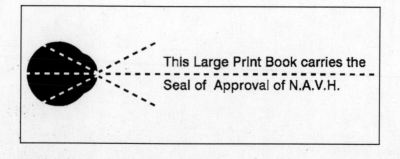

This Large Print Book carries the
Seal of Approval of N.A.V.H.

A MAN'S HEART

LORI COPELAND

THORNDIKE PRESS
A part of Gale, Cengage Learning

GALE
CENGAGE Learning

Detroit • New York • San Francisco • New Haven, Conn • Waterville, Maine • London

GALE
CENGAGE Learning™

Copyright © 2010 by Copeland Inc.
All Scripture quotations, unless otherwise indicated, are taken from the Holy Bible, New International Version®, NIV®. Copyright © 1973, 1978, 1984 by Biblica, Inc.™ Used by permission of Zondervan. All rights reserved worldwide.
Thorndike Press, a part of Gale, Cengage Learning.

Thorndike Press® Large Print Christian Historical Fiction.
The text of this Large Print edition is unabridged.
Other aspects of the book may vary from the original edition.
Set in 16 pt. Plantin.

LIBRARY OF CONGRESS CATALOGING-IN-PUBLICATION DATA

Copeland, Lori.
    A man's heart / by Lori Copeland.
        p. cm. — (Thorndike Press large print Christian historical fiction)
    ISBN-13: 978-1-4104-3573-6 (hardcover)
    ISBN-10: 1-4104-3573-3 (hardcover)
    1. Single women—Fiction. 2. Parents—Death—Fiction.
3. Farm life—Fiction. 4. Large type books. I. Title.
PS3553.O6336M36 2011
813'.54—dc22   2010050262

Published in 2011 by arrangement with The Zondervan Corporation LLC.

Printed in Mexico
2 3 4 5 6 7 15 14 13 12 11

A Man's Heart

PROLOGUE

Washington State

Jules's breath caught in her throat. The lights in The Grille dimmed; heat rushed to her cheeks. She had to run. She had to get out of here! Sliding out of the booth, she fled.

"Jules!"

"I'm sorry! I'm so sorry . . ." Her breath came in ragged spurts. *Poor Cruz.* Why would she do this to him a second time? She loved him. She adored him, but she couldn't marry him. Not tomorrow. She needed more time. She couldn't be married, help Pop run the farm and go back to college. She wasn't Superwoman.

"Jules! Hold it right there!" The force in Cruz Delgado's tone stopped her dead in her tracks.

Drawing a deep breath, she held to the door frame. Jukebox music filled the background. Don William's voice in the background sang something about "some broken hearts never mend." She sensed Cruz stalk toward her. *Think of a sane reason, Julianne Matias, some logical, justifiable circumstance that you would walk away from this man a second time.* Visions of the hours and previous months that she'd spent winning back his confidence formed a gray aura around her.

His surprisingly gentle touch stopped her plight. Closing her eyes, she allowed him to lead her out of the local watering hole to the parking lot. Bitter cold air caught her breath and she took deep drafts of foggy night air.

"It's okay, sweetheart. It's just a panic attack —"

Just! She shrugged free, fighting a sense of impending doom. The kind of dread that some terrible calamity was about to befall her. "Sorry . . . I can't, Cruz —"

"We've been through this a hundred times, Jules." His impatient tone penetrated her angst. "What's wrong now?"

"Nothing's wrong. I realize I needed more time."

His eyes pinpointed her. Hurt filled their depths. "What do I have to do, Jules? How do I prove that I love you — more than life itself?" He turned her around to face him, his breath a vapor in the nippy weather. "You can commit to me. I'm not going to hurt you or abuse your trust."

Shaking her head, she tried to talk between gasps. "It isn't a matter of trust —"

"Bull!"

"It isn't, Cruz. It's just . . . not right yet. Pop needs my help —"

"Pop was growing Blue Bayou potatoes long before you were a twinkle in his eye, and he always managed to make ends meet. I can't see how your going back to college now is going to help a blessed thing."

He was right. Her crazy idea that with more education she could get the farm in better financial shape was crock. She was looking for an excuse out and picked a poor one. She took a couple more deep breaths, squeezing her eyes shut, wishing the dread away. "I can't explain . . . I wish that I could, but I can't. It just doesn't feel right . . ."

"Okay." He released her so swiftly that she lost footing. A calm hand steadied her. "So the wedding is off again."

No, not okay! Her heart screamed the silent rebuke. *Calm.* All she had to do was excuse the panic attack and pretend the incident never happened. They could continue with dinner, talk about last minute

9

wedding preparations. The ceremony was at four o'clock tomorrow afternoon. Sophie's lovely teal blue maid-of-honor dress hung in Jules's closet. The cake was baked; flowers scheduled to be delivered to the church in the morning. She reached out and touched his arm and he drew back. "Please, Cruz . . ."

"Not this time, Jules." The street light above the brick building illuminated his face. Anger. Disbelief . . . disgust played across his rugged features and she couldn't fault him.

"Anytime you think about marrying, a steel gate slams into place. I want marriage, Jules, and kids."

"And that's what I want." She held up a pleading hand. "It's exactly what I want, but . . ." She paused. "The time doesn't feel right."

"This is the second time you've changed your mind at the last minute," he snapped.

"I know . . . I'm sorry. Perhaps in a few months . . ."

Settling his hat back on his head, he said quietly, "Obviously, you don't know what you want. Your problem, Jules, is you've convinced yourself that you're not capable of making a marriage work. You think since your folks' marriage was a disaster, yours is doomed to suffer the same fate."

"That's not so."

"It is so. You got yourself tied in knots thinking if you marry me, we'll end up trying to outshout each other."

"That's not fair, Cruz." Especially in view of the fact that her parents' marriage had been a truck wreck. She knew she would never cheat on Cruz like her mother had on her father. The thought would never enter her mind.

"Then what *is* your hang-up?"

"I . . . need more time to work marriage into my life." She looked up. "Why do you keep pushing?"

"Pushing?" He shifted stances. "That's what you think I'm doing? *Pushing* you into marriage?"

"What's the all-fired hurry? We're young; we have all of our lives." Marriage would come. Eventually.

Irony dripped from his eyes and she turned away. "We've been dating since we were teenagers. You're what? Twenty-six now and I'm looking at thirty. I'm tired of waiting for you, Jules."

She whirled to face him. "You know that deadlines freak me out —"

"Problems," he corrected. "You have problems with commitment, Jules. That's

11

when you freak."

"So not true. I commit: the farm, you, staying with Pop after Mom left. I can commit."

"To a movie, not to me."

"That's ridiculous." She drew a deep breath. "Okay. We'll just forget all about this. I'm fine now." The panic hadn't subsided, but she could do this. She could make herself go through with the wedding this time. Lifting her chin, she smiled. "Let's go finish dinner."

"You're good now? You're okay?" He slipped on his hat.

"Yes. Thank you." She loved him and she could commit as well as the next person.

"Okay. Let me know when you can make a commitment and keep it."

"Now what's that supposed to mean?" The dripping sarcasm in his tone stunned her. She'd just said to forget it. It was only a case of pre-wedding jitters.

"It means that I'm tired of waiting for you to make up your mind whether you love me enough to marry me."

"That's crazy talk. I adore you. All I'm asking is for a little more time."

"To go back to college. For four years."

"Not that much time. I want to go back and complete my education. WSU is doing

12

cutting-edge work in potato nutrition; I talked to a friend and she says I can sign on as a lab assistant — or maybe get special dispensation to do a private study. You know how I love to experiment, and Pop could sure use the help. With an Agricultural Biotechnology degree, I can grow Blue Bayou's business." She reached out to console him. Her heart ached. She wanted to marry him . . . she wanted this terrible sense of panic to dissolve.

"Didn't we have this conversation when you went to college the first time?" He started to walk toward his truck.

"Yes, but you didn't object then. And that was for Crop Science."

"Because 'then' it was sensible. Now I want to marry you, Jules, and I'm not waiting another four years." He shook his head. "I don't think so."

She fell into step, dogging him, anger rising. "*You* don't think so? You're breaking up with me?"

"Take it however you want."

She reached for the sleeve of his coat. "You can't break up with me."

"Yeah? Who made that rule?"

"We're getting *married* tomorrow!" She couldn't breathe. Who stole the air? He couldn't walk out on her . . .

He reached to open the truck door. "I think not."

"Cruz! You can't do this — what about our friends? The church, Reverend Williams — we'll look like complete fools — stop!" She stepped in front of him. "Stop." Their eyes locked.

"Step out of the way, Jules."

"You can't leave — not like this."

"I'm supposed to stay and let you keep walking out on weddings?"

"I haven't walked out. I'm right here — and I love you." She reached out to touch him, loving him with her eyes. This was her Cruz. Understanding. Patient. He was always there for her. He understood her.

His features sobered. "You need two years? You got it."

Relieved, she tried to kiss him but he eased around her and opened the door. "But I won't be around."

She stepped back, her mind whirling. What just happened? Had he broken up with her? Cruz? The only man in the world that she would ever love? Panic then regret choked her.

Or had she broken the engagement a second time.

She put her hand across her mouth and watched the taillights of his truck disappear

14

into the foggy night.

She'd broken up with him, she decided. Yes. For the second time in as many years, she'd jilted him.

CHAPTER 1

Almost four years later

Im·pos·si·ble. a: incapable of being or of occurring. b. felt to be incapable of being done, attained or fulfilled: insuperably difficult.

Jules tossed the paperback dictionary aside, took a sip of hot tea, and then yawned. *Yeah. That one.* Insuperably difficult. That was her to a T. Reaching for another seed potato, she dropped it and two mixed seedlings into the hole she'd finger dug in the dirt tub. She should give up. After years of trying to grow the perfect potato she was no further along. She'd gotten her wish; she'd attended WSU for almost four years and she'd been involved in exciting research. Last year she'd been granted special dispensation to conduct a private project for her thesis. The experiment gave her extra time to complete the document: *How to Grow the Perfect Potato.*

She must have been intoxicated with sleep deprivation the day she thought of the idea. So far no mixture of hybrid had panned out. The dissertation was done and only needed a satisfying conclusion.

Of course she'd lost Cruz in the process.

She moved to the futon, lined with dirt tubs.

She couldn't grow a "perfect potato." She couldn't even hold on to a man's heart. Cruz Delgado's to be exact. Resting her head on a sofa pillow, she pictured the good-looking potato farmer. Delgado men were large, over six feet tall, dark hair and complexion. Did he ever think of her in the gut-wrenching, totally sold out on love way she thought of him?

Shoving the past to the back of her mind, she stood and brushed graham cracker crumbs off her pajamas before she tackled the stack of plastic TV dinner containers piled high in the sink. Finals always left her trying to manufacture time.

The crowded living space was starting to grate on her nerves. Five wooden half-barrel tubs littered the living area. All filled with tubers — potato experiments. The tubs, a worn black sofa, an overstuffed chair piled with textbooks, a table with two chairs and a kitchenette had been her home the past four years. By choice, she lived off campus of Washington State University. At thirty, she didn't exactly fit in with dewy-eyed eighteen-and nineteen-year-old college students, and socializing wasn't her thing. She longed to go home, to be back on Blue Bayou, ride her horse, and raise potatoes. See Cruz. Catch a glimpse of him.

She wasn't a city girl; college had proved that. She loved Pop's old farm where they scraped by selling Ranger Russets to a factory up north, and a few local markets, but it was barely a living. Lack of rainfall was a big factor in these parts; farmers had to irrigate and irrigation cost money.

After running a sink full of steaming water, she washed the disposable containers and a few coffee cups. She didn't own a dish. She drank from accumulated McDonald's cups, and ate from sandwich wrappers and carry-out paper plates. Every chance she got she headed home, but Pullman, where the college sat, was a hundred and thirty miles from Blue Bayou and she was usually buried in experiments.

Around midnight, her cell phone played a jazzy version of Beethoven. Jarred awake, Jules closed the book she'd been studying and reached to answer. A phone call this late at night either had to be a wrong number or bad news. She relaxed. It couldn't be Pop; she'd talked to him this morning and he would have been in bed hours ago.

"Jules?" The voice of Pop's foreman, Joe Fraker, came over the line.

A shiver raked her spine. "What's wrong?"

"It's your dad, hon. He took a hard fall late this afternoon. We were planting the north field and he went a little too far out on a ridge. The tractor overturned — now they don't think he's hurt badly. I'd have called sooner, but you know how clinics are. We've been waiting on tests and he didn't want me to call you until we knew something for certain."

Jules struggled to clear her rattled thoughts. *Clinic.* The injury couldn't be too serious, or they would have moved him to Pasco.

"Where is he?"

"He's lost a lot of blood. Hit his head on a rock and cut about an inch slash in his noggin. They want to move him on up to the hospital in Pasco. If I have your permission, I'll give the go ahead."

"Of course. Is he stable for now?"

"I have to go, hon. I've called your sister."

Crystal. He'd called Crystal? The fall must be more serious than Joe was saying.

20

"I'll start now, Joe."

She sensed a nod in his tone. "I think you'd better."

It took all of five minutes to throw a few things into her backpack, and lock up. Her gaze fell on the potato tubs. Who'd look after her experiments — and she needed to record the last hybrid mix . . .

Hang the experiment.

Locking the door, she headed for her Geo Tracker. The apartment complex was quiet this time of night. Pop was hard-headed. A little fall wasn't going to stop him, so why did Joe have to bring Crystal in on this?

CHAPTER 2

Franklin County, Washington
May

Cruz Delgado hefted a fertilizer sack and pitched it to his brother, Adan. The Delgado truck sat in front of Mayse Feed and Seed this morning.

Any mention of Jules Matias set him off. When her Tracker pulled up to the mortuary, he looked the other way. He had to hand it to his brother; it took Adan a good five minutes before he mentioned the fact that the irritant had arrived at Mellon's.

Adan swung a bag in the pick-up bed, head bent, lips sealed. The truck's worn springs sagged beneath the weight. Then the elephant waltzed into the room, as it usually did. "You didn't expect her to skip her dad's funeral, did you?"

"With her you never know."

Grinning, Adan shook his head. "You're never going to get over her. Face it." A sack of fertilizer caught him mid-section. He grabbed for support. "Hey!"

"Hey yourself. I'm over her. Got it?"

Adan ducked when another sack whipped through the air. The men paused for a breather. Cruz averted his gaze when Jules got out of the vehicle but Adan lifted a friendly hand.

"Can't you at least offer your sympathies?"

"I'm going to Fred's service."

"Yeah, but you won't say a word to her." Adan's gaze followed the petite figure walking up the mortuary's flower lined sidewalk. "Sure is a shame about Fred. An aneurysm to the brain, and bam, he's history."

Cruz shook his head. No, he wouldn't say a word to Jules. He'd said all he was ever going to say to that woman four years ago. Pitching the last sack on the truck, he pulled the brim of his Stetson down over his eyes, and then climbed into the cab. Truth was, he would miss ole Fred. He was a good neighbor, and if you needed something, Fred had it. Shame the farm he'd worked for over forty years would fall into strangers' hands. The rural community was tight knit; neighbors were extended families. Most had been born and raised in the county. Nearly all raised potatoes, unlike the apple growers in other parts of the state.

Cruz started the truck. *Face it, Delgado. You're not worried about Fred's potato patch. You're worried that when it goes, Jules goes.* The admission caught him unawares. A hot branding iron rammed in his eye couldn't have stung worse. *Count your blessings.* She and Crystal would sell out and that would be the end of Blue Bayou. Jules had been back in town less than twenty-four hours and already she had his mind going nuts.

Adan climbed in the cab, and Cruz backed out of the feed store lot and shifted into first gear. *Well not this time, Miss Matias.* He glanced at her car, once a sight that sent his heart into overtime.

Twice stung, and you've made your point.

Jules stepped out of the funeral home, shading her eyes against spring sunlight. The community where she'd been born and raised sat twenty miles outside of Pasco, Washington, deep in the heart of the Tri-Cities area. She loved everything about the community with the exception of the Hanford Nuclear Reservation outside of Pasco. Anyone could have lived without those 586 square miles. The fiftyish spring air had a bite to it this morning. The past thirty minutes had been the most trying in her life. Joe offered to come with her, but she'd

24

refused. She needed a strong arm to lean on, but Pop's foreman's wasn't it.

An ache latched onto her heart when Cruz had driven away without a word of condolence. They'd been friends a lot longer than the state they now found themselves in, which she couldn't identify if she tried. Jilting a man twice was admittedly hard on the ego, but in her mind she had never jilted him, simply postponed the inevitable. She could not ever imagine herself married or having children with any other man. To this day, that was her goal.

He was the one who jumped the gun, acted with pure egotism. Cruz knew that she didn't *jilt* him; that she longed for a solid marriage — maybe not as badly then as now, but her needs seemed to be more pressing at the time. She'd been crowded too often and she hated the feeling.

Sliding into her vehicle, she snapped her seat belt in place and turned the key, listening as the old truck sprang to life. Crystal wouldn't make it to Pop's funeral. She'd bet a bushel of spuds on that. Joe said she promised to come, but Crystal's promises were like Mom and Dad's marriage. Empty.

What she needed now was a strong dose of her best friend, Sophie.

Cruz Delgado's sister.

CHAPTER 3

"Jules!" A spoon of oatmeal sailed through the air when Sophie bound to her feet to hug her. "It's so good to have you home." Pausing, she drew back and her features distorted in a heartbreaking expression. "I'm so sorry about Pop. Everyone prayed so hard; we thought Fred's injury was minor."

"I know." Jules patted her on the back, shed another bucket of tears. She reached for the oatmeal-covered Olivia. "Livvy's growing so fast."

"Like ragweed." Grinning, Sophie wet a washcloth and cleaned the toddler's face. "She's twenty-two months now and you won't believe her vocabulary. She must take after her father's side. She's almost two, going on nine."

Time sped by too quickly. Jules had been with Sophie through labor and delivery, but a week later she'd returned to college and the winter session. Last summer flew by and she was back in college before she realized it. Sophie emailed pictures, but there was only so much to be said in cyberspace and even harder to imagine that this chubby angel was growing up fast. Sophie motioned to a chair. "Tell me what's happening. I know you're reeling with Pop's death."

The dam burst and Jules stepped back into her friend's arms and poured out her heart. Once the flood of emotion subsided, she wiped her nose and concentrated on happier days. "I'm graduating in a couple of weeks."

"I know. Pop and I . . ." Sophie paused. "I'm planning to be there."

"He almost lived long enough to see his dream realized." Jules sighed and reached to butter a piece of toast. "Pop was really looking forward to the event." He'd been proud of her accomplishment and rooted for the experimental potato; he'd also been grateful because he knew she'd sacrificed Cruz's love with her unselfish act.

Nodding, Sophie said, "I was going to drive, and then we were going to take you for a celebration dinner at Holliman's."

"Ah. I'd have loved that."

Silence closed over the kitchen as Jules fought back tears. Pop had to scrimp to send her to college. The money could have gone toward a new irrigation system, but he figured her education would pay off more in the long run if they could grow the business, and growing the business took more educational savvy. With Pop gone, enlarging the business made little sense. Crystal hated potato farming. She'd want to sell the operation as soon as possible and split the proceeds.

"Crystal coming to the funeral?"

Jules smiled. Sophie was always tuned in to her thoughts. "She told Joe she was. I haven't talked to her."

"When is the service?"

"Day after tomorrow." Jules reached for a napkin and dabbed the corners of her eyes. She hadn't seen Pop yet, just taken his clothes to be buried in. Sunday suit. Blue tie. White shirt. She'd shined his best shoes to be set at his feet. Seeing him would be hard; he was always so full of life.

"As sad as it is, you wouldn't wish him back," Sophie comforted.

"No." She glanced up and smiled. "Everything okay with you?"

"The usual. Money is so tight right now."

Jules didn't know how Sophie kept a cheerful spirit; she'd married two absolute losers.

She flashed Jules a grin, a grin from a woman who had been unlucky in love more times than Jules could fathom. "Ethan's dad isn't exactly Father of the Year, but he pays support on time. The kids and I make it. Barely, but we survive, and Cruz says the crop looks pretty decent this year —" Her tone caught and she sheepishly glanced away. "Sorry."

Jules could read her like a book; they both tried to avoid her brother's name but it naturally came up. "I saw him and Adan earlier when I was making Pop's arrangements."

"You spoke?"

"Ha. He didn't glance my way. Is he still struggling to keep the farm afloat?"

"Oh, you know that old farm. Never did produce much. Don't know why Dad held onto it, but Cruz and Adan can't sell it, so they've moved back to the house. Cruz has the lower floor and Adan took the second one. They're making ends meet."

"Pop mentioned that they hit a rough patch these past couple of years."

"You know my brothers. They don't give up easily. We'd have been okay last year, but then we got tuber-moth infestation and it ruined the crop. It's zero tolerance in tubers headed for the processor these days. Nobody cares to find a worm in their fries."

Nodding, Jules finished the toast. "I hate myself for what I did to Cruz, Sophie. I love your brother with all my heart, I just get . . .'"

"Cold feet when you think about marrying him?" Her friend smiled. "I know my ordeals haven't been the best influence for matrimony — or your parents' marriage. I'd like to tell you that Cruz will eventually get over it, but he was pretty ticked at you this time."

She wasn't telling Jules anything she didn't know. Four years and they still were ignoring each other. That was the worrisome part. And yet she sympathized with Cruz. If Mom and Pop's turbulent marriage hadn't soured her, Sophie was living proof that a woman ought to think before she leaped into matrimony.

Sophie glanced at the clock. "Oh great. I have two doctor's appointments. Livvy has a check-up and I have one."

"Are you sick?"

Her friend grinned. "Yes. The thought of a physical makes me ill, but since I skipped the last one, I figure I'd better show up for this one. Come by later tonight and we'll have supper."

Jules helped her clear the table. "Can't, but thanks. The church is bringing in all

kinds of food. I need to be there with Joe —
and Crystal, if she shows up."

"You think she will?"

Lifting a shoulder, Jules rinsed a cup and
stuck it in the dishwasher. She thought of
her drop-dead gorgeous, blonde haired,
blue-eyed, year-round-tan sister, the picture
of the quintessential "love child." "I'd be
surprised if she did. She loved Pop, but they
lost closeness a year or two after she and
Mom left."

"That's sad." Sophie lifted Livvy above
her head and grinned. "You're a good girl.
Yes you are. You're a —" A blob of oatmeal
hit Sophie between the eyes. She lowered
the child, wincing. "Rats. I know better than
to do that."

CHAPTER 4

It was close to ten when Cruz removed his hat, and stepped into the Mellon Mortuary foyer behind Adan and Sophie. As he'd figured they would be, gleaming oak pews were filled to capacity. Fred was well-respected in the community, and his death came as a shock to his neighbors and friends. If it weren't for Fred's friendship over the years, Cruz sure wouldn't put himself through the ordeal. He stepped to the guest book, scrawled his signature and then followed the crowd to the chapel, searching for Sophie and Adan, whom he'd lost in the shuffle. They promised to save him a seat.

As he passed the west entrance, the door opened and the family began to file in. Hat in hand, he stepped back and cleared the way as Fred's brothers, sisters, aunts and uncles filed past. Jules, on Joe's arm, brought up the rear. He searched for Crystal but Jules was last to exit the family car.

She briefly met his eyes when she passed and he looked away, unable to bear the raw emotion he saw.

He waited until the family seated themselves before he stepped to the chapel door. Adan and Sophie sat to the far left between two women. His brother and sister appeared to be holding their own, saving a ten-inch square on the padded bench.

Celebrating Fred's life was easier than Cruz figured. The minister spoke about the good the potato farmer had done in the community, his gift for compassion, his unwavering love for God and his fellow man.

Midway through the service he had the mourners laughing over the time Fred chased a couple of pigs through town one Fourth of July.

Cruz determined he wasn't going to look at Jules, wasn't going to witness her grief, but more than once he caught his gaze centered on her, smiling through tears when someone told a story about Fred that she hadn't heard. Okay, Fred was a good guy. He'd just raised a selfish daughter. His eyes scanned the crowd packed in the hallway. Two selfish daughters. Crystal hadn't made it.

An anchor dropped from his neck when the service ended. He decided not to file by the casket. He'd never forget Fred, and the long late night talks they'd had the two times he'd sought Cruz out to reason with him on Jules's behalf. He'd talked long into the night, trying to make him understand his very complicated daughter, and his personal need to grow the farm. Said Jules was like her mother; mulish, and Cruz knew that if Jules heard that, she'd come out swinging. She resented her mom's leaving, resented the choice between mother and father forced on her.

Stepping into the bright sunshine, he put on his hat. Cars were already lining up for the cemetery service. He pictured Jules and Fred's family gathering around the flag-draped casket, saying their final good-byes. Fred served in Viet Nam and was allotted full military honors. This nagging feeling that somehow he should be beside Jules at the cemetery when Taps sounded to show respect to the fallen, supporting her, irked him. Fred might be like family, but it was a family he could lay no claim to.

On the other hand, he wouldn't step ten feet within Jules's range if she'd asked. She would sell-out shortly after Fred was in the ground, and he wouldn't have to put up with these old feelings. She'd move on, buy a new place up north, and use her fancy education to grow bigger and larger crops.

As far as he was concerned, that day couldn't come fast enough.

The family exited the church and he focused on a blooming bush. *No way was he going to let her get to him this time.* No way.

Mid-afternoon, Cruz and Adan were putting a new clutch in a tractor when Cruz glanced up to see a young woman walking toward him, carrying her shoes in her hand. Blonde, loose fitting skirt and blouse, bracelets lining tan, slender arms. Crystal was here. He glanced at his watch. Six hours late.

Face flushed, hair hanging in curly strands, Jules's sister approached the men. Adan straightened to meet her. "Hey, Crystal." The two were about the same age. They'd gone through kindergarten, first, second, and part of third grade together. "Adan." She glanced at Cruz. "Is Jules angry?"

Turning back to the tractor, Cruz muttered, "You'd have to ask her."

"I was going to be here." Crystal pitched her shoes and oversized purse on the ground and sat on a discarded tire. Sweat rolled down her temples.

Adan glanced at Cruz, then broke the uneasy silence. "What happened?"

"The cab broke down. By the time they sent another one, the second one had a flat and the spare was missing from the trunk. They sent a third cab, and he's new to the area and finally I told him to let me out and I'd walk the rest of the way." She glanced at the red five gallon water cooler. "Can I have a drink of water?"

Adan poured water in a plastic cup and handed it over. "Why didn't you call one of us?"

"I don't have your cell phone numbers. I did try the house and nobody answered." She drank thirstily and lifted her cup for more. "I suppose they didn't postpone the services until I got here."

Cruz bit back a snort. "No. The funeral went as planned."

"Then Pop's already buried?"

He nodded.

She sighed. "I tried my best."

"That's all a person can do." Cruz straightened from the engine, wiping his hands on an oily cloth, then he looked at Crystal as tears rolled down her cheeks. "Adan, why don't you take her to Fred's place?"

"Where's your luggage?"

She motioned to a large purse. "I didn't have time to pack much. I wanted to be here . . . honest. Did you go?"

Nodding, Cruz set the rag aside. "It was real nice. Chapel was filled — some had to stand in the hallway."

"Did he have enough flowers? I was going to buy fresh ones when I got here . . ."

Cruz wasn't sure how much was enough, but he had a bunch. "Lots of flowers. He had a good burial, Crystal. Don't beat yourself up. You made an effort to get here. That's what counts."

"Thanks." She wiped her nose. "Jules isn't going to see it that way."

"Your sister isn't an ogre. She'll understand."

"Is she taking Pop's death hard?"

"I haven't spoken to her. I've been busy."

Adan's cell phone rang. He flipped it on. "Yeah." After a minute he glanced at Cruz. "It's the parts store. They've got the clutch in stock. You want to drive into town or do you want me to go?"

Cruz didn't want to spare the half hour into Pasco and then back. Fred's place was closer. "You go, and I'll run Crystal over to Fred's."

Adan relayed the information, and then

hung up. "Crystal, I'll put your things in the truck." As he walked past Cruz, he grinned. "Good luck."

Cruz ignored the gibe. Luck wouldn't factor into it. He'd drop Crystal off and be on his way. *Lord, please don't let her be home when I get there.*

Crystal rose and trailed Adan to the white pick-up. Cruz heard her chattering. She chattered. Jules spoke succinctly. "How's the shell business?" Adan asked.

"Wonderful. It's so lovely in Destin, you must come visit sometime."

"I'll have to do that."

Cruz stored her bag in the pick-up bed, his mind drifting back to Jules. Picking a casket, family flowers, pall bearers, and memorial acknowledgment weren't the easiest things. He should have offered a hand. Pop's plot was separate from his folks, the headstone already set. Cruz had no responsibility to be with her in her time of need. He needed her plenty of times . . .

Crystal was still talking. "I live in back of the shop. Small quarters, but sufficient. The shop is right on the beach. Lovely sunsets, peaceful waters."

"Sounds nice."

Cruz grinned. He wouldn't visit her. Adan stuck close to home. He was a man set in his ways. Besides potatoes, about the only thing that caught Adan's eye was the Smith girl, and he wasn't overly fond of her. She was pretty enough, but she was the intellectual type. Her idea of fun was a visiting lecturer, spelt bread, and bamboo shoots. If Adan had his way, he'd be a bachelor the rest of his life, and living in a community as small and as tight as this one, was a distinct possibility.

The farm was all he and Adan had, and it was starting to get real cramped financially. Potatoes were flowering in the west and north fields, putting off pretty white blooms. The smaller three fields rested in an effort to ward off disease. This year's crop, so far, looked to be a first-rate one and it sure better be. He was down to less than five thousand in his business account.

Straightening, he shook his head when he saw Crystal was still yakking. Unless he missed his guess, she'd favor no-caffeine, whole food products, and never dream of eating a Ho-Ho, unlike her sister who had the metabolism of a tape worm. He'd once watched Jules down two Cokes and three Snickers and never break a sweat.

CHAPTER 5

Jules stepped off her mare, and approached the fresh grave site. Hours ago the community cemetery filled with mourners, cars and trucks lining the dirt road. Now, silence settled over Pop's final resting place. Golden-crowned sparrows flitted in and out of aspen and tall goat-chicory. Pop visited here only when necessary. Memorial days, Jules would coerce him into putting flowers on Grandpa and Grandma's graves, but he never stayed around long. He wasn't afraid of death; but like everyone else, he wasn't necessarily eager to board the bus.

She knelt, rearranging a gladioli spray. So many flowers. She had given some to the nursing home and sent a couple over to the medical clinic, but still the mound of fresh dirt was piled high with floral offerings.

"I thought I'd find you here."

Startled, Jules turned to see Crystal approaching. She glanced toward the empty road. "How did you get here?"

"Cruz brought me."

Jules turned back to the grave, shifting sprays, rearranging pots. "You're too late."

"I know . . . please, Jules. Don't be upset."

Pushing to her feet, Jules dusted her hands. People must think she was a cold person. "What happened?"

"The cab service out here is awful."

Jules couldn't argue. Getting a cab from here was like pulling goat's teeth. A little hairy. "You could have called. I would have picked you up."

"I did call the house, but by then you'd left for the services. I ended up walking the last mile." She brushed long silky tendrils out of her eyes. Bracelets jingled. "It's hot. I don't remember it being this hot this early in the year."

"It usually isn't." She finally met her sister's eyes. It had been years since she'd seen her — how long? Mom's funeral? Years fell away and Jules recalled the morning Mom got up and announced that she'd had enough. She gave her daughters a choice: stay with *him* or go with her. An hour later she took Crystal and deserted the battle front.

Jules stayed because she thought Pop couldn't make it alone, but there hadn't been a day since that she hadn't wondered if she'd betrayed Mom, if her life wouldn't be different if she had gone with her and Crystal. Over the years, they wrote and talked on the phone, and Mom didn't resent Jules's choice, but eleven years old is young to be stuck in the middle of your parents' failings.

Crystal visibly squirmed under her appraisal. "I got your Christmas cards."

"Yeah. I got yours."

"You look good." Crystal smiled. "Not aging a bit."

"Thanks. You too — you look the same." Not true; her sister was even prettier wearing a long, gauzy skirt, oversized blouse and large jewelry. Lots and lots of big, flashy sundials glistened around her neck. Jules owned a pair of diamond studs Pop had given her one Christmas and rarely wore them.

"I talked to Cruz and Adan when I came into town."

She was way ahead of her. Jules moved to her grandparents' graves. Crystal trailed behind, chatting. "Cruz took me to Pop's and when you weren't there he suggested you'd be here. So, here I am. Oh gosh — this is Granny and Paw Paw's grave." The young woman knelt, running her tanned hand gently over the grassy surface. "I barely remember them."

She wouldn't. She had been eight when Mom took off, and Mom hadn't brought her back when Buck and Sue Matias died within a few months of each other. "Cruz brought you here?"

"Yeah. He gets better looking every day."

Jules forced a tolerant smile.

Crystal glanced up. "Sorry. I guess . . ."

"I haven't talked to Cruz lately." If you could call four years "lately."

"He wasn't at Pop's funeral? He said he was." "He was there. I just didn't get an opportunity to visit." And how did she know so much about she and Cruz's past? Had Pop written and told her?

Crystal answered the thought. "Sophie writes a lot — and sends the local paper." She patted Granny's grave and stood. "What do I need to do?"

"Nothing. Everything's done. Tomorrow morning Pop's attorney will read his will. The place will be ours. We'll need to agree on terms."

"Terms. Such as?"

"Such as, I'll buy you out."

"Oh. Those terms." Crystal fell silent.

"You don't plan to come home, do you?"

"No, I love Florida, the sun and surf. You

know me. I won't eat potatoes, let alone grow them." She flashed another smile.

"You still buy into that myth that potatoes are fattening?"

"No, I don't like the taste."

Frowning, Jules avoided her gaze. Didn't like potatoes. She didn't know a person alive other than Crystal who wouldn't chow down on fries or a big Baker loaded with sour cream and chives.

The women fell into step. Maddy grazed, bridle dragging the ground. How did Crystal intend to get back to the farm? "Is Cruz picking you up?" That's all she needed after the trying day. It hurt enough when he hadn't spoken at the funeral home.

"No, I told him I'd either hitch a ride with you or walk."

"In this heat?"

Crystal's gaze sized up the mare. "Sophie says you and she ride the barrel races."

"We did until I decided to go back to college. Now we ride the annual Fourth of July rodeo."

"I remember that! Mom and Pop used to take us every year. We'd eat corn dogs, cherry snow cones and funnel cakes." She shuddered. "I can't believe I'd eat a once living thing."

"It's a wiener, Crystal. When you eat a

wiener your last concern should be that something in it once had a face. Unfortunately, everything in meat was once something." They approached the waiting mare and stood for a moment, uncertainty shadowing Jules's mind. "Do you want a ride?"

"Sure." Gathering her full skirt, Crystal hooked her sandaled foot in the stirrup and climbed aboard, bracelets tinkling. Staring down at Jules, she grinned. "I haven't forgotten how to ride."

No, she wouldn't. When they were kids, the two girls had lived on ponies when they weren't working the potato fields. Her sister reached to stroke Maddy's neck. The gentle mare had been Jules's constant companion before she left for college.

Jules was never more aware of the two sisters' diverse differences. Jules's dark, short cropped hair, petite build, hazel eyes and tenacious approach favored the Matias side, while Crystal's long-legged beauty, fair complexion and bohemian lifestyle flaunted Mom's Swedish heritage.

Cruz once said that because of Jules's dogged nature she would make a good Apache, while Crystal would be hard put to swat a moth. Well, if perhaps she'd been the one to go and Crystal had stayed to work the farm, she wouldn't be so stressed and hardened. Surf and sand was a long way from dirt and potatoes. Wonder if *Mr.* Delgado had thought of *that?* She grabbed the reins and swung into the saddle.

Jules and Crystal made the thirty-minute drive to Pasco the next morning, and by ten-thirty occupied the two leatherback chairs sitting in front of Jack Meddleson's massive cherry wood desk. Office walls tastefully contained the attorney's framed accomplishments. Rich sea green carpeting set off paneled oak walls. Stylishly structured pictures of Jack's grandchildren and wife lined the console behind his oversized chair. Jack handled Fred's business matters since the day Pop bought the potato farm. Joe Fraker, Blue Bayou's foreman, stood behind the sisters' chairs at Jules's request. Joe had been with Pop since the two started the business. Pop wouldn't forget Joe in the will.

Last night had been awkward. The sisters shared a plate of food from the massive casserole and meat dishes lining the kitchen counter. Crystal picked out meat and set it aside without fuss. The two had gone to bed early. Crystal's old bedroom had long ago been converted into a guest room. This morning Jules told Joe to take the remain-

46

ing food and floral offerings and distribute them among the employees. Two women — one a vegetarian — couldn't make a dent in the overwhelming show of appreciation for Pop.

Jack's secretary laid a folder on his desk. "Would anyone like coffee? Perhaps a cold drink?"

When the offer was refused, she quietly left and Jack opened the folder. "I know this has been a trying time for your family, so we'll get down to business." He cleared his throat. "I, Fred Matias, being of sound mind . . ."

Jules's brain registered her father's last will and testament, picturing Pop, worn WSU Cougar ball cap in hand, twisting the fabric, wearing bib overalls, hoping to get his "business" over with as quickly as possible. Pop loved the Lord so the first request was allotted to the church. He gave five thousand, a tenth of cash on hand.

Joe got four thousand dollars. When the amount was announced, the older man's jaw went slack.

The attorney read on. "Joe, you're probably here supporting Jules, so just let me say I couldn't have left this without all the years you've given me, years when you never complained, some years when we both didn't get a red cent for all our hard work, but you've earned this and more, friend. I'll be waiting for you at the Gate."

He left his father's watch to Cruz. Jules sat up straighter. Jack glanced up and continued reading. "By now Jules will be on point, but you tell her that I find the man worthy, and I want him to have the watch to remind him that time goes by too fast. I regret the sacrifice the boy's made on my behalf."

Cruz's sacrifice? What about me, Pop? Jules shifted in her chair.

The attorney turned a page. "He left a particular hoe to Miles Ledbetter. Said Jules would know why."

She nodded. "He broke the blade and never got around to buying Miles a new one." That had been last summer.

Nodding, Jack sobered and read on. "By now, you know that I had a burial plan and plot so you aren't out that expense. Other than that, I leave the farm and all my worldly possessions to my daughter Jules."

Jules's jaw dropped. She sensed Crystal's swift intake, then silence.

Closing the folder, Jack cleared his throat. "Short. That's how Fred liked things." His gaze focused on Crystal and then shied away. "Everything's in order. The estate should be settled without a hitch." Pushing back, he stood and shook Jules, Joe, and Crystal's hands.

Crystal's expression remained pleasant. "Thank you, Jack. I barely remember you, but I know Pop thought the world of you."

"It's good to see you, Little One."

Jules sensed that he wanted to apologize for Pop's oversight, but didn't trust his judgment. But then there were no words or reason why Pop had excluded Crystal from his estate.

Outside, Jules sat in the Tracker organizing her thoughts before she turned to Crystal. "I don't know what to say. Maybe Pop . . ."

Crystal smiled. "What's to say? Pop wanted you to have the farm, and I think that's only fair."

"Fair?" Jules didn't see anything fair about it, but Crystal appeared unfazed.

"Pop was a good man, but you know his weakness was forgiveness. That was evident with Mom."

Yes, Mom's one indiscretion with a young farmhand during a turbulent time in her early marriage had led to the fights. One was enough. Pop was a God-fearing, God obeying man in every way but forgiveness. You did the crime; you served the time.

There were days when Jules feared she had the same unreasonable trait. "Rest assured that half the farm is yours. I wouldn't think of taking part of your inheritance."

"You will think of it. I would have it no other way. End of subject."

When had she become so virtuous? And so insightful. Jules couldn't figure her out. Give away half of what she owned? That made about as much sense as leaving a daughter empty-handed. Fred Matias would have given you the shirt off his back, but he could carry a grudge to his death, which apparently he'd done. But why resent Crystal? She was an innocent pawn in a war that she'd had no control over.

CHAPTER 6

What could easily have been an awkward silence turned out to be a pleasant ride home. Jules's mind spun at the turn of events. Crystal couldn't be that complacent that Pop had left her out of his estate. Not that he was a millionaire, but Jules considered the oversight to be an insult. Crystal was his child, for gosh sakes. Just because he and Mom couldn't get along, why did he take it out on his own flesh and blood, especially when he'd loved his daughters, or claimed that he did.

He sent Christmas gifts to Crystal every year — or had Jules do it. Birthday cards. Sometimes Easter greetings. Yet Crystal sat on the passenger's side quietly humming "In the Sweet By and By" under her breath as though she hadn't a care in the world. She'd matured. When Mom died, she'd left nothing but bills. There was no estate to settle. So the shell shop had to be running on a wing and a prayer.

Pulling into the farm yard, Jules spotted Sophie's car. *Thank you, Lord.* When Pop's exclusion finally penetrated Crystal, she'd have someone to help calm her. She slid out of the Tracker and went inside.

The Matias home, a simple rock farmhouse, a couple of barns, machinery shed and the potato cellars — underground storage units, was always open to Sophie. She'd had a back door key since she was nine years old, and she came and went as she wanted. It wasn't unusual to come in from a cold winter's day and find a couple of fresh loaves of Sophie's bread waiting on the stove. For someone so domesticated and loyal, Jules couldn't understand why the woman couldn't keep a husband, other than her best friend had an uncanny knack for picking louses.

"Hey."

"Hey."

Crystal came in and closed the door. "Hi, Sophie!"

"Crystal." The two women embraced. "Great to see you. It's been a long time."

"Too long, but I don't feel that I've missed a —" Crystal drew back. "What's wrong?"

Jules opened the refrigerator for a cold drink, turning when she heard alarm in her sister's tone. A red-eyed Sophie seized her attention. She'd been crying. Streaked make-up and runny mascara marred her features. Closing the door, Jules approached the table.

"Better sit down." Sophie lifted a tissue and dabbed her eyes. Dropping into a chair, Jules faced her. "Is it one of the kids?"

Sophie shook her head.

"What is it, honey?" Crystal eased to put her arms around Sophie's shoulder. "Whatever it is, we're here with you. God's in his heaven."

"I just got a call from my gynecologist."

Jules tensed. *Sophie's annual physical.* They'd found something unusual — maybe an abnormal pap? That happened. "Oh hey, whatever it is I'm sure it's simple —"

"It's uterine cancer."

Silence seized the room. The ticking wall clock penetrated the thick air. Jules swallowed. "Scary, but they can —"

"Stage three. They took a biopsy. It came back positive."

Bringing her hand to her mouth, Jules swallowed back panic. *Stage three.* The abysmal number rang in her ears.

"Oh, honey." Crystal held Sophie closer. Jules waited for the usual platitudes to follow: "It'll be okay. They can do a lot these days — they've come so far." But none of that happened. Crystal held her while the dam broke and Sophie cried, agonizing sobs that clawed at the heart.

Sophie accepted a handkerchief from Jules and rubbed her eyes. "What's going to happen to my children?"

"Don't even think that way." The thought of losing Sophie was intolerable. She was twenty-eight years old. She'd barely begun to live her life. "Maybe there's a mistake. Get a second opinion."

Wagging her head, Sophie declined. "They want me in the hospital today."

Jules's head spun. Her mind couldn't grasp the turn of events. First Pop. Now Sophie? She struggled to wake from the nightmare.

Crystal broke the stagnant silence. "What can we do to help?"

"I need someone to look after my children. Cruz and Adan said they will take them, but I need yours and Jules's help. You know men." She blew her nose. "My brothers don't know beans about taking care of children. The big lugs are kids themselves."

"We'll keep them," Crystal offered. "I can hire someone to run the shell shop. There's no reason I can't stay here for awhile."

Sophie met Jules's eyes. "I know what I'm

asking is a lot — you'd have to be around Cruz more often than you'd like, but —"

"I'll do it," Jules confirmed. Dread filled her. Not only would she be forced to deal with Cruz on a daily basis, she'd have to adjust to having Crystal around. She and her sister had been so distant — so foreign to each other. They were strangers with nothing in common but the blood running through their veins.

"There's treatment —"

Sophie dismissed the hope with a wave of her hand. "Surgery first, then chemo and radiation."

"You can beat this." Jules reached for her hand. "I know you. Right now you're terrified, but we'll fight this. Miracles happen every day in the medical field."

Nodding, Sophie wiped her eyes. "The children's fathers are not to know about this. I don't want Matt or Jake coming around if this doesn't turn out the way we hope. They might try to get the children though that's laughable. Cruz says he won't let that happen, but you may have to help him fight, Jules. You know both my ex-husbands are no good. They've relinquished all paternal rights."

"Isn't Matt in jail?"

"Usually. I don't know where he is right

now. I don't think you'll have to worry about him or Jake, but whatever happens, those two men are not to have custody of my children. Nor the grandparents." Sophie sniffed. "I want those children to remain here."

Jules wasn't sure what she could prevent, but she'd give it her all. "I'll protect the children, I promise, but you have to promise me that you won't give up. This is going to be a hard fight, Sophie, but you've weathered some tough times."

Biting her lower lip, Sophie faced her, tears spilling down her cheeks. "I'm scared, Jules. I'm so scared."

"You can do it, honey." Crystal drew Sophie's head to her shoulder. "We'll pray, and God will hear our prayers."

Shaking her head, Sophie buried her face in her hands. "It's hard to believe in God right now."

"I know," Crystal soothed. "I'd feel the same, but every day brings new hope."

And when had Crystal become so virtuous? Smart. Savvy. What happened to the old airhead Crystal? Jules shifted Crystal aside. Sophie didn't need a sermon. She needed comfort. Pop had always seen that Jules went to church — God would hear her prayers. In truth, her spiritual life had slipped a little. Weekends she studied, but the times she came home she always accompanied Pop to church.

"I'll help Cruz and Adan with the children until you recover. When are you expected at the hospital?"

"I'm supposed to go home, pack a bag, and check in."

"Who has the children?"

"Ann Ramsey."

"Crystal will collect the children from Ann, and then I'll go with you to your house and pack a bag, then on to the hospital."

"I'll bring the children over here," Crystal offered.

"No, Cruz wants them with him, for the time being."

Jules knew the next answer before she asked. "He agreed to let me help?"

"Not exactly — but I convinced him it was the sensible way to handle this."

"Cruz and Adan are struggling with old equipment and potato fields. They'll want to spend time with you." Crystal straightened. "I'll talk to Adan and see if he doesn't think it wise to bring them here for now. You're not to worry about anything but getting better."

Now she was stepping on her feet. Jules turned to face her sister. What made Crystal

57

think she'd have more sway with Adan than Jules would? A heifer would have more credibility with Cruz than she would, but that wasn't the point. She and Cruz had far more history than Crystal and Adan, and Jules resented Crystal's interference. She'd left years ago; she didn't know these people like Jules did. What right did she have to step in and be Florence Nightingale?

Sophie pushed back from the table and stood. "I don't want the children told yet about my condition."

"Whatever you say." Jules's mind raced. What day was it? Graduation was this Friday night. She had to return to Pullman, attend graduation ceremonies, and close the apartment. "School . . . I graduate the end of the week."

"Don't worry. I'll be here." Crystal smiled. "I'll make a few phone calls and we'll be fine."

"Jules." Sophie's face sobered. "Make me a promise."

"Name it."

"There may come a time when I'll ask you to take the children indefinitely. It . . . depends how this all works out."

"Everything will be fine, Sophie. You know I'll do anything you ask — if it comes to that."

Crystal broke the weighty tension. "I'll take over here until you get back. You graduate; it's what Pop wanted. Then come home."

The joy from all her hard work was gone. Jules didn't give a whit whether she walked down the aisle and accepted her diploma, but the apartment had to be closed by the end of the month.

"I'll get you settled, Sophie, then return to Pullman Thursday, graduate, close the apartment and move back home."

Sophie nodded. "Thanks — I love you."

"I love you too, kiddo."

And I can't lose you. The idea was inconceivable. Crystal was staying. Cruz would be around a lot more than she liked, Pop had excluded Crystal from his will, and Sophie was facing a ghastly fight for her life.

Exactly what was the proper course of action when in hades?

CHAPTER 7

"Adan!" Cruz stalked through the house tracking dirt. The kitchen was empty. Dirty dishes filled the sink; a large yellow cat lounged on the sofa littered with newspapers.

Eventually his brother's voice came from upstairs. "Yo!"

"Come down here!"

Adan descended the stairs, frowning. "What's up?"

"Have you talked to Sophie?"

"Nope."

"She's got cancer."

His brother's face drained. "She's got what?"

"Cancer." Cruz strode to the kitchen and yanked open the refrigerator door. How did you tell a man that his sister has cancer? There was no way to soften the blow.

Stuffing his shirt into his pants, Adan entered the room behind him. "When?"

"She just called. Her biopsy came back bad. She's got stage three uterine cancer."

Leaning against the table, Adan swore.

"You better be on your knees praying."

"Sorry. Can they do anything?"

"They darn well better be able to do something." Cruz slammed the door. He'd forgotten what he was after anyway. Sophie didn't deserve this; she was a good mother, and she was the glue in the Delgado family. She couldn't die. Cruz swallowed back a sense of helplessness.

Adan spoke softly. "Is she going to die?"

"No."

"Then it's not serious —"

"It's serious, but she's not going to die." Maybe if he said it enough the conviction would come true.

Come on, God. You wouldn't take Sophie too. If you're God, make this a mistake.

One big, ugly mistake.

Taking his hat off, he wiped his forehead with his sleeve then replaced the Stetson. "Come on. She's on her way to Pasco now. The doctor wants her in the hospital tonight."

Adam reached for his hat. "Who's driving her?"

Who indeed.

From the moment Sophie called thirty

minutes ago, he had a hunch that his luck was about to take a turn for the worse.

And sure enough, it had.

CHAPTER 8

Hours passed in a blur. Jules's mad rush to Sophie's house, packing, consoling the children when Sophie told them that she was going to be gone for awhile but that Uncle Cruz and Adan would bring them to see her in a few days. Jules suggested that when Sophie was better they break the news that she was in the hospital. For now, they should remain calm.

Yet Jules would never forget the stricken look on the children's faces when she drove off with their mother in the Tracker.

Cruz had said little to her when Adan put Sophie's overnight bag in the truck. Jules avoided his eyes and he avoided hers, a device she knew she couldn't keep up once Crystal was settled. However major their differences — and they were large — Sophie's needs came first.

By late afternoon, Sophie was settled in a private room in Lourdes Medical Center in

Pasco. Jules was haunted by her friend's now composed acceptance of the situation. Her hands shook when Jules helped her remove her clothing and climb into the long narrow mattress with the blue disposable pad on it. All sorts of scary looking equipment encircled the bed. IV pumps attached with clamps to rolling poles. A blood pressure cuff. Some sort of canister attached to the wall. A huge water jug sat on the bedside table. Jules purposely avoided staring at the visible proof of the fight yet to come. She adjusted a light blanket and put the call button attached to the sheet closer.

"I'll be back the moment I rent a U-Haul and close the apartment."

"I wish I could be at your graduation. I was going to drive your father —"

"Shhh. I know. Life has a way of throwing curve balls." Jules fluffed a pillow and made her comfortable. "Better?"

"Just like a Marriott."

Jules grinned, relieved to see that she'd regained her sense of humor. "You're going to make it. There's no way on earth you're going to leave me alone to fight my battles."

"Your battles?" Sophie snorted. "What about mine?"

"There's no way I'm going to leave you alone to fight yours."

64

Sophie sighed. "Crystal's changed. She isn't the way I remember her. The last time I saw her she was a little pest that tagged after us everywhere we went."

"Yeah, she was a real fungus. Always asking questions and threatening to rat us out." Jules straightened and the words tumbled out, words she'd wanted to say from the moment she'd left the lawyer's office. "Pop left her out of his will."

Sophie cocked her head. "He what?"

"Left the farm and everything to me. What was he thinking?"

"You're not going to take it, are you?"

"I don't have a choice. I own it now." Events had happened so swiftly that Jules hadn't had time to consider what she would do. What would she do? Give half to Crystal anyway? Ignore Pop's last wishes?

Wearing a wan smile, Sophie closed her eyes. "You'll figure it out. I'm very tired."

Jules's hand closed over her friend's. "I'll stop by in the morning before I leave for campus. I should be back no later than Sunday. You know I'd be here for the surgery if I could."

"I know you would, but I'll need you more later."

"I'll be right here."

Once Jules got back, she'd make the

thirty-minute drive to the hospital twice a day if necessary. She blinked back threatening tears. "You'd better be." Sophie was her rock, her emotional support. She couldn't make it here, with Cruz so close-by but so distant, without her. Sophie's children needed her, but even more important, she needed them. She hadn't realized until now those children felt like hers.

As Jules left the hospital, she uttered a prayer that God didn't need Sophie worse.

She walked out of the hospital and encountered Cruz coming in the entrance. For a moment their gazes locked. The last time they faced off was the night before the second planned wedding.

Her throat seemed to close and air left the foyer.

Brown eyes dueled with hazel ones and won out. Jules dropped her gaze. "She's settled and resting."

He nodded and was about to walk on when she reached out and caught his sleeve. "Can I have a word with you?"

Surprise dominated his nut-brown features. He stepped back when she motioned to the quiet foyer. The hush settled over her like a shroud.

"What do you want?"

She was so nervous in his presence that

she struggled to find her voice. He still had the same unsettling effect on her he'd always had. "We have to put aside our differences and concentrate on Sophie." She swallowed. "She's in for the fight of her life, Cruz."

Pain reflected in his eyes. "Has she got a chance?"

"Of course, God can do all things, but knowledge tells me she's fighting an uphill battle."

"Sophie's a tough opponent."

"She'll need to be even tougher now."

They stood in the whispered stillness. He removed his hat and her heart caught at the sight of black curly hair, slightly damp from the headband. Once those curls were as familiar as her hair, and the thought made her heart thump so loud she imagined that he heard the beat.

"So."

A skeptical dark brow lifted. "So?"

"Do we agree to set aside our differences and look after Sophie's children without all this hostile animosity between us?"

A dark gaze skimmed her. "I don't know what hostility you're referring to, but yes I agree that Sophie's needs come first."

He didn't know what hostility she was talking about. When they were near each other you couldn't cut the air with a chain saw. She pushed a wispy bang out of her eye. She was weeks overdue for a haircut. "I'm leaving first thing in the morning for Pullman. I have to close my apartment."

"Oh right. Pullman. Big college town. You're graduating."

His patronizing tone irked her. "Yes, but that's secondary. I have to close the apartment and get back here. Crystal's agreed to stay and help for awhile."

"I bet you're nuts about that idea."

She refused to meet his mocking eyes. "We'll get along."

"Rumor mill says Pop left her out of his will."

The rumor mill. She gritted her teeth. Was nothing in this community sacred? "I should be back by late Sunday afternoon."

"You won't be here for the surgery?" His frown deepened. "Sophie leans on you for emotional support."

"We've discussed it, and she agrees that I should attend graduation services. She knows I'd rather be here but it's not possible."

"Whatever."

"The surgeon that she wants is going out of town for a week, and Sophie pleaded with him to perform the surgery before he left.

He agreed partly because Sophie begged him and mostly because he's a decent man and didn't want her to sweat this for another week. Of course the surgery is serious but he thinks she'll do fine — with the surgery part."

"And the 'other' part?"

She shook her head. "He doesn't know, but he gave me no reason to lose hope."

His gaze skimmed her and his features softened. "Sorry about your dad. He was a good man."

She'd heard the sentiment repeated at least a hundred times the past twenty-four hours, but coming from him the certainty of Pop gone overwhelmed her. Her breath caught and she bit back hot tears. "He left his watch to you. I'll deliver it later."

Cruz settled his Stetson on his head, then nodded and stepped away. She stood for a moment gaining composure before she left the hospital. Nothing about death was easy, and yet facing Cruz after all these years could run a tight second.

But Sophie came first, and he'd best plant that in his stubborn mind.

CHAPTER 9

The stench of a closed room filled with dirt tubs hit Jules the moment she opened the apartment door. Dust filtered the air, evident from the crack in the blinds. Wrestling three empty toilet tissue cardboard boxes, she wedged her way through the doorway and closed the door with her foot. Similar boxes sat in the back of the Tracker.

Exhausted, she dropped down on the futon and took a nap.

Thirty minutes later she stirred, checking her watch. Sophie would be out of surgery by now. She reached for her cell phone and called Adan. He answered in a hushed tone.

"Is she out of surgery?"

"The doctor was just here to speak to us."

"And?" She held her breath, praying.

"It was more extensive than he thought." Adan sounded very tired. "He says he wants her to start treatments as soon as she can get over the surgery, hopefully next week."

Jules closed her eyes. At least she was past the immediate danger. They could work all kinds of miracles these days. With time and treatments, Sophie could beat this.

Once she clicked off, her gaze roamed the cramped room, the habitat where she'd spent the last four years. Nothing but books, dirt tubs, random pieces of clothing draped over furniture met her eye. Good ole "Wazzle." Everything was orderly, just neglected. She was almost obsessively self-controlled about neatness, yet for lack of time she'd let things slide.

Time was never on her side.

Sliding off the futon, she began to pack. Books, knickknacks she'd gathered over the past four years. A picture of her and Pop, Pop with his arm around her in front of the Christmas tree. A photo of Old Jack, a retriever they'd had until last year. She picked up the near-complete thesis: *The Perfect Potato and How to Grow It.* Her gaze shifted to the dirt tubs, pausing to rest on one. Stepping closer, she eyed the plant shooting out of the dirt.

On closer examination, she noted the shoot was blooming earlier than usual. This was the tuber she'd planted the night she got the call about Pop's accident. Reaching for her scissors, she snipped a leaf sample

71

to chemically analyze for the amounts of essential nutrients. Once the tub of tubers used up the originally applied fertilizer, she would apply more to the plants. Plants needed lots of water, but could survive periods of dry soil. She hoped these particular tubers followed their predecessors because they'd been severely neglected the past few days. Yet they appeared to be thriving. Strange.

By late afternoon Saturday, the rented U-Haul was packed. She scrubbed the apartment clean, and then carefully showered, put on her makeup, blow dried her hair, and then drove to the college for graduation ceremonies. The long anticipated event was bittersweet without Pop and Sophie in the audience. Many, like her, had gone back to school after years of absence to get degrees. The ceremony was long and poignant. At the end, Jules walked across the stage, received her diploma from Dean Strauss, and then walked off the stage with friends cheering. She still had to complete her thesis, but by all standards she now had an agriculture/ biotechnology degree.

Early Sunday morning, she climbed into her vehicle, settled her cup of coffee in the console, and prepared to drop the apartment key in the complex drop-box. Her business here was finished.

Sophie was incoherent when Jules called her last night. Cruz had taken the phone and reported that his sister had made it through surgery fine but she was still drowsy from the anesthetic and pain medication.

Closing her eyes, she had listened to his voice, aching for him — aching for her. They might have their differences but they both loved Sophie. Funny how life sorts one's priorities into place. She thought having a degree would be the Mother of Satisfaction. Sadly enough, the ceremony felt just like any other she'd endured. Lengthy. Sophie, not irrigation systems, filled her thoughts. Cruz, not accomplishment, drew tears.

Father, I would trade everything I've inherited to have Cruz back and Sophie out of danger.

She braked at the gate, dropped her apartment key into the lock box, and drove on. But she doubted that God would heed her pleas, since she hadn't been exactly the most obedient sheep in his flock. When Mom and Crystal left she'd been mad at everyone — including God. She believed in him, because you can't be mad at something or someone that you don't think is there, but she'd had some hefty reservations about his ways over the past four years.

Was she still mad at him? No. She, unlike Pop, didn't carry a grudge — or at least she didn't think she did, but right now God seemed so far beyond her reach she might as well be an atheist.

CHAPTER 10

Cruz slammed on the brakes when a Tracker pulling a U-Haul streaked through the four-way stop without braking. Muttering under his breath, he reached to the floorboard and set his overturned coffee upright.

Jules was back.

The woman was going to get herself creamed one of these days. From the day he'd taken her to get her driver's license, he'd warned her that STOP meant Skid Tires on Pavement. Obviously the advice hadn't stuck.

Pulling into the local grill, he cut the engine and got out, adjusting the brim of his hat. At two in the afternoon, the place was quiet. He ordered a burger and fries, and then moseyed to the pool table where he shot a few games. His banker, Lex Hughes, walked in, ordered a cold drink, loosened his tie and joined him at the table. Chalking his stick, he grinned. "Was that

Jules's vehicle pulling a U-Haul?"

Cruz racked the triangle of multi-colored balls. Lex nodded for him to make the break. The clack of balls overrode the juke box. Bending, he positioned for the push out. "You saw her? All I saw was a blur."

Chuckling, Lex bent when it was his turn. "Four side pocket." The ball shot into the hole. "The community is going to miss Fred. Has Jules said what she and Crystal plan to do?"

Switching to the right side of the table, Cruz said, "Nine center, four side pocket." Balls clacked and found their target. "Not to me, she hasn't." Lex was on a fishing expedition. He'd heard the rumors about Fred excluding Crystal from the will and wanted to know why.

The banker studied the green felt. "Still feuding? Thought you might be a Good Samaritan and help her unload the U-Haul." Bending, he said, "Ten in the left pocket."

"Haven't talked to her in years — unless you count the other night when I bumped into her coming out of the hospital."

Lex sobered. "How is Sophie? I'll stop by the hospital, but I thought I'd wait until she felt up to company."

"Four and six ball, side." Clack. "Surgery

went well. She has a chance. The cancer has spread, but she has a great gynecologic oncologist."

"I hear the cancer was worse than first thought."

"Sophie's a fighter." Cruz bent and shot. "Adan mentioned that we might have to move her to a larger facility . . . maybe in Kennewick or Richland."

Lex shook his head and bent. "Four, center. That she is. How are you and Adan making it with the kids? How old are they now?"

"Ethan's five and Livvy's twenty-two months." More stuff came out of that kid's orifices than Cruz thought possible. This morning she'd spit oatmeal twenty-five feet — he'd measured. What didn't go on him hit the wall. He called another shot, sank it, and changed the subject. "I planned to catch you in the office tomorrow. What are you doing working on a Sunday afternoon?"

"This housing market is crazy. The refi's have me covered. I'm taking the afternoon to get caught up on paperwork." He called the shot, bent and played. The ball bumped the eight and rolled to within a hair's length of the back pocket. "What'd you need?"

"A week's extension on my loan." He straightened, meeting the banker's eyes. "I know you've been patient, Lex, and I hate to ask, but I'm expecting a check from an account up north sometime by the end of the month."

Lex frowned. "You know your credit's good, Cruz, but this past year you're getting in pretty deep."

Cruz knew only too well. Last year's moth infestation wiped out half his crop, and Sophie didn't have enough health insurance. Real estate bombed, and he and Adan couldn't sell Mom and Dad's house — who in this community needed a house with fourteen rooms? About the only thing the home was good for was a restaurant, with its big windows and wraparound porch, and this area sure didn't have the clientele to keep a business that size going. If this year's crop failed . . .

He shook the thought aside and smiled as the waitress brought the burger and fries. He'd work it out; he always did. At the moment, he wasn't sure about anything other than he had to keep his distance from Jules or risk falling in love with her again. How many times did it take for him to get it through his thick skull that she was history?

Twice bitten, and he'd learned to stay clear of women with sharp teeth.

The game ended. The two men shook

78

hands. "I have to get back to the bank."

"Sure thing. Catch you later." Cruz hung his stick on the rack and returned to the bar where a burger and fries awaited him.

He took a bite, wincing. Just like his life. Cold.

CHAPTER 11

May gently folded into June, bringing light showers and blooming flowers. With three hundred days of sunshine, the sports enthusiasts came out. They liked to fish, walk, and bike riverfront paths. Jules and Crystal took the children to Pasco on the weekends to take advantage of the large sport complexes — six softball fields, batting cages, playgrounds adjoining soccer fields or to catch a game with the Tri-City Dust Devils Single A baseball team. Often the entourage would windsurf, water-ski or take a leisurely hike in a nearby natural habitat for deer, Canada geese, quail and Chinook salmon.

"Can we have hot dogs tonight?" Ethan asked one afternoon.

Jules caught the child into her arms and hugged him. "We've eaten hot dogs every single night this week."

The child squealed with delight when she tickled him. Jules wasn't sure how they managed, but between her and Crystal they had kept the kids' minds off their mother and on a normal routine.

"Can we visit Mommy tonight?"

Crystal tousled the boy's hair. "Sure. Would you like to take her a pretty flower?"

"Yeah!" The child broke away and headed for one of the petunia beds.

"Crystal, he's not supposed to pick the flowers."

"Nonsense." Crystal smiled at Jules. "What are flowers for other than to be enjoyed by a sick mommy?"

Pesky complications kept Sophie in the hospital. Prolonged bowel obstruction slowed her recovery. The need for nasogastric suction kept her in the hospital. Jules was relieved that her spirits were still intact. Every day she made the drive to Pasco and visited while Crystal occupied the kids.

"You can't tell me that by now you're not pulling your hair out. I know what a handful Olivia can be." Sophie forced a wan smile.

"Honestly, she wears me out, but Crystal and I love it."

Her friend cocked her head swathed in a doo rag. Sophie was particular about her long, thick hair, and a hospital bed did nothing for her beautiful locks. "Are you and Crystal getting along well?"

"We barely see one another. I'm so busy trying to help Joe keep the farm running while Crystal watches the kids. I see her in the evenings for a few minutes, and we take the kids into Pasco often."

"I thought by now you two would be at sword's point."

"She's messy," Jules confided. "She doesn't know how to stack the dishwasher, and she can step over clutter as though it isn't there. I nearly broke my leg stumbling over one of Livvy's toys last night."

"Does Crystal help with the cleaning?"

"Cleaning?" Jules laughed. "I'm not sure she'd recognize the word. She's in her own perfect world. Flowers, fauna, peace, love and goodwill to all men." That was Crystal's focus and admittedly, her strong points. Jules envied her ability to let Rome fall while she puttered in the flower beds. Dirty dishes and dust balls under the bed didn't faze her.

"Pastor Williams stops by every day."

Sobering, Jules met her eyes.

"We pray together."

"That's good. Do you want me to pray with you?"

"Do you pray alone for me, Jules?"

Jules squirmed. She did, but on the run. Drive by prayers. *God bless Sophie today. God make Sophie comfortable. God heal Sophie.* Of course she prayed. "He's answering my prayers."

Sophie caught her hand. "Oh, Jules, I worry about you."

"For goodness sake, why?" As far as she knew, she was the same ole Jules. Dull. Hard-working. Loyal. Short nails with potato dirt under them.

"Because I know if this turns out differently than you expect, you'll be mad at God again."

"Again?"

"Oh, Jules. You've been angry at God since the last time you broke up with Cruz."

The last time? That was unnecessarily frank. "I wasn't angry at God. I was mad at myself. You know how I hated what Mom and Pop did to each another — to our family. I need to be certain when I marry, and, at the time, I wasn't certain."

"Yeah." Sophie sighed. "It's hard to imagine your mom having an . . ."

"Affair?" Jules provided.

"Was it a full-blown affair, or one regrettable indiscretion?"

"One indiscretion that ruined her life. Pop never forgave her."

83

"Odd. He was such a good, tolerant God-fearing man. You would think that forgiveness would come naturally."

Jules smiled though tears welled in her eyes. Not having Pop around was going to take adjustment. She missed his cheery smile every morning, his voice calling to her from the potato fields. "We're forgiven by the grace of God, Sophie. That doesn't make us perfect in human form. But yes, Pop's inability to forgive Mom not only destroyed his life, but it took mine and Crystal's childhood."

"And now?"

"What?"

"Are you ready to marry and settle down now?"

"Yes — if there was a man in the picture." She was ready; she'd love to have her own children. Caring for Ethan and Livvy made her realize that she wasn't getting any younger. Her maternal clock was ticking.

Sophie laughed. "Twice I thought I was ready. You'll never be absolutely certain about the man. You might think you are, but then he'll do something so entirely foreign to what you expect or thought you knew about him, and you realize that you can never really know a person. You have to accept the good with the bad unless the bad outweighs or endangers you. I chose men who met both criteria." She sighed. "I know people must wonder about my destructive choices."

"People love you, and if anyone would dare criticize your choices you have two brothers who would defend you 'til death."

The wan smile surfaced. "Yeah, they are great brothers."

Jules watched as Sophia's strength visibly drained. She pushed back from the bed. "Can I bring you anything special tomorrow?"

"No . . ." She caught Jules's hand. "What day is it?"

"Twenty-eighth of June."

"Are you riding in the Fourth of July rodeo this year?"

Jules had thought about signing up for the event, but it seemed inconsiderate of Sophie, and it wouldn't bring the same joy. "I think I'll skip it this year. The potatoes take up so much time — did I tell you someone stole one of our tractors over the weekend?"

"You mentioned it." Sophie closed her eyes and rested her head on the pillow. "Do they have any idea who took it? Cruz and Adan can't afford to lose any machinery."

Jules shook her head. "Machinery theft is

rampant. Our old potato planter is making a racket. Maybe they'll steal that." Her thoughts turned to the dirt barrels sitting in Pop's tool shed. The one promising experiment had now bloomed, and the potato was growing. She maintained a daily check on its progress. The other four tubs had ordinary looking plants, but the fifth tub . . . She didn't want to get her hopes up, but there was definitely something unusual about that fifth plant.

"I want you to."

Jules glanced up, drawn back to the conversation. "To what?"

"Ride the barrel races this year."

"Oh, Sophie, I don't —"

"For me." She reached for Jules's hand. "Do it for me. I don't want this stupid cancer to interfere with tradition. I'll be there with you in spirit. I don't want you to miss the fun."

Jules had no heart for the event, but if it meant so much to Sophie she'd ride. "Okay. But you'll owe me one."

Smiling, Sophie nodded. "I'll lie back next year, let you win."

"Lie back, my foot. I always beat you by a couple of seconds."

"Not always."

"Oh right. Four summers ago you got

lucky and won by a millimeter."

"Still won, didn't I?"

Jules bent to kiss her friend's forehead. "You still won. And you'll win this one too, Sophie." Jules gently readjusted the doo scarf, willing strength into her friend. She knew the long odds were against the fight, but anything could happen, and Sophie was responding to treatment and chemo would start soon. Other than the pesky surgery complications, she was doing great. She'd known people who'd beat this disease and if anyone could, this brave young mother would. Sophie had endured two deadbeat husbands. She could whip a disease.

Sophie caught her hand and held on tightly. Jules could feel the tremble, both in her heart and Sophie's fingertips. "You keep praying," she whispered. "God's mercy is the only thing that's going to pull me through this."

CHAPTER 12

Arriving back at the farm, Jules got out of her vehicle and headed straight for the tool shed. Tub five plant was practically shooting out of the container, so much so Jules couldn't wait to see the product. An ordinary potato would be months away from harvest, but judging by the sheer size of the tub plant, Jules had a hunch if she gave in to her curiosity she'd find a sizable potato under the dirt. She reached for her trowel and turned when Crystal appeared in the doorway.

"Hi. I thought I heard you drive in." Her sister picked her way through the crowded tool shed, side-stepping picks and rakes. Jules gaze swept the small area. Pop had three different size lawn mowers in here, one that didn't run, one that did, and one that he refused to discard. The stench of oil and pesticide hung in the air. Crystal paused before the tubs of dirt. "Why are you growing potatoes in tubs? Isn't a couple hundred acres enough for you?"

Stepping around her, Jules pulled on her gloves. "They're experimental plants."

"Like how?"

"Like, they're different from the others, Crystal."

Her sister eased around the tubs, studying the shoots. "What are you trying to grow?"

"French fries. Pull them out of the ground, heat them, and they're ready to eat."

Crystal's gullible side flared. "You could do that?"

"Of course not." Jules left the fifth tub alone and started on the smaller ones. Crystal didn't need to know about her experiment. No one did. After a spiral notebook full of failures she expected more of the same, no matter how good tub five looked. "Where are the kids?"

"Napping." Crossing her arms, Crystal leaned against a rickety potting table. "How's Sophie today?"

Jules stuck a trowel in the dirt. "Weak, but she's coming along. I wouldn't be surprised if she didn't get to come home soon."

"Really?" Crystal's features softened. "But stage three, Jules. That means it's spread —"

"And that's the reason she'll go through radiation." Jules rammed the tool into the dirt and loosened the soil. Sophie had years ahead of her with proper treatment. "When did you become such a pessimist? Didn't Mom take you to church — teach you the power of faith?"

"Not often. Mom was a free-spirit. She drew her strength through the things God provides. The wind, trees, and all living things. She didn't trust people."

Jules straightened to face her. "Mom didn't believe in God?"

"She did, Jules. She didn't believe in religion. She believed God was God and his ways, though different from ours, need no explanation, and someday, if it's important, we'll understand why some prayers are answered and others aren't."

Jules dropped her gaze back to the potato plant. Well, the reasoning wasn't exactly flawed. "What was Mom like?"

Crystal smiled. "You don't remember her?"

"I remember her." Jules had lain awake nights picturing the blonde, petite woman who always smelled of Red Door perfume. "I remember her soft voice when she came in at night to hear our prayers."

"Yeah. And that voice could be shrill as a

harridan when she and Dad were fighting."

"That I remember all too well. Fred, I'm going to leave you!" Jules mocked.

"Go ahead! Make my day!" Crystal could sound exactly like Pop. Angry, hurtful words that can never be forgotten.

Jules couldn't find a big enough pillow to block the angry voices, accusations and horrifying threats. Alone, Pop was mild-mannered and easy going, but with Mom he lost it. "Why do you suppose they hated each other so much?"

Crystal sighed. "I'm not sure she hated him. She spoke of him often — and she grieved that you were caught in the middle."

Jules pitched a trowel of dirt into the tub. "That's why she wrote or phoned me so often?"

"She didn't call or write because she didn't want to further tear you apart. She always planned to make it up to you, and she would have if it weren't for the car accident."

"Maybe." Jules rammed the trowel in the dirt and reached for the fertilizer. "I hear Olivia."

"She didn't sleep very long." Startled, Crystal headed back toward the house.

When her sister cleared the shed, Jules returned to tub five. With Christmas-like anticipation, she took the trowel and loosened the dirt around the plant. Even at this distance, she could see a potato, a very large potato.

Working more quickly, she turned the dirt and her eyes widened at the sight of a perfectly formed Russet Burbank. Smooth, about the size of two fists held together. Lifting the jewel out of the dirt, she held it for closer inspection. She examined for green peach aphid, a disease that doesn't affect people but causes tubers to have brown internal markings called net necrosis. The potato in her hand showed no sign of the insect pest.

Excitement grew as she picked up a knife and sliced into the potato and again, the white flesh was flawless. No brown spots. She took a bite and savored the extraordinary flavor, fresh, meaty. The tuber had grown in six weeks compared to the normal growing season from planting in late May until harvesting began around the Fourth of July and continued through late summer. This particular tuber had survived on neglect, little water in the beginning, and minimum fertilizers.

Jules's brain spun with the realm of possibilities. Fields could be used more than once during the season. The need to "kill" off the ground — stop all irrigation or spraying with special chemicals that kill the leaves and stems before the harvest, might be eliminated. Her hand came up to cover her mouth. Now all she had to do was wait a few days and see if the potato would rot, grow eyes and sprout roots. If this potato failed to do that, then she had created the perfect spud.

Turning to her notebook, she thumbed through the pages, impatient when her notes stuck together, the result of too many nights of peanut butter and jelly sandwiches while she worked. She reached the date of planting: May 25. The page was blank.

She flipped back a page and glanced at the date. May 24. She turned back. May 25. Blank. Where was the data for May 25? The night Pop died.

Blood pumping, she stepped to the John Deere calendar Pop kept over his work bench. Leaning on her tiptoes, she flipped back to May and studied the date.

Her mind reeled, going back over that evening. She'd planted the experimental tubers. The phone rang. Her heart double-timed. The awful news that Pop had been in an accident. She was brain dead from finals and lack of sleep —

She hadn't written down the hybrid mix.

Impossible! She always wrote down the experimental tubers. She returned to the notebook, dumping it upside down in hopes that she'd penned a note and left it inside the book. Nothing fluttered out. Shaking the spiral pad, she willed the combination to come out, but nothing materialized but dry crumbs.

She lowered the notebook to the bench and sat down, dropping her face into her hands. She had created the perfect potato. A few days under a heat lamp and she'd know if the product was perfect. And if it were . . .

She'd forgotten to write down how she achieved it.

CHAPTER 13

Gunshots pierced the air. The annual Fourth of July rodeo galloped into full swing. Red, white, and blue banners draped the outdoor stadium. Fireworks popped and sizzled in the distance.

The sleek mare bolted from the start gate and Jules mentally prepared for the pocket. She knew Maddy's speed like the back of her hand; was she feeling frisky tonight? Settling deeper into the saddle, she gripped the pommel, legs tucked closely to the horse's side; her leg to the inside of the turn, supporting the animal's ribcage to assist her to effortlessly make the tight turn. Maddy cleared the barrel.

The crowd roared as Jules flanked the mare, focused on the second barrel sitting across the arena. Taking the turn in the opposite direction, she shifted her weight to the left side. *This one's for you, Pop.*

Barrel two cleared, she galloped headlong

to the back of the arena amid cheers, hoots and whistles.

"Come on, girl, make this one for Sophie," she whispered as she aimed for the final goal. Racing against the stop watch, she let Maddy do the work. The animal turned opposite the second barrel turn, completed the final turn and headed for home as the crowd swelled to their feet with applause. Horse and rider raced across the center of the arena.

Falcon Merit hit the stopwatch, a grin breaking across his rugged features. "13 seconds! Hot diggity!"

Jules reined up, breathless. "That's a record, isn't it?"

"It shore is, girlie! Best of the season!"

The crowd roared its approval as Jules reined and accepted her victory. Sweeping off her hat, she waved to the crowd.

Jules felt the cloud of doom that she'd been living with lift. She flashed a grin at the crowd. Day five and the experimental potato looked even better. No rot. Root free. Sophie was looking forward to eating her first real meal when the tube came out. Jules had learned to not look at Pop's chair at the table or his old recliner — it made the days easier. Breathing in victory, Jules whooped!

She reined Maddy back to the corral,

dismounted, and gave the horse an affectionate pat. "You're the best!"

She spotted Joe Fraker from the corner of her eye and she whirled to hug him. "Didn't I tell you Maddy was the best little mare around?" Her gaze skipped to the stands where Cruz and Adan sat with the kids. Did Cruz even notice her performance? He appeared to be unusually absorbed with the kids, trying to control them on the cramped bleachers.

Joe returned the embrace. "Your pop would be proud as punch of his little gal."

"Thanks!" She grinned. "I can't wait to phone Sophie and tell her."

"Wanna brag a little, huh?"

"A little." She flashed another grin. "Next year she'll whip my fanny."

Joe fell into step with her. The arena sat in the middle of a dusty field, and rodeo nights could be hard to catch a breath without a breeze. She took a deep breath, thankful to be home and to have college behind her. Ride horses, feel the wind at her back.

"Thought Crystal would be here tonight," Joe mused.

"She didn't say anything about wanting to come."

"And you didn't invite her." Joe glanced her way. "You better put that stubborn streak aside. I know you and your sister ain't close, but you're a big girl now with big girl responsibilities. Crystal didn't have much choice in the situation, and neither did you."

"I know that." Her gaze caught the holding pen that restrained a big, black snorting bull. Black Devil. "I'd still love to ride that animal."

"You're joking. Tom only brings that old bull to events for sentimental reasons. Black Devil's son, The Terminator, is the one to ride these days."

"The Terminator, huh?" She eyed the massive bull. Ladies didn't ride bulls. Wasn't that Pop's philosophy? The community agreed, but not Jules. Like God would strike her dead if she dared to enjoy the life he had given her?

Joe's voice broke through her resentment. "Back to your situation. You're heir to the Blue Bayou whether you like it or not."

She didn't like it. The more she was forced into the role, the more she resented it. She could use some help, thank you. She had helped Pop all of her life, knew her way around a potato planter, but raising a crop, keeping house, managing the bills and settling the estate wasn't easy. If Crystal would do something other than play with Sophie's children! Pick up after herself, run a load of wash, cook a meal. Instead, she stood back as though she were a guest in the house.

Sometimes she wondered if God was punishing her for her aimless spiritual drifting. She'd sure done nothing to grow in faith these days, but God had no reason to be angry with her. She skipped church pretty well on a weekly basis, but she intended to get back in one of these days. She didn't talk vile like some she knew, and she honored Pop until the day he died. She'd done her duty; she had stayed at Blue Bayou.

Her gaze drifted back to the bleachers where Cruz and Adan corralled the kids. Most certainly she'd given Cruz a reason to resent her. Her eyes skimmed the once cocky teenager that had grown from an awkward teen to a good-looking man who attracted women like flies to honey. Sophie's letters said women adored the single bachelor. And Adan had his fair share of female admirers. A group of young women surrounded the bachelors, taking charge of the children.

Cruz ignored her every possible chance he got. When they passed at the hospital, he barely acknowledged her presence. Lately she went early afternoons so he and Adan could have evenings with Sophie. Tension was starting to wear thin. The brothers talked of moving Sophie to Kennewick, but she begged them to let her stay closer to the children.

So all right. Cruz was never going to forgive her; she was spoiled and bratty, if you believed his former accusations. Her attention remained on the bleachers where he was now holding up little Olivia so she could see the bronc rides. She'd been the fool; knew it from the moment she broke the second engagement, known it for certain a year into college but pride had anchored her to her goal. She didn't want more education; she wanted Cruz and babies and a home of her own. For the first time, she allowed the implication of her need to sink in.

She wanted nothing more in life than Cruz and his babies.

It was the first time in a very long time that God clearly revealed the missing element in her life. She had been grasping for years to wrap her fingers around this bizarre, unexplainable curse called indecisiveness, and now, in the middle of a rodeo ground, on a hot summer night, he'd addressed her prayer.

Joe's voice drew her back. "Saddle up. Calf roping coming up next."

Shaken, Jules led Maddy to the pen, her eyes still on Cruz.

CHAPTER 14

Tucking her gloves in her back pocket, Jules made her way to the concession stand. She'd taken second in calf roping; Sophie would get a kick about that one, but she'd been busy the last few years and she was a little rusty on her skills. Plus she was getting older. The old bones weren't quite as limber as they'd been in her teens. *Teens.* She grinned. That had been over a decade ago.

The concession line was backed up to the porta potties, which were backed up to the arena entrance. Jules threaded her way into line and waited. Up ahead she spotted Cruz holding Ethan by the hand. He looked as tight as one of Pop's hatbands. Biting back a grin, she pictured him wrestling a five-year-old around in a tight, stinky space, trying to help him "go wee wee." The picture didn't compute. Cruz had a weak stomach and the second image she got wasn't pretty.

She stepped out of line, pushed her way to the porta potties, and approached the tall good-looking man. "Want me to take him?"

Relief flooded his features. "Would you?"

"Sure." She extended a hand. "Come here, big boy."

Ethan stepped to her side. "Hi, Aunt Jube!"

"Hey there." She glanced at Cruz. "I'll bring him to you when we're finished."

He walked off, but not without a backward glance and a hint of a grin.

Thanks. No problem. Be glad to help. Would it have killed him to thank her? Would he choke if he congratulated her on the win?

Twenty minutes later, Jules burst out of the porta potty and released her breath in a gasp. Ethan wrinkled his nose. "Shooeee."

"Shooeee is right, sweetie." She hitched up the little boy's jeans and secured them. Fresh air was wonderful.

"Aunt Jube?" Ethan said.

"What is it, honey?"

The child pointed to the concession stand where the line had thinned. Children were carrying fat cherry snow cones back to the bleachers. "You want a snow cone?"

He nodded.

Jules reached for his hand and they approached the concession line. Later, she steered Ethan and balanced two cherry snow cones back to the stands where Cruz, Adan and Livvy sat near the top. She climbed the metal riser, steadying the little boy and snow cones.

Cruz glanced up when she approached, horror forming on his face. "What's that?"

Jules led Ethan to his lap, spilling sticky red liquid on his snakeskin boot. He glanced down.

"Snow cones. Ethan wanted one so I knew Livvy would too." She smiled and handed the little girl her treat.

"Aunt Jube!" Livvy reached to hug her, snow cone in hand. Jules winced as the red liquid seeped down her back.

"You bought the kids snow cones?" His tone indicated that she had lost her mind.

Loosening her blouse, she shuddered as ice trickled down her back. "It seemed like a good idea at the time."

Livvy climbed from Cruz to Adan, dripping red juice. Flies buzzed Adan's head. He took a swipe, and then reached in his back pocket for a handkerchief. "Thanks a lot, Jules." He flashed a grin.

She reached to position both kids between her and Cruz. "Stay," she ordered. The children settled down, licking their cones.

She glanced at Cruz who was now fixed

on the bull rides. *Well, how awkward is this?* Her sitting here next to him as though they were all one big happy family.

Adan shattered the palpable silence. "Congratulations on the win!"

"Thanks. I thought I was a little rusty. I haven't ridden much in the past few years."

"Nah, you're still in great form." Her eyes met his dancing ones. He could always lighten the mood. "Been meaning to stop by and give you my regrets. Your dad was a great man."

"Thanks."

"It's good to have Crystal back."

Jules nodded. Cruz, Crystal, Adan, and she had spent many a summer evening chasing fireflies and eating watermelon. They'd ridden the school bus and attended church together. "She's decided to stay and help until Sophie comes home."

"That's what she said." He nodded gravely. "We drop the kids off, but I haven't had a moment to tell her how much we appreciate her help."

He'd left the obvious unsaid; a moment without Cruz present. The thought that he was forced to accept anything from her had to irk him.

Of the two, Adan was closer to Sophie than Cruz, maybe because Cruz was older and Adan spent more time with his sister in their younger years, but both men would do anything for her. The past few weeks had made that apparent. Two young children to care for was trying for a saint, and neither Cruz nor Adan had an abundance of patience.

Livvy tipped her cone and sticky liquid gushed out covering Cruz's left foot. He sprang to his feet, reaching for a napkin. "Come on, Livvy." Spectators turned to locate the ruckus.

"Sit down," Jules muttered. "You're making a scene."

"I just bought these boots a few months ago."

"A little snow cone juice isn't going to hurt them." Cruz didn't have the money for expensive boots, nor would he settle for something he didn't want, so the boots were important to him, but if he was going to have the care of a two-year-old he'd have to make sacrifices. Still . . . A moment later she weakened. "I'll go get wet towels and clean them."

His eyes fixed on the arena. "I'm perfectly capable of cleaning my boots."

"Fine."

He scooted away from her and hugged the bleacher rail.

"Fine." She crossed her arms. She'd scoot away if she could, but she didn't cherish the thought of tumbling out of the bleachers.

The remainder of the ride they sat in stony silence.

Sometime after midnight, Jules pulled the Tracker into the farm lot. After the rodeo she'd hung around with a few old friends and reminisced, turning more than once to share something with Sophie, but she wasn't there. Instead, she was lying in the hospital, battling surgery complications. Years away from her best friend, Jules had learned, even understood herself better. She always told people the truth, however painful. She had a tenacity to push herself and others beyond their limits to help them grow, see things in black and white, but doubted herself far too often. Sophie was always positive, uplifting, and had an answer for anything. Only now her best friend was starting to question God's intentions. The bowel obstruction was still there, and the daily treatments were dragging Sophie down. But she was strong and gut-determined to start her chemo and come home before summer's end.

Switching off the lights, she climbed out of the truck and hit the lock button, a habit she acquired with all the theft going around.

When she walked into the house, she heard the sound of Daffy Duck drifting from the den television. Peeking around the corner, her jaw dropped when she spotted Crystal, Olivia and Ethan cuddled beneath a large throw. Daffy lisped "th-his is a downright diss-grace!"

"Crystal!"

Crystal started, her hand flying to her throat. "Jules. For goodness' sake. Are you trying to give me a heart attack?"

Jules entered the room like a bull out of the shoot. "What are the children doing up this late? What are they doing here at all? Adan and Cruz had them earlier."

"I know. I got lonesome, so I called and asked if the kids could spend the night. Cruz didn't mind, said he had to clean his boots anyway and he'd prefer to do it in peace."

Guilt flooded Jules's mind. She had thoughtlessly not asked Crystal to the rodeo. She'd spent the whole night alone.

"Those *stinkin'* boots." Jules switched off the lights, kicked a throw pillow aside. The man cared more about his boots than his niece and nephew. She caught her thoughts. That wasn't true. He adored Livvy and Ethan, but he was fastidious and kids were messy.

She walked through the house turning off lights. Every bulb in the back part of the house was lit. Crystal had no sense of responsibility or the high cost of utility bills. She stepped into the kitchen and paused. Apparently the gang had popped corn. Oil splattered burners; kernels, popped and raw, littered the floor. Kitchen cabinets stood open. Dishcloths hung out of the drawers.

Crunching across the vinyl, Jules swallowed her anger. *She's trying, Jules. You have to give her that.*

Crystal appeared in the doorway. "What's wrong?"

She whirled. "Look at this mess! Has the house been ransacked? Burglarized?"

Her sister's eyes skimmed the clutter. "I'll clean it up."

"*Why* would you leave it like this? Is this how you keep house?"

Crystal assessed the damage. "Pretty much."

"Well it's not how I do it." Jules slammed the corn popper into the sink and turned on the hot water. Steam bellowed up.

"Did you lose tonight?"

"No." She turned to face Crystal. "I won. Why?"

"You're in such a temper."

"Look at this house, Crystal! I've been

patient but this has got to stop. I can't run this farm, raise potatoes, help with the kids and oversee the household. If you want to help, you're going to have to do your share." Jules hated the aggressively direct and insensitive tone that now crept into her shout. Yes, shout. And she never shouted. She was tired, had red sticky syrup dried to her back and was in no mood to deal with this tonight, but resentment poured out. If Crystal thought she was a guest here, she was sadly mistaken. Blue Bayou was her home too. Guilt swamped her. But it wasn't her home. Pop had seen to that. She brought her hands to her temples. "I'm sorry. I shouldn't have spouted off like that."

When she looked up she saw the doorway was empty.

Sinking into a kitchen chair, she buried her face in her arms. Why did she resent Crystal so much? She wanted the warm, fuzzy relationship other women had with their sisters, but she didn't have that with Crystal. Crystal was an irritant, and she was powerless to know why. She didn't blame Crystal for choosing Mom over Pop — if anything she blamed herself for letting Mom down, but Pop seemed to need the help and Mom and Crystal had always been close.

Over the years Crystal had written letters, childish, girlish ramblings that more often upset Jules than drew her closer. She rarely wrote back. Other than parents, the two shared nothing in common. Their nature and personalities mixed like sugar and vinegar. As they grew older, Crystal once confided that she'd like nothing better than to share a bottle of wine and talk all night. Wine gave Jules a headache, and she was dead on her feet by 10:00 p.m. Running a shell shop in Florida was less taxing than working ten hours in a potato field.

Face it, Jules. You consider yourself more dependable. You have never tiptoed through the tulips of life. Crystal's laid-back tendencies irked her, and she didn't know if she was judgmental or envious of her naiveté.

Jules's boot encountered an unpopped kernel. She couldn't live in this pig sty! And yet, in her own screwy way, she loved her sister.

How schizophrenic was she?

Reaching for a broom, she allowed her temper to cool. Once she finished cleaning up, she'd take Crystal a cup of that flowery smelling tea she drank. And apologize.

Yes, apologize, Jules.

It seemed that was all she knew how to do.

111

CHAPTER 15

Haute Peterson was a "catch" by any woman's standards. Not only did he own the biggest farm in the area, but he was easy on the eyes. He stood just under six feet, had a stocky frame that carried nothing but hard muscle. No fancy gyms for Haute. Handling a hundred bales of hay a day took care of his physical needs. Cap that with feline green eyes, and blond hair — not to mention an outgoing personality and a perpetual friendly grin — and most women found the farmer irresistible. The puzzle was why he'd managed to stay single for thirty-four years. Haute's diesel sat at the gasoline pumps when Jules pulled her Tracker into the convenience store to fill up.

Haute flashed a grin when he spotted her, and walked over. Uncapping her fuel tank, he winked. "How's it going, babe?"

"Good. Sorry I didn't get an opportunity to speak to you at the funeral."

"You were a little preoccupied." He stuck the hose in the tank, flipped the lever and gasoline ran into the tank. Leaning against the truck, he boldly assessed her. "You get prettier by the day."

Heat flooded Jules's cheeks. Pretty wasn't exactly how she'd describe her boyish looks, short cropped hair and freckles. "You have me confused with Crystal."

"Hey, heard your sister was back. How is she?"

Jules shrugged. "Different."

"How so?"

"When she left here she was a little girl. Now she's turned into a nurturer. You know the kind, driven to help people, generous to a fault." Jules's face turned hot. Those were wonderful traits, so why did she resent them?

Haute chuckled. "I saw her briefly going into the grocery store a couple of days ago. She's a looker."

"That she is."

"Hear Sophie's coming along."

Jules beamed. "She's having a few complications from the surgery but the doctors hope to clear those up soon. I'm on my way to the store to buy spelt flour. She's requested some of my banana nut bread."

"She's eating already?"

"Not yet — she still has a feeding tube but that will come out any day."

"Think she's going to beat this?"

"Absolutely. As soon as the complications clear up, she'll have chemo and radiation, and hopefully she'll be home for that."

The pump cut off and Haute topped off the tank before he replaced the hose in the pump stand. He screwed the cap back on. "You up to doing dinner one of these nights? I thought we'd drive to Pasco, have dinner, take in a movie. Is Saturday night good for you?"

"Saturday's great. Thanks." She and Haute had always gotten along well. Over the years, they'd gone out when she was back to see Pop. Haute was great company, and she could talk to him as easily as she could Cruz. In fact she had, many times, trying to explain her side of the troubled relationship. Haute knew about the two broken engagements and the fact that Jules was still in love with Delgado; that's why she enjoyed Haute's company. There was no pretense. No explaining sudden mood changes when they bumped into Cruz. Just comfortable companionship. Jules wasn't looking for anything more.

Later she pulled out of the convenience store and headed for the only large grocer

114

in the area. She parked, grabbed a cart and wheeled into the store, intent on purchasing the flour and then heading home. If they didn't have it, she'd have to drive to Pasco to a health food store. As she rounded the cookie aisle she heard a child's scream. *Olivia.* She'd recognize that high-pitched squeal any day.

Cruz and the two-year-old were in gridlock over a package of cookies. Livvy clutched a package of those marshmallow chocolate things to her chest, holding on for dear life. Every attempt to take them from her proved useless. The more Cruz pulled, the louder Livvy screamed. Fellow shoppers paused to watch the growing fracas.

Pushing her cart up to the pair, Jules reached over and took the cookies out of the child's unsuspecting hands. Olivia looked up with wide-eye astonishment. "Sneak attack," Jules told Cruz. "The only way to deal with her when she gets in this mood."

"Thanks." He set the slightly dented cookies back on the shelf and reached for ginger snaps. Jules shook her head.

He touched chocolate chip.

No.

Oatmeal.

No.

Lemon.

Absolutely not.

Vanilla wafers.

Jules nodded.

He dumped the box in the cart, along with a package of oatmeal cookies, which he carefully settled in the basket beside Livvy. She supposed the treat was for him. Jules's eyes accessed the cart contents and she felt faint. Ice cream bars. Bite size Snickers. Potato chips. White bread. Four boxes of sugary cold cereal. Some cheap brand of lunch meat she wouldn't feed her animals. Ranch dip. Microwave popcorn. Two cans of pork and beans, and chocolate milk. "Is this what you feed her?"

He lifted an eyebrow. "It's what she'll eat."

"Have you thought about throwing in a few carrots? Maybe some broccoli —"

"Neither she nor Ethan will eat broccoli."

"They do, and they love it."

Livvy lifted her palms and wiggled her fingers.

"See." Jules turned to the two-year-old. "You like broccoli, don't you?"

The little girl wiggled her fingers more enthusiastically.

Jules bent to give her a kiss as she pushed her cart past.

"Hey. Hold on."

She turned to face Cruz. "What."

"What does she eat that isn't so messy?"

Jules shook her head. "She likes to feed herself, and she is messy."

"With everything?"

Jules nodded. "What can I say?"

"Will she eat scrambled eggs instead of oatmeal? She spits oatmeal on me and the walls."

"Sure, eggs, fruit. Have you tried yogurt?"

"She spits that too." He pushed his cart in line with Jules and they continued down the aisle. Occasionally Jules reached for something in more solid form for Livvy's meals, but the child was a spitter. Jules reached for a jar of peanut butter.

"Oh, that'll be great," Cruz said.

"She can't spit peanut butter and jelly as far."

She added a can of ravioli and spaghetti.

"Nothing messy about those."

Jules paused. "Look. You asked for things she couldn't spit as far. Messy you'll have to deal with. It's known as 'kids.' "

"I've raised hogs that were cleaner."

She picked up a sack of spelt flour.

He observed her purchase. "Are you going all 'earthy' like Crystal?"

"I'm baking banana nut bread for your sister, if you must know."

"Oh, I *must* know. Your every move fascinates me. And Sophie can't eat banana nut bread through a tube."

Jules shoved the cart faster down the aisle, tossing over her shoulder, "I thought we agreed to keep this civil for Sophie's sake."

"You agreed. I listened. Sophie can't have banana nut bread."

"*You* agreed."

"Whatever."

Biting her lower lip, Jules paused. Turning, she marched back over to his cart, lifted her fist and smacked his package of oatmeal cookies.

He stared at the carnage. "Well that's real adult."

Her lips firmed and she reached for the milk. His hand blocked her. Their eyes met and dueled. "Don't you dare," he warned.

"That's right. You detest messes."

"That's right. I do." His dark stare said they were no longer talking about smashed cookies.

She set the milk back in the cart, in doubt about whether she would have followed through on the visual threat. If she was trying to retain harmony with him, she wasn't scoring any points today. Olivia sat in the cart, blinking her eyes during the exchange.

Lifting her chin, Jules regally grabbed the

cart handle and wheeled off. When she left the store she heard Olivia's high-pitched wails. Undoubtedly, they had reached the candy aisle.

Real adult, Jules. Now he will go home and celebrate the day you broke the second engagement.

CHAPTER 16

Adan spotted smoke mid-morning. Stepping out of his truck, he studied the rising black fumes, deciding it was somewhere near the Matias place. Getting back in the cab, he spun off.

When he pulled into the farm lot, smoke poured out of the tool shed. He grabbed a hose and raced to the outbuilding, shooting water on flames creeping up the side wall. Another ten minutes, and the whole shed would have been up in flames.

Crystal moseyed out of the house, carrying Olivia on her hip. When she spotted the flames, she squealed.

"It's okay! I've got it under control!" Adan drenched the building, hitting every ember twice. Dragging the hose back to the well house, he frowned. "Did you call for help?"

"I wasn't aware anything was wrong." Her features sobered. "Jules's potato plants — are they okay?"

Adan stepped in the shed to check. A moment later he returned. "No harm done. Just smoked up the walls a little."

"How did it start?"

Adan focused on Ethan, who was standing next to Crystal holding a box of stick matches in his hand. "Know anything about that, buddy?"

Ethan shifted the matches behind his back. "No."

"Ethan?"

"No."

Crystal reached for the matchbox. "I've taken these away from him twice this morning."

Rolling up the hose, Adan grinned and winked at Crystal. "Reminds me of the time I tried to burn off a potato field without Dad's supervision. My backsides stung for a week." He glanced at the smoldering shed. "Why is Jules growing potatoes in the shed? Isn't two hundred acres enough for her?"

"They're another one of her experiments." Crystal fell into step as Adan prepared to leave. "She's out here piddling into the wee hours of the morning. I've never known anyone so fascinated with a tuber."

His eyes skimmed her. "You're looking great."

"Thanks. So are you." Color tinged her

tan features. He'd forgotten just how pretty she was. When she'd left she'd been a kid, one he liked to tease. This woman barely resembled the young girl he'd known. She'd cornered the market on looks, but she had a knack for being at the wrong place at the wrong time.

"Guess you're anxious to get back to Florida."

"Not really." She took a messy cookie away from Olivia and pitched it to the dogs. The little girl set up a wail and reached out for Adan. He took her and carried her to the truck.

"Thought you hated potato farming."

She flashed a grin. "I don't like potatoes, but I'm enjoying my stay. I miss the beach, but it feels rather nice to be home." She said the word "home" with a possessive emphasis, but Adan knew Fred had left her out of the will. Pretty rotten deal in his opinion. Why would Matias want to split the girls further?

Reaching the truck, he playfully tossed Olivia above his head, eliciting giggles. "Time for me to go, Cricket."

The little girl shook her head. "Stay."

"Nope, have to go." He lowered her, ruffled her hair, and then handed her back to Crystal. Meeting the blonde's eyes, he

122

grinned. "See if you can keep from burning the place down."

Flushed cheeks darkened. "I will. Thanks for coming to the rescue."

Climbing into the cab, he rolled down the window. "No. Thanks to you. What you're doing for Sophie is real nice."

"It's nothing, really. The shell shop is doing fine without me, and with the economy in recession, I don't expect a big season." Olivia reached out to grab him around the neck for another hug. He returned the sticky sentiment.

"Sorry." Crystal drew the child back. "Livvy, your hands are sticky from cookie."

As he backed up, Adan focused on the two. Crystal might be a throw back from a love child, but she was going to make some lucky kid a good mom one of these days.

He adjusted the side mirrors, keeping an eye on the young woman and child as he drove off.

Darn straight, she would.

Sophie wasn't in high spirits for someone who was beating cancer. When Jules took the banana bread to her late that afternoon, the young mother was resting. She wasn't wearing the scarf around her hair today. When Sophie didn't care about her appearance, she was mighty sick. The stagnant situation hit Jules like a baseball bat. In spite of her family and friends' optimism, Sophie was still fighting a grave battle. Swallowing a knot in her throat, Jules sat the bread on the bedside table. "This will keep for a while. When you feel better and the tube comes out it will be waiting for you."

With a wan smile, Sophie closed her eyes. "That might be awhile."

Jules's eyes traveled her body, outlined by the sheet. Her small frame had withered to nothing. Sophie was never heavy, but this stage worried Jules. She'd have to fatten her up with fried chicken and hot fudge sundaes when she got home.

Pulling the chair closer to the bed, Jules reached for Sophie's hand, paper thin now. "Has the doctor been in today?"

Sophie nodded. "Early this morning."

"And?"

"He says stay the course. I need to be patient — sometimes complications happen."

Relieved, Jules patted her hand. "I saw Cruz and Livvy at the store earlier."

Sophie shook her head. "I bet that was a riot."

"They were in hand-to-hand combat over a package of marshmallow cookies."

Another smile broke across Sophie's pale features. "And Livvy won."

"Nope. Aunt Jube rode to the rescue."

"My hero," Sophie teased, then sobered. "How are you and Cruz getting along?"

"We're not. We're on speaking terms, but barely." After a moment she added, "How I wish I could turn back time."

Sophie's voice caught. "Yeah, I've been wishing the same thing. What would you do differently?"

"Hire a good psychiatrist, one that could help me figure out why I walked away from Cruz, not once, but twice."

"No need to hire a professional. I could tell you that."

"Then why haven't you. You know what? The other night at the rodeo, I think God spoke to me."

"Literally?"

"In my head. All of a sudden, I knew what I wanted, Soph. I want your brother and his children."

"You've thought that twice before."

"I've always loved him; but that night, it hit home how much and how my life will never be complete without him. Heck of a spot to be in — especially when he runs from me like I'm a rabid skunk."

Sophie struggled with the nose tube. "God

and I have had a few moments together like that. And I didn't say anything because Cruz warned me to stay out of his business."

"I didn't warn you to stay out of mine." Jules scooted onto the bed and held her. "So, Doctor, why do you think I am clueless to know why I do the things I do when supposedly I'm quite bright for my age?"

"You've got commitment issues."

"No kidding. The Amazing Doctor Freud."

"Serious commitment issues. I, on the other hand, have committed twice to two losers, so that makes me what?"

"Certainly without commitment issues."

"True."

Jules released her and slid off the bed. "I suppose you'll use the same tired excuse for my behavior. Pop and Mom instilled the fear of failed marriage into me."

"See. You know more than you let on."

"I refuse to blame my parents for my problems. I'm a grown woman, capable of making choices. Admittedly, I doubt myself more than I should, but honestly, Sophie, I have no idea why I've backed out on Cruz twice. I love the man —" She caught her admission, then figured Sophie knew anyway. "Idolize the man. Why would I fear him?"

"You don't fear him, you fear yourself. You think love will fall by the wayside if you marry him — or worse that he would cheat on you like your mom did on Pop. But that wouldn't happen, Jules. I know Cruz. He's solid as they come, and he has a deep love and respect for God's teachings."

"I couldn't stand to marry Cruz and then lose him." The admission slipped out in a whisper.

"There you go, doubting yourself. You're not your mom or your pop. And who knows the issues they had between them that caused the continual battles."

Oh, she knew the issue; Mom had cheated on Pop once and Pop wouldn't let her forget it. Everything set them off. Arguments and accusations were a way of life. It is said there's a fine line between love and hate, and that line was even narrower between the Matiases. The only reason they stayed together as long as they did was for the kids. "Regardless, I pray that Cruz will find someone and be happy."

"You do not."

"I do — sometimes."

"Then forget the shrink. You're nuts. He might be my brother, but he's one good-looking hombre, plus the fact that he has values and morals, Jules. Do you know how hard that is to find these days?"

"I have a date with Haute Saturday night." Men didn't come any more honorable than Haute.

"Really? You guys seem to have fun together."

"We do. He's good-looking, a deacon, prize catch."

"But he's not Cruz."

Resting her head on the side of Sophie's mattress, Jules reached for Sophie's hand and tightened her hold. Sophie was her anchor. Without her she'd fall apart; at times her failures drowned her. "He's not Cruz."

"No. He's not my big brother."

When Jules left the hospital later, Cruz was coming in the front door. He held it open for her, briefly acknowledging her presence.

"Sorry about the cookie thing." The incident weighed heavily on her mind. She'd smashed his cookies. How could she do such a childish thing?

"There were a couple still whole."

"I'll buy you a new package."

"No thanks. I buy my own cookies."

She exited the entrance, and he walked to

the elevator and pushed the button. The scent of his after shave filled her senses long after she got into her car and drove off.

Why didn't she offer to *bake* him cookies? Bet he didn't do that on his own.

CHAPTER 17

Saturday evening Haute picked Jules up at six. She flipped down the visor to shade her eyes from the orange ball in the west on the drive to Pasco. "I've made reservations at an Italian place. Hope that's okay."

"Spaghetti sounds good."

Jules sat back and relaxed, letting the air conditioner wash over her. She'd spent ten hours in the fields, and temperatures had warmed today.

Her thoughts drifted to the shed fire. She'd come home yesterday and found the singed building. She'd frantically checked her experimental plants and the potato lying beneath the heat lamp, but there'd been no damage. She couldn't believe Crystal had let Ethan near a box of matches. It was an act of grace that he hadn't burnt the shed down, and the experimental plant with it. If Crystal only knew how close Jules was to growing a miracle, she'd take her supervisory responsibilities more seriously, but she didn't know, and Jules had no intention of telling anybody until she produced the actual plant. Another week and she'd know how quickly, or if the potato would rot. So far it showed no evidence of decay. It was still a perfectly shaped, flawless skinned baker. Jules was making history, and Crystal couldn't keep track of a five-year-old.

Over plates of spaghetti, Jules caught up with Haute's life. Admittedly nothing happened in the community other than an occasional church function. There wasn't much to catch up on.

Later they took in a "chick flick" as Haute bemoaned good-naturedly. In general, the date was comfortable.

When Haute walked her to her front door, he kissed her. Returning the friendly gesture, she realized that she felt nothing. Funny thing was she could sense he experienced the same non-responsive emotion.

"This has been fun. Let's do it more often."

"I'd love that. Thanks, Haute."

And that was that.

The following Saturday night, Jules came in from the fields and Crystal was dressed to the nines. Jules stepped to the back porch to wash up. "Going somewhere?" Of course she was "going somewhere"; she didn't often wear heels to fix supper.

Jules tripped over a scatter rug and checked her tongue. Crystal's housekeeping hadn't improved. The place was a cluttered mess. Toys littered the floor, Cheerios strung throughout the house, sticky spilt milk spots — black ice, she'd come to think of them, places where someone had tried to ineffectively wipe up the spill, stuck to the heels of her boots.

"I have a date," her sister called. "And we have the kids tonight."

You have a date. Great. Thanks for telling me. The thought of a hot bath and early bed went down the drain. She'd have to give the kids their baths and tuck them into bed.

"With whom?"

"Haute!"

Haute! She stuck her head around the kitchen opening. "With who?"

"Haute Peterson. You remember him — he used to —"

"I *remember* him. I'm dating him!"

Crystal dropped a fork on the table, her face going blank. "Oh you are not."

"I am so, Crystal. We went out last Saturday night."

"Well I'll call and break the date. I understood that he wasn't seeing anyone seriously."

"We're not *serious*." By no stretch of the imagination were they serious, but Crystal had no right to hog in on her territory.

"Okay. I'll call him. Sorry." Crystal poured Ethan a glass of milk.

Jules's conscience cut in. She wasn't romantically interested in Haute Peterson. So why would she object if he went out with Crystal.

Because it's Crystal.

That is not true. I'd feel that way about any woman —

Well, no I wouldn't.

"Fine. We're not serious . . . but we are dating."

"It's not a problem. Relax."

Jules started up the stairs. She never understood Crystal. She leaped before she thought. Just like Mom and Pop, leaping, leaping, and leaping. When she reached the landing, she paused, her temper cooling. *Haute will think you've lost your mind. You can't let Crystal call and break the date.* That would practically commit her to Haute, and she had no romantic expectations for the man. *Darn it.* She smacked the corner post with her fist. "Crystal?"

"Yes?"

"On the other hand, Haute and I are not a 'couple.' Go ahead. Have fun."

"Are you sure?"

"I'm sure."

Stark fear assaulted her. What if Crystal decided to date Cruz . . . ?

She shoved the thought aside. Then she would have to put her foot down.

Sunday morning Jules drove into the church parking lot and searched for an empty space. Her spiritual life had to change. She wasn't sure if God was putting her or Sophie through this ordeal, but she'd been too lenient in her college years about church attendance. She was going to do better. She was going to consider others more often and make church friends. Losing Pop and then watching Sophie's illness had formed a hunger in her to draw closer to God, consult him more often about her life and where it was going.

When she entered the hushed foyer, organ strains already filled the building. The packed rows offered few seating selections, so she picked a vacancy closest to the back. Excusing herself, she made her way down the long row and sat down. When she glanced around, her heart sank. Cruz and Adan sat a seat away. She'd had to step over

134

their feet when she entered the row.

Soon Jules focused on the music director and sang the praise refrain. From this distance she heard Cruz's baritone, strong and confident. Years dropped away and she was a teenager, sitting beside him during youth activities. He liked to sing but resented the fact that he had a good voice. He was singled out too many times for youth solos, which he detested. Cruz wasn't a man who liked the spotlight, all the more reason Jules's twice humiliation had hit so hard.

During the morning offering, Cruz leaned over and spoke to Adan in a tone loud enough for her to hear. "Hear Crystal and Haute are dating."

A slow burn started at the nape of Jules's neck. She pretended to read the church bulletin.

Adan shifted. "Yeah? I hadn't heard that."

Cruz straightened and focused on the organ music. After the offering, the pastor asked that all stand and give their neighbor a handshake. Jules shook the hand of the older woman sitting on her left, then on her right. Cruz stepped around the woman on his right to shake her hand. "Jules! Good to see you here. It's been awhile."

She calmly shook his hand. "So nice to be here, Mr. Delgado."

"I was just telling Adan — did you know that Crystal and Haute were dating? Saw them together in Pasco a couple of nights ago."

She didn't dignify the taunt. Instead, she smiled and shook Adan's hand. "Good to see you, Adan."

His eyes excused his brother. "Glad you're here, Jules. I didn't like seeing your empty seat."

The greetings died away and the congregation settled into their seats. Jules was not going to let Cruz's remark upset her. She was here to worship. Biting her lower lip, she lifted her chin and concentrated on the Scripture reading.

Shifting, she crossed her right knee. Moses. Red Sea. God's children, wandering in the wilderness. That's how she felt. Wandering in the wilderness — without a clue of where she was heading. Perhaps if she were more dependent on God and less on her own meager attempts, she wouldn't be so lost. He had to be disappointed in her. He'd sent Cruz, hat-in-hand, twice, and twice she'd backed away. Maybe he wouldn't send another mate the rest of her life. Single wasn't a bad state. She loved the farm, found joy in the fertile earth. God had blessed her. She was content with life.

Leaning slightly back in the pew, she whispered around Adan's shoulder, "Not that it's any of your business, but Haute and I are *not* a couple. Crystal can date anyone she wants."

Adan glanced at Cruz, whose eyes were fixed on the podium.

Trust God. Have faith that he is in control of all situations. She was getting all the sermon points.

Cruz leaned back and said from the corner of his mouth, "That's not what I hear. I hear that you see Haute when you're back on vacations."

Steam rose from the top of her head. She leaned. "Then something's wrong with your hearing."

"My hearing's fine."

Drop it, Jules. You're here to worship, not spar. She cleared her throat and focused on the message. Everything was fine until the reverend got to the part about meekness and humbleness. She leaned. "I said I wasn't dating *him*."

Cruz stiffened. "You're in church. Show some respect."

"How *dare* you! You started this conversation."

"I was talking to Adan. Do you mind?"

"Yes. When it involves me."

Adan intercepted the argument. "Knock it off, you two!"

The lady beside him muttered, "Amen to that."

CHAPTER 18

When Jules entered the shed to check the plant, heat blasted her. This was the hour she most looked forward to in the day, the magic potato's progress.

Every day her enthusiasm and complete awe overwhelmed her, but when she stepped into the moist greenhouse, she frowned. From this distance she could smell the distinct odor of rot. Beneath the lamp her magic potato laid, bluish purple, emitting a foul odor. Crushing disappointment filled her. What happened? Last night the potato was perfect.

Pulling on gloves, she gingerly removed the stink and dropped it into a plastic trash bag.

Crystal appeared in the shed doorway. "Dinner's ready."

"I'll be there in a minute."

Holding her nose, her sister entered the shed. "*What* is that stink!"

"You've never smelled a rotted potato before?"

"Many times, but never anything like this."

Jules did have to admit that she'd created something: the smelliest potato in history. She turned to the four tubs of dirt with the same blooming plant and jerked them out.

"Why did you do that?"

"I'm trying to grow a perfect potato; not a perfectly obnoxious one."

"A perfect potato? There isn't such a thing."

"That's why I'm growing one. I was so close — so close . . ." She reached into her hybrid mix and changed the formula a third time that week. She recorded the change. The phone rang and Crystal turned to leave. "Good luck."

"Yeah. Thanks." Jules planted the new mix, sick at heart. The recent experiment had looked so promising. She might have to conclude her thesis by stating the obvious: a mere mortal cannot raise a perfect anything.

Seconds later Crystal appeared in the doorway. "It's Adan."

Jules glanced up. "What's wrong?"

"Sophie's had some sort of set-back. Adan thinks you need to come."

"Sophie?" Her pulse skipped a beat. "Tell him I'm on my way."

The Tracker covered the thirty minutes to Pasco in record time. Pulling into the parking lot, she braked, swung out of the truck and ran to the entrance. Cruz was standing at the elevator.

"What's wrong? Has something happened?"

"She took a turn for the worse early afternoon."

"But that can't be. I was with her this morning and she was fine."

He met her gaze. "Come on, Jules. She hasn't been fine since the surgery."

"But the surgery was successful —"

"And the complications continue. Adan says her vitals have gone nuts."

They stepped into the elevator and Cruz punched the button. "Let's not borrow trouble until we see what's going on."

Covering the polished corridors, Jules kept step with Cruz as they headed for Room 326. Adan got to his feet when they entered the hospital room. Sophie had tubes running in every arm, machines beeped. Cruz removed his hat. "What's going on?"

"Her temperature's up; her kidneys are in trouble."

"How high?"

"103."

Jules slumped against Cruz and he steadied her. The warmth of his arm felt so natural she leaned into his support. "They can fix that, can't they?"

"They're trying." Adan stepped aside when a nurse brushed past him.

Jules fumbled in her bag for a tissue. "She was doing so well this morning. What happened?"

"Don't know," Adan contended. "We were talking and all of a sudden an alarm went off. Nurses came running. Then the doctor. They've been working on her for over an hour."

Jules glanced at Cruz. "It's a temporary setback, right? This type of thing happens all the time?"

"I don't know, Jules." Cruz's strained features revealed more than his answer.

Sophie was in trouble.

The three huddled near the doorway, watching the activity, dodging nurses and carts. Finally a nurse ushered them to a small family waiting area. A couple of couches, some chairs. Various sections of the *Tri-City Herald* strung about on tables littered with half empty sodas and cold coffee.

"I need to call Crystal and tell her what's going on." Jules rummaged through her purse for her cell phone. First try, there was no signal. She had to walk partway down the corridor to get a bar on her phone.

When she returned, she recoiled at the sight that met her. Both brothers, hat in hand, staring at the waiting room floor. The sobriety in Cruz's dark features broke her heart. She sat down beside him.

He glanced up. "Did you get her?"

"Yes, she's putting the children to bed. I told her I'd call when we knew anything for certain."

The hands on the large overhead clock crept by. After an hour of repetitive cable news, Jules finally located the TV remote and switched off the set. Night sounds greeted the silence. Nurses going about their work. A meds cart rattling down the hallway.

Was Sophie scared half out of her mind? The notion hit Jules like a wooden mallet. She'd never once seriously given thought to losing her best friend. Sophie could beat this; she'd overcome every other obstacle in her life.

Sometime around eleven a nurse appeared to tell them that Sophie was being moved to Critical Care. They retreated to the unit waiting area and resumed their vigil.

Hours dragged on. Jules determined to keep her eyes open but by midnight she was dozing. Head bobbing. She faintly remembered Cruz wadding a blanket someone had left into a pillow and laying her head down on the sofa. His familiar scent washed over her.

"You always smell so good," she murmured. She reached up to touch his face before she drifted back asleep.

Around two-thirty, footsteps awakened her. Sitting upright, Jules pushed back her hair, noting the stern look on the doctor's features. "Sophie's stable."

A sigh of relief left Jules like the air from a pricked balloon.

Cruz released a pent-up breath. "She's going to make it?"

"She's gravely ill, Mr. Delgado. She's been responding to treatment well, but as you know, we're fighting serious complications. We'll watch her closely." The doctor shook his head. "I wish I could tell you more. Go home, get some rest. We'll call if there's any change."

Adan spoke. "I'll stay with her the rest of the night. You two go home and get some sleep."

"I don't want to leave her." Cruz turned to Jules. "Go home. She'll need you in the morning."

"Only one of us can go in there at a time,"

Adan argued. "Both of you leave and come back in the morning."

Cruz nodded and took Jules's arm and they walked out of the room and to the elevator. "I'll follow you home."

"Thanks." It was very late, and the highway would be a lonely one. Jules climbed into the Tracker, wiped her eyes, and then pulled out of the hospital parking lot. Adjusting her mirror, she saw Cruz's pick-up pull in behind her, a sight she hadn't witnessed in a very long time.

God, I've asked for many things: Sophie's full recovery, Cruz's forgiveness. I know that you're not a grocery store and I can't come to you with a written list. I guess this plea ties in with Cruz — doesn't everything that I ask lately? Let me find a way to win back his love. I promise the third time I'll take better care of your blessing.

A sense of peace drifted and settled around her shoulders with the weight of a feather. Sophie had a minor set-back — that was to be expected. Everything would be fine.

Just fine.

CHAPTER 19

In both good and bad ways, Jules decided that night was a turning point. Two days later, Sophie returned to a private room. Jules resumed her daily visits, and Cruz and Adan battled the continuing drought. Eastern Washington was never known for sufficient summer rains, so every farmer had an irrigation system. Center pivots that could water fields well over 100 acres in size. Both the Matiases and Delgados had old systems that struggled to keep up with the crops. With harvest coming up, the daily battle for sufficient water supply and Sophie's illness took its toll.

Joe Fraker shook his head when Jules told him their system had broken down in the west field.

"We've got to replace that one, honey, or we're not growing potatoes next season."

"I know," Jules sighed. Her mind pictured the tubs of dirt in the shed. The new tubers were doing well, but it would be weeks before she knew if she'd hit on the right formula. If she had discovered the perfect spud, money would be flowing like wine.

Ethan burst out of the house with Crystal on his heels. He raced for "Aunt Jube" wrapping his arms around her legs.

"Ethan! Come back here!"

Crystal stood in the doorway, hand on her hip. "You come back here, dirty boy!"

Jules glanced at her sister. "What's wrong?"

"It's his bath time and he doesn't want to cooperate."

Bending to meet the child's eyes, Jules said sternly, "You have to mind Crystal."

"You hafta mind, Crystal," Livvy parroted.

Sighing, Jules realized that the kids were with her and Crystal more than their uncles.

"That will be quite enough from you, young lady." Jules shooed her into the house and turned back to the boy. "Ethan?"

He shook his head and clutched her jeans tighter. "Don't wanna take a bath."

Crystal approached, giving the ranch foreman a smile. "Hi, Joe."

He tipped his hat. "Miss Crystal."

Ethan stepped in back of Jules.

"Honestly," Crystal exclaimed. "He's been in a rebellious mood lately."

"Want Mama!"

Jules sighed and patted his head. "She'll be home soon, sweetie."

Crystal focused on the trowel in Jules's hand. "Working on your experiment?"

Nodding, Jules hoped to avoid the subject in front of Joe. But Crystal blurted, "Joe, did you know she's working on producing a perfect potato?"

Joe frowned. "That a fact?"

"Crystal!" Jules mentally groaned.

"She is." Crystal sounded proud as a newborn's parent. "And she's very close. So close you had it last month, didn't you, Jules?"

Jules shook her head. "Not even close."

"But the plant under the light —"

"Rotted."

"But you're close."

"I've . . . planted other versions. We'll see." She reached for Ethan's hand and ushered him to the house. "Mind Crystal. Take your bath." When she returned to the yard Joe was waiting.

"Need something else, Joe?"

"What's this about a perfect potato?"

"Nothing. Really. I'm doing my thesis on potatoes and I thought I'd try to grow a perfect one."

"And you came close?"

"I thought I'd found one that showed real promise. It grew quickly, had beautiful spotless skin, needed little water and fertilizer, but overnight the thing turned a strange gray purple and put off this noxious smell." It had taken days to rid the shed of the last experimental stench. "I've planted another mix."

Removing his hat, Joe scratched his head. "Now ain't that something. Don't know of anyone around here that's ever tried anything like that."

"Probably because everyone but me has better sense."

"Well." Joe settled his hat on his head. "I need to see if I can get that irrigation system going again. Need anything from the store?"

"No, don't believe we do."

"I need to get some chaw before I go back to work."

"You know that's a nasty habit."

"I do."

It was hard to argue with someone who wouldn't.

Late afternoon, the phone started to ring. Three calls in less than an hour. Two from guys Jules dated in college who were now divorced and on the prowl. One from a widow man who lived three counties away.

At first the friendly chats puzzled Jules until the dinner invitations followed — and they mentioned that they'd heard she was working on some kind of "experimental" plant?

Jules had closed her eyes and wished a pox upon her sister. News about her project had gotten out. Apparently Joe had innocently shared Jules's experiment when he bought his chaw. By now the whole county had to know what she was working on.

She smacked the plaster board beside the wall phone. Suddenly she was the most sought after single female in Franklin County.

Cruz studied the dry field, hands on hips, surveying the crop. Beside him lay the old irrigation pump, dead as a doornail.

Adan arrived in a cloud of dust. Climbing out of the truck, he said, "Can you fix it?"

"Not this time. The thing's gone for good."

"Man!" Adan jerked off his hat and slapped the felt on his thigh. "And we're only a few weeks from harvest."

"What harvest?" Cruz glared at the crop. "If this field doesn't get water soon, there'll be nothing to harvest."

"Two years in a row, Cruz. We can't hold

out if the crop fails this year."

"What do you suggest that we do?"

"Get a bigger loan at the bank."

"Can't. We're over extended as it is."

"Can we rent a system?"

Cruz turned to give him a cynical look.

"I know — we don't have the money. What about borrow one?"

"How many farmers do you know that have a spare irrigation system lying around?"

"Martindale put in a new system last year. What'd he do with his old one?"

"Haven't heard, but if I were guessing, he got rid of it. If it worked, why would he have bought a new one?"

"Updated? A lot are doing that."

"I'll call him, but don't get your hopes up. You talked to Sophie today?"

"This morning." Adan shook his head. "She's so weak, Cruz."

"Keep praying. She's going to make it."

Adan's eyes scanned the field. "Lord's going to think I've got a lot of favors on my list. Sophie's health, new irrigation. Might as well throw in a new Diesel and a turkey dinner."

"He's a big God."

"Yeah." Adan studied the dry soil, and then turned on his heel. "I'll drive over and talk to Martindale. If we're lucky, he's still got his old system."

"Right," Cruz grunted. "Just lying around for the taking."

Adan tooled down the road, jacking up the truck radio. Hank Martindale's place sat about a mile from the Matias spread: a modest spread but a good producer. Hank raised half the french fries eaten in the Northwest.

Adan spotted a streak, and swerved to the right to avoid hitting it. Heifer? Had to be a small one. He slammed on his brakes, got out of the car, and watched Crystal running down the lane.

"Ethan! Have you seen him? He's wearing nothing but boots. I've lost Ethan!"

Turning, Adan wasn't sure if he had. "I saw something. Had to throw on my brakes. What's going on?"

"Ethan won't take a bath." She swiped blonde hair out of her eyes. His gaze focused on her short shorts and a T-shirt and he found it hard to concentrate on her problem. She sighed. "We go through this every day. He hates baths."

"I think I saw him." He turned and pointed to a bunch of weeds gracing the riverbank. "He went that-a-way, ma'am."

She struck off and he followed. It only took a minute to locate the naked boy huddled behind a tree. Adan scooped him up and carried the boy to the truck and draped his shirt around him. "Climb in!" he told Crystal. "I'll run you back to the house."

Stepping into the truck, she eyed the child. "Ethan. What am I going to do with you?"

"Ever try swatting his fanny?"

He met horrified eyes. "I would never strike a child."

"You'd rather him run off and be hit by a truck?"

He drove up the rutted lane and into the farm yard. His gaze fixed on a stream of water pouring out of the kitchen doorway. "Were you drawing him a bath?"

Her hands flew to her mouth. "Oh goodness!"

Adan climbed out of the truck carrying Ethan. He handed him to Crystal before wading into the kitchen. Water stood on the kitchen and den floor. He sloshed his way to the bathroom, switched off the faucets, then stood for a moment to catch his breath. He wouldn't want to be Crystal at this moment.

"Is it bad?" Crystal's voice drifted from

the back door.

"Define bad."

"Is everything soaked?"

"Not everything. The stool and sink aren't overflowing." Wading through two inches of liquid back to the kitchen door, he took pity on the now tearful woman. "Grab some mops. I'll help you clean up before Jules gets home."

Relief lit Crystal's eyes. "Thank you. It seems everything I do back fires."

He knew the feeling. If they lost this year's crop, they couldn't stay in business. He needed water, and Crystal had more than she could handle.

"I'll put Ethan down for a nap, and then get the mops."

"Where's Cricket?"

Her voice came from the front part of the house. "Mrs. Fielder stopped by and wanted her to come over for an hour or so."

Great. His hands came to his hips and he studied the flood. It would take all afternoon to clean up this mess.

Crystal swung back through the kitchen. As she passed, she paused to kiss his cheek. "Thanks so much. After we clean up, can you stick around awhile? I'll fix a pitcher of lemonade."

He glanced at his watch and decided he

could spare a few minutes. "Sure."

They spent the next hour mopping up water. Finally Crystal said, "That's it. Why don't you wait on the porch and I'll make the lemonade."

"Sure." He meandered to the wide concrete porch where roses trailed the banisters. As a kid, he'd spent many an evening in the farm yard with Jules and Crystal. When Crystal left with her mom, the place never seemed the same. He'd stopped coming around, but Cruz had it bad for Jules. Back then he was over here every day.

Adan located a wicker chair near the steps, lifted a long-haired tabby off the cushion, and sat down. Propping his booted feet on the railing, he relaxed.

Crystal appeared carrying a large tray with a pitcher and two glasses on it. Smiling, she balanced the load, her pretty features red from exertion. "Hope you like it extra sweet."

"The sweeter the better."

She started across the porch, caught her sandal on the corner of the welcome mat and pitched forward. Lemonade hit him full in the face. Gasping, he sprang to his feet, swiping at lemon chunks dotting the front of his shirt. He heard her squeal about the same time he heard the tray hit the porch and glass shatter. Reaching out, he pulled her back from the sticky mess.

"Oh! I'm so sorry!"

"Hey, no problem. Are you hurt?"

"No — look at you. Let me get you a towel."

"Thanks."

She left and returned with the item. "I'm so sorry! That's the second time I've done that. You'd think I'd have enough sense to move that mat."

"No — really. It's okay." He mopped the front of his shirt.

"I'll make another pitcher —"

"That's not necessary, Crystal. I can't stay long. I'm on my way over to the Martindales."

"Oh? Well." She surveyed the mess. "I'll clean up later."

He took a chair away from the broken glass, near the end of the opposite end of the porch where the railing ended and open space allowed for a breeze. He grinned. "So. How does it feel to be home?"

She paused, and then said quietly, "I'm enjoying it. I thought I wouldn't, but I realize now that I missed the solitude here." Leaning back in her chair, she drew a deep breath. "Do you remember Heaven's Rise?"

"Sure, drive by the rise two-three times a week."

"I often wake early and go there to watch the sunrise." She leaned back and closed her eyes. "It's the most peaceful place on earth."

"Yeah, it's one of Sophie's favorites." He studied her. "You haven't changed a bit."

A blush touched her cheeks. "You've become even more handsome." She glanced away and breathed deeply of the fresh air. "I do love the air here."

"You didn't think so at one time. I remember how you always wanted to live by the ocean."

Nodding, she smiled. "That's why Mom took us to Florida. I love the ocean, but after all these years, I've discovered there's no place like home."

"I believe I've seen that on a pillow or two." He grinned.

"Have you heard about Jules's experiment?"

"The perfect potato? Yeah, I've heard the rumor."

"She thought she had it, but then the plant proved disappointing."

Her gaze fixed on something above his head. Tilting his head, he glanced up to see a hanging fern.

"Honestly." She sighed. "Another dead frond." Getting out of her chair, she approached him. "I don't think the plant is getting enough sun." Reaching out, she tried to latch onto the dead leaf. After a couple of failed attempts, she eased closer, fingers probing the air. Adan leaned back as far as possible to give her access. With a lunge, she secured the leaf, but in the process knocked him off balance. Arms flailed when the chair toppled over the edge of the concrete porch, landing him in a petunia bed.

She bound off the porch to assist. "I am *so* sorry."

He sat up, head reeling. "No — no problem. Did you get it?"

Setting back on her heels, she grinned and displayed the dead frond. "Got it."

Later he limped to the truck in a lemonade soaked shirt, wondering what hit him.

No doubt, the woman was a charmer but she was a little on the dangerous side.

CHAPTER 20

Lunch business at The Grille slowed to a trickle by one o'clock. Jules pulled up in front of the local hang-out and got out of the Tracker.

Inside, bamboo blades lazily turned the air. The corner jukebox played a version of Linda Ronstadt's 1977 hit, *Blue Bayou.* Jules's stomach lurched when she heard the familiar lyrics . . .

I feel so bad I got a worried mind . . .

Her and Cruz's song. They had spent hours in this room swaying to the singer's voice. Not only was it their song, it brought back sweet memories of Pop. He'd named the farm after this hit.

Proprietor Nick Olsen noticed her. "Jules. What can I get you?"

"A tall ice tea, plenty of ice."

Music stirred old memories, painful but sweet ones.

She dropped on a stool and sank in the

cool air.

"The perfect potato, huh?" The crack of a pool ball hitting a pocket caught her attention. Her eyes adjusted to the dim lighting and she swiveled the stool to see Cruz shooting pool in the back corner.

He'd heard the rumors. She decided to ignore the jibe. Turning back to face the counter, she concentrated on the Willy Nelson autographed picture hanging over the bar.

To Nick: Best chicken-fried-steak sandwich I've ever tasted. Willy.

Balls hitting pockets. Jukebox singing its heart out. Jules shifted. She should have gone home and eaten a baloney sandwich.

"I'm in sort of a hurry, Nick."

"Cold tea coming right up."

She closed her eyes to the achingly sweet steel guitar strains that now held her captive.

Nick set a tall paper cup in front of her and she reached to pay. Handing back her change, the owner then disappeared into the back kitchen.

Grabbing her keys, she headed for the doorway as the singer promised to come back someday.

Halfway out the doorway, the song got to her. Closing the screen, she turned around and walked to the back of the room and confronted the man who occupied her every waking thought.

"I *almost* had it."

"Yeah." He shot an eight ball. "So I hear."

"I'm close, Cruz." He might not believe her, but he would when he saw the proof of her potato experiment. The newest plant was looking more promising every day. A few more weeks, and she would be able to announce her success. The thought was still bizarre. She, Jules Matias, creating the perfect potato.

Cruz lined up for a pocket shot. "Why don't you invent an infallible irrigation system?"

She'd heard the talk. Cruz and Adan were in bad shape. Their old equipment had broken down, and there weren't enough funds to fix it. Nobody had an extra system, so Cruz's crop was dying in the fields. Her heart ached. In addition to a failed crop, he had to be worrying about Sophie and mounting hospital bills.

"No luck finding a workable system?"

He pocketed a ball. "Not on my budget." He straightened. "How about you? Any luck choosing a new husband? I hear with that potato experiment that you could have your pick of any eligible man around."

"Not *any*." She lifted her chin to meet his eyes with a challenge. For a moment their gazes locked and the music swept them back. Steel guitars, promises of some sweet day they'd be taken away . . . The feel of his arms around her, holding her as they moved as one to the music . . .

He broke contact and made another shot. "You know what those men are after."

"No. Clue me in." Did he think she'd lost her mind? Of course she *knew* the sudden overwhelming interest was in her magic potato, not her. If the experiment worked, she'd be wealthy beyond words. Their gazes held again and she felt herself falling, falling . . .

"Be careful, Jules." His eyes held more than a warning. They mirrored real concern.

"Of what? You know me. I couldn't make a commitment if my life depended on it." Breaking eye contact, she turned, picked up her drink and left.

As the door closed behind her, she heard the song start over. Gritting her teeth, she blocked out the refrain.

She glanced back. Cruz stood at the jukebox, dark eyes centered on her.

CHAPTER 21

Jules made the hospital drive early the next morning. Today would be a long one in the fields, and she might not make it back to visit Sophie later. The thirty-minute drive allowed time to drink coffee and watch the sunrise, spreading golden rays across the potato fields.

It's a glorious morning. What's it like up there? Down here things are going pretty well. Crops are looking real good this season. My experiment is coming along well. Every eligible suitor in the county wants to date me — or the magic potato. Sophie's coming along slow, but sure. Guess I've got about everything I need to be content.

Everything but one thing. Cruz.

She nearly spilled her coffee when the admission slipped out. Thank goodness she was talking to Pop, and not to the Lord. The Lord might have choked on the thought. How many times had he given her

163

the love of her life and she pushed it aside?

Her thoughts turned to when she'd left the house this morning. Crystal was up scrambling eggs for Livvy. The little girl was an early riser. When Jules had pretended to eat part of the child's breakfast, the toddler squealed.

"Stop! Aunt Jube!"

Pouring coffee, she'd said over her shoulder to Crystal, "I'm having the church book club in tonight. Make sure the house is clean."

Crystal glanced around her. "Is it dirty?"

It was. Always, if not dirty, more like ransacked. Jules's sister was trying but her skills hadn't improved. "Just spruce it up a little, and would you mind sticking a cake in the oven? The women will be over around seven." Setting the cap on her thermos, she started to leave.

"I'll be happy to. I planned to bake Lucille something and take it over later."

"Lucille Miller?" When Crystal was little, Lucille had taught her Sunday school class. For some reason, her sister had latched onto Lucille and the two became close friends. Lucille grieved when Crystal moved to Florida. "Have you seen Lucille since you've been back?"

"The kids and I drive by and check on

164

her nearly every day. She's getting a little feeble now."

"Mmmm." Jules was so busy she'd neglected Lucille. She hadn't visited her in months. "Be sure and vacuum around the sofa. The kids have spilled Cheerios."

"Are the women in the study group around our age?"

"Pretty close." Crystal was attending church lately. Jules didn't know if it was for the children's sake or hers, but she had to give her an A for effort. She didn't appear to have formed any relationships, but perhaps that was her choice. Jules never asked. A knot formed in her throat. Now why had she mentioned the book club? She should have straightened the house herself and baked the cake. Now Crystal would want to join in.

"That's nice." Crystal set a sippy cup in front of Olivia.

"Are you and Haute going out tonight?" Jules hadn't seen the man around in awhile, and hadn't given him much thought.

"No. Actually, we only had the one date." She left unsaid, *you put up such a fit I didn't want to antagonize you.*

"You could have dated him all that you wanted." Jules started out the door when she heard the wistful sigh. *Ignore it. She*

165

*wants you to invite her to the book club. You
know that she'll only embarrass you with her
"I'm okay, you're okay" thinking.* Jules caught
her thought. *You should be ashamed of
yourself, Jules Matias. Crystal is your sister,
not some stranger living in this house.*

"I'll bake the cake — and I'd be happy to
squeeze lemons for lemonade," Crystal said.

Closing her eyes, Jules relented. "Care to
join us?"

"Honest? I'd love to! What are you reading?"

"It's a Christian bestseller fiction. Large,
weighty stuff."

"Doesn't matter. I'll catch up." She
grinned. "Thanks, Jules. I'm sure I'll enjoy
the company."

She had no doubt that Crystal would
enjoy the company; few things displeased
her. The question was: would Jules survive
the event?

The hospital parking lot was nearly empty
this time of morning. A few scattered
vehicles dotted the parking spaces. Locking
her vehicle, she spotted Cruz's diesel and
Adan's Chevy pick-up. That was strange.
They visited in the evenings when the work
was finished. Her pulse quickened as she
walked into the hospital and took the eleva-

tor to Sophie's floor, thinking how her friend still had a long road to travel. Once the doctors were able to overcome the surgery complications, chemo loomed in her future.

Sophie was dozing when she entered the room and quietly approached the bed. She spotted Cruz in a corner chair, asleep. Adan sat nearby. Sophie opened her eyes and reached out to clasp Jules's hands. Pain-filled eyes stared up at her.

"How's it going, sweetie?" She glanced at the brothers.

Shaking her head, Sophie's hold tightened. "Not so well, Jules Bug. I'm glad you're here."

Jules smiled when she heard the affectionate nickname. Sophie hadn't called her that in a long time.

Sophie struggled to sit upright. "What time is it?"

"Very early."

"Oh?" Her head dropped back to the pillow. "I've lost all track of time."

"What's going on?" Jules's eyes indicated Cruz and Adan as she pulled up a chair and sat down.

Sophie's eyes filled with tears and she shook her head, pointing at all the medical apparatus now attached to her. "I had a bad

167

night. I'm not improving."

"Nonsense. You're getting stronger every day." Jules bent close and kissed her forehead. "This too will pass."

Tears spilled from the young woman's lids. "I'm not going to overcome this, Jules."

"Yes, you are." She glanced at Cruz who was now awake, watching the conversation. Sophie couldn't give up. Not now, not when she'd fought so hard. Was that the reason her brothers were here? To support this crazy reasoning?

"I'm tired, Jules. Really, really tired. I've fought the good fight, and I'm losing. It's time to let me go."

The thought was so foreign and out of the blue Jules couldn't compute the request. "Has something happened overnight?"

"Something different?"

"Yes."

"Nothing's different," Cruz argued. "She's had a rough night. She's still making progress."

Sophie shook her head. "I'm not, Cruz. I've spent the same tortuous night I've spent every night since I came here — what? How long? I've lost track of time. It gets dark, and then it gets light. I don't know if it's Monday or Saturday. Are the flowers blooming? Is fall approaching? I don't know anymore. All I know is pain and it's not getting any better. We're all kidding ourselves. The cancer was too far spread. I'm going to die and I think I should choose how that happens."

Jules stiffened. "No. You've had complications from the surgery. The doctors will get that under control. The doctors —"

"Are doing all they can and they can probably keep me alive another few months, but at what cost? I've known almost all my life that I have an eternal home waiting for me, one free of pain and illness. My only qualm is leaving Ethan and Olivia, but I know that you will take care of my children."

This was medication talking. This wasn't the Sophie Jules knew and loved. The fighter. The do-or-die Sophie. "Don't talk this way." She glanced at Cruz. "Tell her this is all nonsense, and the doctors will have the complications under control soon." Jules's hold tightened and Sophie winced. She relaxed her grip. "You can beat this —"

"I can't do it this time. This is life, Jules. God didn't promise it would be a walk in the park. I don't know why he chose to end mine so soon, but I trust what I trust, and believe that I'll know more on the other side." She opened her eyes to meet Jules. "Let me go, honey. I love you more than a

169

sister, and I know life's going to be tough for you without me around to cheer you on, but let me go."

Hot tears rolled from Jules's eyes. She turned. "Cruz?"

Cruz stepped to the bed. "Sophie has something she wants to ask you."

She touched a tissue to her eyes. "What?"

Sophie spoke softly. "I want to remind you of your earlier promise."

"Regarding what?"

"That you'll take care of the kids until you decide who gets them. Cruz or Adan."

"Hey!" Cruz objected. "If anything happens to you, Adan and I will take care of the kids. I didn't know you wanted to ask something crazy."

"It's not crazy."

"It is!"

"I want Jules to care for them." Sophie's features hardened. "When they're a little older and the farm is in better financial shape, she can decide which of you gets custody. Right now, I don't think you or Adan are in a position to assume full care of the children. Kids need lots of care and attention."

Cruz's features tightened. "That's a heck of an insult, Sophie."

"I don't mean for it to be, and I've thought

170

a lot about it, Cruz. I love you, big brother, and you too, Adan, but I want Jules to care for them in the immediate future. Later, when they're more adjusted to my death, Jules can make the decision."

"Well that stinks." Adan tossed his blanket aside. He got up and approached the bed. "Don't punish us just because we haven't married yet —"

Sophie shook her head. "I know that you will, in your good time. And I know Cruz loves Jules more than he loves life, but he's a stubborn fool. He's letting emotions rule his life, and you, Adan, aren't through sowing wild oats, my love."

Jules refused to meet Cruz's eyes. *He was in love with her?* The declaration rang in her ear.

"You're mistaken, Sophie," Cruz spoke stiffly. "I run my life just fine, and Jules isn't in it."

"No, not now — not ever if you both continue to ignore what's right under your nose, but that's neither here nor there. Right now, Jules is settled. You guys aren't — you're on the ledge about to go over, and Ethan and Livvy need security. Without rain, you'll lose the farm this year, so for now, the kids stay with Jules until she says otherwise."

"Those children are our flesh and blood. They belong to us."

"I'm not arguing that; but Jules will keep them until life returns to normal for them. It'll be almost like having me — Jules has been around them since the day they were born."

"Jules was off to college for four years," Cruz snapped.

"I sent her pictures every day via internet. She sent them toys and cards — they love her like family, Cruz."

"I won't take them." Jules dabbed at her streaming eyes. The moment she agreed to take them, Sophie *would* give up, and she couldn't give up. Jules wouldn't allow her.

"You will. When I'm gone, you will."

"No, I won't."

Sophie went on as if Jules was mute. "I don't want any of you crying and going all freaky on me. Dying is a natural process, and you're going to experience it yourself one day, but not until you've raised Ethan and Olivia to be upstanding citizens in the community. Of course until it happens, I want to spend as much time with them as possible."

"Sophie —"

"Shush." Sophie enfolded Jules's hand, holding strong. "We've done a lot of nutty

172

things together, Jules, and now we have one more adventure to share." With her other hand, she reached for Cruz. "When it's time, you help me step over gracefully. And for heaven's sake, Cruz, don't let anyone see me looking like I do right now. I want to be cremated. Once I die, this body will go back to ashes anyway. When the time comes, I want Olivia and Ethan sitting right here on the bed beside me, sort of like a family picture. Will you see that it happens that way?"

Cruz nodded. Jules turned away when she saw a tear course down his cheek. She shook her head. "This is like a bad dream —" When she'd started out this morning it was to visit Sophie, cheer her up, and not speak of gloom and doom.

"But you'll indulge me? When it happens, you'll carry out my wishes? And you'll make the decision on who gets my children. Cruz or Adan."

She glanced at the brothers. "They'll both hate me if I do that. Right now, I only have Cruz's disgust to contend with."

Cruz looked away.

"My brother doesn't hate you. He loves you. That's his problem. They say that hate and love are a fine line. It's up to you to help him step over his boundary."

"Come on, Sophie. You're talking out of your head. And I'm standing right here. I'm not deaf. If you two are hatching up some plan —"

"I'm dead serious, Cruz." Sophie fixed a stern look on him.

Sophie sighed. "The day will come when loving each other again will come as effortless as eating cotton candy." Sighing, she closed her eyes. "I adore you, Jules, and if possible, I'll be waiting at the Gate when you join me someday."

Jules's expression broke. "I love you, Sophie. My life will never be the same without you."

"That can be good, can't it?" She smiled. "Knowing some of the hare brained tricks that we've played on people, that can be especially good."

It was close to noon before the doctor came in and Sophie made her request to cancel treatments. No more nasogastric suction. No more antibiotics. No more tubes or noisy machines hooked to her.

The doctor shook his head. "We can beat this, Sophie. I know that you're discouraged, and the complications are worrisome, but you can't give up."

174

"Will I ever be any better than I am today?"

"We can give you a few weeks, maybe months . . ."

"Can you make me comfortable?"

"We're doing all we can; I can't up your dosage much more —"

"Then let me go. At best, the cancer will take me soon and my quality of life will be nonexistent. Send me home with hospice and let's get this over with. I want to spend my last days with my children."

Cruz snagged Jules's arm and as they stepped into the hallway, where he turned her to face him. His distorted features pained her. "I don't believe you!"

"What!"

"You *refuse* Sophie her last request, to take care of the children?"

"If I agree she'll die tomorrow, Cruz. I know her. She's given up and it's too soon to give up."

"Children." Adan stepped out of the patient's room to intervene. "Knock it off. This is the last thing Sophie needs. For once, put aside your petty feelings and do what she wants."

Whirling to face him, Cruz seethed. "You want *her* to raffle off which one of us gets

175

our own flesh and blood?"

Adan nodded. "If that's what Sophie wants."

Jules intervened. "You just berated me for not doing what Sophie wants!"

"Stay out of this, Jules."

"I don't have to stay out of this! You just said —"

"Stop!" Adan ended the ruckus. "Promise Sophie the moon, if that's what she wants! We'll sort it out later."

"She can give up all that she wants; it doesn't matter," Cruz stated. "She's not leaving this earth until God says she does." He stalked off, leaving Jules and Adan standing.

"You knew he'd be resentful about the situation," Adan reminded as they watched him walk away.

Jules focused on Cruz's tall, achingly familiar form stride down the hospital corridor. "I never thought it would come to this."

Settling his hat on his head, Adan nodded. "Sophie was right about one thing."

"What?"

"He loves you, Jules, and it's eating the man's heart out."

"And I love him, but he *refuses* to acknowledge that I'm still here. What am I supposed to do? Club him down and make him marry me?"

Adan settled his hat, jaw muscle flexing. "If that's what it takes. Have at it."

CHAPTER 22

The book club was the last thing on Jules's mind when she pulled into the farm yard later. One glance at her watch and she knew she didn't have time to cancel the event, but she was still reeling from Sophie's numbing announcement that morning.

God, help me accept her wishes — but please don't take her. I know that you can work miracles, and we're all in bad need of one right now.

God could do all things and be all things, yet she'd also come to believe that his ways were not always her ways, and she could only trust that he knew best though it was unimaginable to think of taking two small children's mother.

The aroma of baking brownies greeted her when she entered the kitchen. Olivia and Ethan ate their dinner, a nice grilled cheese instead of something they could stir or dump.

Crystal glanced up with a smile. "Hi. Want a grilled cheese?"

"Thanks, I'm not hungry." Jules headed toward the bathroom medicine cabinet. A splitting headache was getting worse by the minute.

"How's Sophie?"

Jules sagged against the sink and relived the awful day. How was Sophie? She'd just sealed her death sentence. "I'll be in there in a minute." She popped the top off the ibuprofen bottle and dropped two capsules into her mouth. When she returned to the kitchen, Crystal had poured her a cold glass of lemonade. "Sure I can't fix you anything?"

"Nothing. Thanks." She sat down, her glance grazing Livvy and Ethan. Right now their innocent lives were untouched, but not for long. Would they even remember their mother, the impish grin that popped out at the most inopportune moments? The way her nose turned up funny-like when she laughed, or got all red and puffy when she cried.

Dropping her head to the table, Jules fought back the urge to wail and beat her chest. Sophie couldn't give up. Jules couldn't imagine her life without her best friend.

Crystal's voice drew her back. "What's wrong, Jules? Is Sophie worse?"

Biting her lower lip, Jules's eyes indicated the children, and Crystal changed the subject. "Want more milk, Livvy?"

The child turned her palms up and wiggled her fingers.

Jules reached for the lemonade in an attempt to loosen the tight knot in her throat. The tart liquid couldn't alter the painful emotion. "Has anyone called to cancel yet?"

"I haven't had a cancellation." Crystal wet a washcloth and wiped the toddler's hands. "You have time for a hot shower."

"Thanks." Jules pushed back from the table. The questions in Crystal's eyes would have to wait. The book club was due to arrive in thirty minutes. Her gaze quickly assessed the kitchen. Everything was in place. "The house looks good, Crystal."

"Thanks. I've worked hard on it." She smiled. "Don't worry. Everything will go nicely."

Could Crystal suddenly read her thoughts? Admittedly, she was worried about the evening. She was new to the club, and Crystal could be such a space cadet . . .

By seven-ten, the den was filled with chatting women. Crystal served coffee and brownies and visited with each member.

Jules caught sketches of conversation, and there was nothing wrong with her sister's hosting skills, but it wasn't etiquette that worried Jules. Mom had been a stickler on etiquette; that much she could remember, so it was only genes for Crystal to acquire those skills. But the constant referral to Florida, sun and white sand grated on Jules's nerves. She inspected lingering dirt under her fingernails. They should all have sunny days and warm surf.

The leader called for quiet, and the women settled down, opening their fiction study book. For the first ten minutes general discussion revolved around the main character and the author's perception of God.

A brunette raised her hand. "I feel the author's perceptions overpowered the real principle of the book, that of love and forgiveness."

"How so?"

"In chapter 3 where the protagonist must choose between his belief and those of his wife's, I think too much of the author's personal opinions came through. I've written various things, and I try to keep my private observations on neutral ground, while this author shoves his convictions in my face."

"I didn't see that," a woman exclaimed. "I

thought he explained very convincingly why he could not tolerate their situation."

Jules listened, but her heart was in the hospital room where she longed to be. How long? Without the treatments, how long could Sophie last? A week? A month? Cruz was right; Sophie wasn't going anywhere until God said she was. Her thoughts focused on the verse in Ecclesiastes, when God says it's time, my time to go, your time, we all will keep that appointment. Did the verse contain "amen," the sealer? *So let it be.* Jules turned in her Bible to locate the passage, but she glanced up when Crystal lifted her hand to speak.

She mentally groaned.

The moderator nodded. "Yes, Crystal?"

"Sometimes I feel that we can tolerate anything that God sends our way. Doesn't he promise that he will never send more than we can bear?"

The leader cleared her throat. "He does make that promise."

Jules closed her eyes. They were discussing a fiction book, not Scripture. While she learned more than she dreamed in fiction, it was still fiction soundly based on Scripture. And they weren't talking about bearing burdens; they were talking about a man's inability to accept.

A woman lifted her hand. "I don't question God or his Word, but sometimes the burdens that are placed upon us are nearly more than we can bear."

"But a loving God offers to carry the grief for us," Jules offered, hoping to move on before Crystal could pursue the subject. But Crystal was like a pit bull with a juicy bone, and Sophie's dilemma too raw in her thoughts.

"I will never understand tragedy or why God permits it."

Jules shifted in her chair, then cleared her throat. "If anyone understood God's ways, trust would become less important." The women would think that Crystal wasn't a believer when Jules knew that she was.

"Yes, that would make sense," a blonde agreed.

Crystal shook her head. "Still, if I were doing it, I would erase all wars, human suffering and disease."

"But God is doing it," Jules softly reminded her. "Now shall we move on to the book?"

Close to ten o'clock, the meeting broke up. Jules said good night to the last one, and closed the door, her mind still on Sophie's bizarre request. Of course she was discouraged. Anyone would be under the circumstances, but the doctors couldn't allow her to give up. Crystal was in the kitchen stacking cups and glasses in the dishwasher.

Yawning, Jules tidied the den and then walked into the kitchen. "Need any help?"

"No, I'm through." Her sister folded a dishtowel and hung it on the hook.

"I'm beat. I'm going to bed." Jules reached for the last brownie and headed to her bedroom.

Crystal's voice stopped her. "You're ashamed of me, aren't you?"

Closing her eyes, Jules experienced a sinking feeling in the pit of her stomach. "Why would you ask that?"

"I may not view life in the same way you do, but I'm not stupid, Jules."

"I've never said that you were stupid."

"Yes. You have. Every day your expressions and your eyes say it."

Jules turned to face her, then sighed. "It's late, Crystal. Let's not pick an argument tonight."

"I'm sorry."

"For what?"

"For embarrassing you at the meeting. I didn't intend to — I intended to guard my every word, but I forgot where I was and what we were discussing. If that makes me stupid, then I am, but I didn't mean to embarrass you."

"Forget it. It was nothing. I don't know those women anyway."

"That's not the point. The point is that I embarrassed you. And that seems to be a pattern lately."

"You don't think before you speak, Crystal. We were talking about a fiction book. How do you go from fiction to being God?"

"I wasn't 'being' God. I was only offering an observation. I spoke before I thought."

"I've wished I could take back my words a million times," Jules admitted. Her life would be different now if she could rein back all the times she'd refused Cruz's wishes. She'd be married to him; they'd be fighting old equipment, lack of sufficient rain and potato infestations together. But idle words couldn't be taken back. "I just wish . . ."

"That I was Sophie."

"No . . ." Even Jules knew that was cold. "I wish that you would think before you speak."

Crystal sighed. "Don't you think I wish the same thing?" She brushed past her and walked to the doorway. "I'm taking Lucille a cake in the morning. I'll give her your best wishes."

"Crystal."

She turned. "Yes?"

"Sophie asked to be taken off the treatments this morning."

"She can't survive without them, can she?"

"No."

Her sister's features softened. "I'm sorry, Jules. I know what Sophie means to you. And this makes my thoughts and observations that much more hurtful."

Blinking back hot tears, Jules swallowed. "God's still in control. He'll have the final say about Sophie's life."

"And if he chooses to take her home, can you live with that?"

"Do I have a choice?"

"I'll help all that I can."

The trouble was Jules knew her sister could never take the place of her friend.

"Funny." Crystal smiled. "Christians strive to reach their eternal home, but nobody's eager to make the trip." Turning, she left the kitchen.

Jules tried to absorb the notion, the first practical thought she'd witnessed from Crystal. Sophie loved God and always talked of heaven and what she and Jules would do there. Tears streamed from the corners of her eyes. Sophie was going to die. She would drift off, and Jules would be left to lie on her back on a blanket spread on the ground on summer evenings and visualize heaven, and what Sophie was doing that day. She figured she'd want to talk to the woman at the well first. Their earthly lives held the same similarity and forgiveness.

Snagging a tissue from the countertop, she wiped the sudden tears that came as if from a cloud burst; both laughing and crying out loud at the image of Sophie sprawled on a celestial conveyor belt eating her heart's content of donuts. She loved Krispy Kreme.

The God Sophie loved and worshiped would meet her at the Gate, take her hand, and lead her into eternal peace.

CHAPTER 23

Opening her eyes, Jules was met with memories of the long night two years ago when she'd held Sophie's hand during labor, and panted, grunted, and cried with her. Toward dawn, on July 26, Sophie held her daughter in her arms, a perfect bundle of grace. Olivia Dawn came into the world weighing five pounds nine ounces, sporting a crown of jet black hair.

Memory of the priceless moment made her laugh. "It's your daughter's second birthday, Sophie. Did you think about that this morning, and reconsider ending your fight?" Surely she must.

No gloomy thoughts today. Today all illness and trouble didn't exist. It was Livvy's birthday. Swallowing the lump in her throat, she wiped back tears and turned to happier thoughts. What's Livvy's favorite cake? Ah, white. Jules sprang from bed and dressed. Even with Sophie's illness, she hadn't forgotten her little girl's special day. She sent Jules shopping two days ago, and the gift was waiting in Sophie's bedside table.

Within the hour, she had the cake in the oven and Crystal busy gathering paper and scissors. "Look at this." Her sister held up a blue-and-white-checked jumper. "Isn't it adorable?"

"Cute as a bug, but somehow I think she'll like the baby buggy better."

"Only because you bought it for her."

Jules noticed that light-hearted banter came easier now. Lately, they could tease each other without one or the other taking offense.

"I wonder what Adan and Cruz will buy for her?"

Jules turned from the cabinet. "Are they coming?"

"Of course. Sophie asked me to make sure they were invited. Livvy couldn't have a birthday celebration without her uncles in attendance."

Sneaky Sophie; she hadn't mentioned a word to Jules about inviting the uncles. "I bet Cruz isn't crazy about the idea." She bit back a grin. Seemed he was stuck with her no matter how hard he tried to avoid it.

She noticed that Crystal didn't immediately jump to his defense. She fashioned a large pink silk bow, her face a mask of concentration. "At first he didn't favor the idea; he thought that he and Adan should have a celebration of their own, but Adan made him see the wisdom of presenting family unity."

Jules's reservations melted. Cruz didn't want to be around her; but family celebrations were practically sacred for Sophie and she would be upset if Cruz wasn't there. The event was going to be hard enough with Sophie's absence. "I'm glad we're taking them to the park. The hospital is too . . ."

"Dismal. I agree." Crystal tied off a stunning pink ribbon.

Later Jules iced the cake while Crystal loaded presents into the Tracker. The dessert had two large relighting candles on it because Livvy loved blowing out candles more than eating cake.

When Crystal came back into the house, Jules remarked, "I guess we can stop by a deli and pick up food."

Crystal reached for the icing laden beater. "Food's taken care of. Adan insisted that he and Cruz bring the meal."

"Oh brother, I can imagine what that will be." She pictured the men's shopping cart with all its junk food items.

"I warned him to bring something

healthy."

"Healthy to Adan is the basic corn dog, catsup and fries for a vegetable, and a drink."

"You don't give those two men enough credit. They're smart and devoted to the children. I think they're doing a remarkable job." Crystal licked icing off the mixer beater. "They're a little clumsy in their attempts to help, but they're always around when we need them. I'd say either man would make a dedicated father." She took another swipe of white frosting. "Yum. This is wonderful."

"Pure sugar and butter," Jules teased. But Crystal's logic remained. At first, Jules had thought that neither Cruz nor Adan would know how to change a diaper; they both not only knew but she hadn't heard much complaint when the often disagreeable task showed up.

Her sister lifted a self-deprecating shoulder. "Tofu makes terrible icing."

On the drive to Pasco, Livvy and Ethan chattered. "It's Livvy's birthday," the little girl sang. "Can we see Mama?"

"We can go to the hospital briefly after the picnic and say hi." She glanced at Livvy and smiled. If they went to the hospital, they couldn't stay long. Yesterday had been a taxing day for Sophie. The doctors were still encouraging her to continue treatments. When she'd spoken with Adan this morning he'd said that a few tubes had been pulled, but she was still on the nasogastric treatments.

When they pulled into the park, Crystal spotted Cruz's truck. Jules drove to the picnic site, a popular and appealing area with blooming flowers and spouting water fountains.

The two men walked to the mini SUV to help carry the children. Cruz nodded at Jules. "Morning. You want to leave the gifts in the back until after we eat?"

"Good idea." Once Livvy saw the presents, her food would be forgotten.

Jules's eyes fixed on the concrete picnic table where the men had spread a gaily colored plastic cloth over the top. Matching cups and dishes with a Cinderella theme enhanced the party atmosphere. A large center piece of pink and white balloons floated overhead. "You guys did all of this?"

Adan grinned. "What can I say? We have talents yet to surface."

"Everything looks lovely." Crystal seated herself beside Livvy and after settling Ethan opposite them, Jules took a seat beside her sister. Adan and Cruz bookended the two ladies. It was a tight fit.

Closing her eyes, Jules took a deep breath, determined to shake the smell of Cruz's after shave, the warmth of his shoulder pressing against hers. Given a few moments, she could overcome the desire to lean and hug him. Not that long ago not a soul would have thought a thing about the affectionate exchange. When Jules and Cruz were together, it was a foregone conclusion that one or the other would steal a kiss or an embrace.

"Now for the pièce de résistance." Adan dramatically whipped the cover off the bowl.

Livvy scrambled to her knees to peer at the offering. "Cheesy!"

Jules's heart sank. Macaroni and cheese. *Again.* Their diet consisted of carbs and dairy. She glanced at Crystal.

Her sister shrugged. "Want to bet chicken nuggets are next?"

"Chicken!" the kids parroted. And nuggets appeared.

Adan started to dish the food, glancing at Jules. "Would you rather they eat their meal or ignore it?"

The meal turned noisy as the party goers ate their dinner. Later Jules lit the two candles, and Livvy blew and blew. And blew.

Cruz winced and leaned close to Jules's

ear. "I hope you brought a second cake for the adults."

Livvy was blowing more slobbers than wind.

"No cake — but we have ice cream."

"Praise the Lord."

The two candles were finally extinguished, and cake was cut. Jules noticed Livvy and Ethan were the only takers. The adults ate ice cream.

While Jules and Crystal cleaned up, Adan and Cruz erected a croquet set. Jules eyed the work and whispered, "Do you think it's wise to hand Ethan a croquet mallet?"

"Adan will watch him. We play all the time at home."

Jules turned. "You do? When?"

Crystal smiled. "Whenever Adan brings the set over. The kids love batting the balls around the yard."

Never once since Jules had been entrusted with the children's care had she taken the time to play with them. Crystal was always involved in some board game: Candy Land or Chutes and Ladders.

The sun climbed higher and the family played soccer, then a rousing baseball game using plastic balls and bats. By now the tension between Cruz and Jules dissipated. Conversation was easier, relegated to friendly taunts. Jules luxuriated in her and Cruz's former relationship, easy, comfortable. It was like old times.

"Aunt Jube's a big ole sissy girl!" Cruz taunted as he and Ethan played field during the baseball game. "She can't hit the broad side of a barn!"

Jules dug imaginary cleats into the tufted grass and affected an exaggerated batting pose. "Come on, Delgado. Let's see what ya got!"

Cruz pitched the plastic ball and she leapt back then sprawled on the ground in an embellished position. "I'm hit!"

"I didn't come within a mile of you!"

Other players giggled as Jules dramatically surged to her feet, spat on the ground and affected a mock dispute. Pitcher and batter came nose to nose.

"You stepped into that ball!"

"Oh yeah! Prove it!"

Crystal pompously assumed the role of umpire. She stalked to the pitcher's mound wearing her most aggravated expression. She parted the two combatants, lightly slapping their cheeks, lifting her knees to their backsides, and then sent them back to their positions.

The kids and Adan rolled on the ground, laughing. As shadows lengthened, the merriment turned to the big hour: presents. Livvy was getting cranky. It was long past her afternoon nap, but when she saw the mound of gaily wrapped packages awaiting her on the picnic table she brightened. "Yea!" She clapped. "Presents! Lots and lots of presents!"

Jules set the camera aside and popped the lid on an ice cold diet Pepsi and watched the fun. If only Sophie could be here to see her daughter turn two; the bloom on her chubby cheeks, the delighted squeals as the wrapping came off the baby carriage, new dolly and board games. Cruz disappeared and returned rolling a new pink bicycle, complete with training wheels, basket and horn. More snapshots of an elated, bubbling Livvy.

The child jumped up and down with glee. "Yea!"

Jules glanced at Cruz and grinned. "You do know it will be two to three years before she can ride that thing."

"One," he corrected. "Our Livvy isn't the ordinary little girl."

Jules laughed, her gaze straying back to the miniature Sophie trying to straddle the bicycle. Livvy *wasn't* the average child. She was smart, articulate and far older in reasoning skills than in years. Sophie would be so proud of her . . .

The sun cast long shadows across the park as Crystal spread a large blanket on the ground and the party attendees stretched out, exhausted. Livvy fell instantly asleep. Jules dozed and listened to Adan tell Ethan horse stories. Cruz lay to Jules's right, hat tipped over his face. Rolling to her side, she studied him: the outline of his strong features, the dark curly hair. She imagined who their children would have favored, and Cruz won hands down. Dark hair, nut brown skin, eyes the color of espresso. By now they would have had one — possibly with a second on the way. She didn't want a lot of years between the children. She wanted them to grow up close. Of course that would mean braces, cars and college relatively close together — and if they were daughters, weddings would factor into the budget.

She tightened her fist that wanted to stray to his jet black hair, shiny in the sun. Rolling back over, she fought the deepening ache. *Lord, I wish Sophie could be here to witness this family unity.*

When she opened her eyes again she started. It was almost dark. Crystal, Cruz, Ethan and Livvy slept soundly, the kids sprawled against Crystal and Adan.

Sitting up, she touched her hair as Cruz stirred. Tipping his hat back, he glanced at his watch. "What time is it?"

"Almost nine o'clock."

Livvy shifted and opened her eyes. When she spotted the new pink bicycle, she sprang to her feet and ran to the new gift.

Crystal, Adan and Ethan stirred. Adan checked the time. "Holy cow. It's late! If we're going by the hospital we have to get cracking."

A scramble ensued to pack up lunch remains and the new toys. Daylight faded; street lamps in the park began to light.

Shaking out the blanket, Crystal folded the mat while Jules wrestled the pink bike away from Livvy. The little girl broke into tears.

Cruz appeared, scooping the child into his arms. "Hey guys! We have one more game before the party's over!"

Everyone stopped what they were doing and turned to look. Setting Livvy on her feet, Cruz then opened a large bag and produced four big bottles.

A smile broke across Crystal's features. "Bubbles."

"I know what Livvy likes." He distributed the party favor and motioned for the others to follow. The summer evening contributed warm air and softly lit lampposts to the festivities. Jules always favored this particular park; she and Cruz had spent many hours here tossing a ball around, lying on a blanket in the sun on mild spring days, planning a future together.

Cruz distributed the soap bubbles. *Did Jules remember the hours we've spent in this park?* The sound of Jules's delight echoed in his ears as one particular afternoon came to mind. They had gone for a walk in this same park, holding hands. Dusk was about to overtake them, but mid-way through the walk they encountered a tiny kitten, obviously lost from its owner.

"Oh," Jules had said as she scooped to rescue the frightened animal. She hugged the cat to her chest. "Are you lost, little one?"

"Don't even think it," Cruz teased. "You have five barn cats right now. Pop would skin you alive if you bring one more home."

"I don't have a single one like this one." She flashed a grin, stroking the kitty. "But when we marry I'd like to have at least six."

He grasped her behind her neck and pulled her forward to meet his kiss. When their lips parted he whispered, "When we're married you can have anything you'd like."

The owner came running, and Jules handed

the kitten over. "It's so sweet."

The relieved woman smiled. "It is precious."

"And so are you," Cruz taunted as they walked on.

"How precious?" she teased back.

His face sobered and his arm tightened around her neck. "You're the most important thing in my life." He drew her close and kissed her long and thoroughly.

Jules glanced up when she felt his gaze on her. For a moment their eyes touched, and then he turned and led the gang to a lamp post beneath a flower garden and paused. After opening Livvy's bubbles for her, he blew several into the light. The big fat shiny globes danced and skipped around the flowerbed, illuminated by the light post.

What was that look? Had he remembered the times they'd spent in this park — crazy in love? Everywhere she looked she saw memories.

The others uncapped their bottles and blew into the wands. Soon the entire flower garden shimmered with iridescent globes, skipping across the tops of coral impatiens and purple pansies. Jules reveled in the children's enchanted cries as bubbles floated overhead, landing on hair, hats, shoulders and faces. Ethan paused and stuck out his tongue to catch a cylinder globe. The soft lamp light turned the world into hundreds of glistening bouncing bubbles.

Jules was about to lift her plastic wand and blow when she stopped, drinking in the surreal scene. Children laughing; family bonding. Cruz. Laughing, helping Livvy chase floating bubbles. A child's delighted cries of joy.

This was the life she wanted, the life she'd always envisioned. Where and why had her dreams gone astray? Her thoughts were suddenly filled with clarity. She had allowed fear to rule her life, not God.

The thought was so heavy she sat down on the end of the brick flower encasement.

Cruz glanced over. "Are you okay?"

Nodding, she slowly capped the bubble bottle. "Just got a little light-headed." Reality sometimes did that to a person.

On the walk to the vehicles, Cruz said, "I know the kids are tired, but we have to run them by the hospital for a few minutes. Sophie's expecting us."

"Sure, we'll follow you. Cruz?"

"Yeah?"

"Do you think Sophie is serious about discontinuing her treatments? Don't you think she's just down right now and can't see any hope? There's always hope."

He shook his head. "I don't know, Jules. I argued with her — pleaded with her to give it a little more time, but you and I both know the cancer was too far spread. She's right. Even if she continues the treatments, she'll only have a few months at most. I can't wish that on her."

"But we can't lose her either."

"Are we given a choice?" His gaze met hers. "I don't know what life will be like without her, can't even imagine not having her around."

She reached out to touch his arm. "I've tried to picture it, and I can't. The world won't be the same."

He nodded. "I know you love her."

Jules's eyes must have mirrored her thoughts. *As deeply and unequivocally as I love you.*

He glanced over. "You holding up all right?"

Her spirits soared. Concern filled his voice. "I have my days. Losing Pop and Sophie so close — sometimes I can't hold back the tears. You?"

He shrugged and parroted, "I have my days. We'll make it through this."

They reached the vehicles and paused. Cruz opened the truck door. "We'll meet you at the hospital. Do you want us to take the children?"

Yawning, Crystal pleaded off. "Jules, can you and Cruz take them? I have a splitting headache. I want to go home and soak in a hot tub." She glanced at Adan. "Can you run me home?"

"Sure, be glad to. I spent the morning with Sophie."

That left Jules to accompany Cruz.

Later they pulled up to the hospital and carried the children up to Sophie's room. She was sleeping when they arrived. Jules stepped to the bedside and gently whispered, "Hey, sleepyhead."

Sophie opened her eyes and smiled. "You've brought my babies. Happy birthday, Livvy."

Livvy squirmed, trying to go to her mother. Wincing, Sophie shifted. Jules drew the child back. "No. Let her stay."

"But she'll hurt your incision —"

"Doesn't matter. Settle her gently."

Cruz lifted the little girl onto the bed, and then set Ethan beside her with the order, "You guys sit still."

Livvy patted Sophie's hand. "Mommy has owwee?"

Her mother nodded. "A tiny one. Did you have a big day?"

"Uh-huh. I make bubbles."

"Really? I know how you love to blow pretty bubbles. And what else?"

"She got a new bike," Ethan said. "She can't ride it."

"A new bike? Hmm — that must be from Uncle Cruz?"

"And cake!"

"White cake?"

"With white icing! And her bike has a horn!"

Livvy nodded. "My bicycle has a horn."

"A real horn? Sweet. Well, young lady, it just so happens that I have something special for you." Sophie motioned for Jules to open the metal drawer sitting beside the hospital bed. She did, and took out the package she'd wrapped in child's paper, earlier in the week. Sophie presented the gift to Livvy.

Ripping into the paper, the child broke into wreaths of smiles. "A Cinderella Barbie!"

Grinning, her mother nodded. "Just what you ordered."

"Thank you, Mommy!" Livvy hugged Sophie's neck tightly. "I love you! When are you coming home?"

"Mommy can't come home right now." Sophie met Jules's eyes over the child's head. The drained expression broke Jules's heart. "I'm sorry that I had to miss your fun, but I was with you in my heart all day long."

Jules's heart ached when she thought how Sophie had spent the day. Praying for her little girl, wishing . . . She reached for Sophie's hand. "Next year Mommy will be there to blow bubbles with you."

Sophie gave her a sharp look.

But Jules held firm. Sophie had to fight and fight hard. Was her little daughter's third birthday motivation enough to make her best friend battle even harder?

As Cruz had so eloquently noted, God still had the final say. Jules determined to hold on to the assurance.

CHAPTER 24

Sophie's battle ended at 12:05 p.m. a week later. Not by cessation of treatments — she'd struggled to the end, but from a sudden pulmonary embolism. Cruz and Adan were beside her at the last; Jules had driven like a maniac to reach the hospital when she got the call Sophie was being rushed into surgery to insert a vein filter to block the clot, but time ran out. Jules cried for hours, knowing that Sophie had wanted Ethan and Livvy at her side when the end came, and Jules had failed her.

Cruz, Adan and she had stood in the quiet hallway and held each other.

"She can't be gone," Jules whispered. But inside the room where Sophie's battle had raged, nurses were preparing her for the cold journey to the morgue.

Cruz's hold tightened on her and Jules wept uncontrollably in his arms.

■ ■ ■ ■

Sunlight spilled over the potato fields when Cruz drove into the farm lot early the next morning. Jules had been up for hours; sleep eluded her. She'd prayed for sleep when she came home from the hospital so she could awaken from the nightmare, but relief failed to come.

Cruz tapped on the back screen and she motioned him into the house. He stepped inside, face somber. Her heart turned over at the sight of worn lines etching his forehead. The feel of his arms around her as she sobbed last night struggled with the stoic look on his face this morning. He'd aged overnight. "Have you had breakfast?"

"I'm not hungry." He reached for a coffee cup and filled it. The familiar gesture tugged at her heartstrings. How many times over the years had he made himself at home in this kitchen?

Crystal wandered into the room, yawning. Early morning could not detract from her natural beauty. Her skin glowed, cheeks naturally pinked.

Jules absently reached to smooth her tousled mop. She'd rolled out of bed and headed for the coffee pot around four that morning.

Leaning against the old counter, Cruz met Jules's eyes over the rim of his cup. "You okay?"

Nodding, she looked away. She'd woken Crystal and told her about the death and they'd had a good cry. She hesitated to speak openly of the death yet; words only made it real.

Crystal heated water in the microwave for herbal tea, and then sat down at the table. For a moment, silence covered the room. Each appeared lost in thought. Finally Cruz spoke. "Someone has to tell the children." They hadn't prepared the children for death, praying it was too soon.

Jules reached for a tissue when tears spurted. He glanced at Crystal. "Can you help me, Crystal?"

"I'll do anything, Cruz, but telling Ethan and Livvy that their mama is gone should come from you and Jules." She reached for Jules's hand and squeezed it. "They love 'Aunt Jube' and the news might be easier to accept coming from you."

Jules brought the tissue to her nose. Crystal was right. She'd developed an uncanny sensitivity when it came to the children's needs. "Where's Adan?"

"He can't handle this." Cruz glanced away

but not before Jules detected moisture in his eyes. "He's taking . . . her death pretty hard."

Crystal rose. "I'll dress and go over. He doesn't need to be alone right now. Is he sleeping?"

Cruz shook his head. "He hasn't slept all night."

Her sister left the room and Jules stood. "The children should be awake anytime."

He nodded. "Should we tell them in there — here?"

"Let's keep a normal schedule. Let them come to us."

Within ten minutes Jules heard the patter of bare feet on wood floors. Livvy was out of her single bed, heading for the kitchen and breakfast. The child, though exceptionally bright, would have no idea what life changing news awaited her this morning. She burst into the kitchen, dragging a blanket, her Cinderella Barbie, all giggles and warm fuzzy smiles. Her face lit when she spotted Cruz and she went directly into his arms.

He caught her up, lifting her over his head, inducing a round of giggles.

Jules was drawn back to the day she had come home. Sophie had done the same thing; lifting her baby daughter over her head and got a face full of oatmeal. Jules watched the playful antics, recognizing Sophie's infectious spirit still flourished in her little girl.

Minutes later a tousle-haired Ethan arrived, joining the rowdy activities. Rounds of tickling and giggling slowed the inevitable, and Jules was grateful. How did they tell two young children that their mother was never coming home?

Finally Jules took control of the situation and sat Livvy in her chair. Cruz settled Ethan at the kitchen table. Sobering now, the two adults faced the children. Jules reached and took hold of Cruz's hand. He didn't pull away.

He began. "I have some sad —"

". . . but happy news," Jules interjected. Kids didn't understand death and dying. They had to make this acceptable to their limited knowledge.

Cruz glanced at her, frowning.

She mustered a smile. "Happy in so many ways, Cruz."

He nodded. "Aunt Jube is right. It is happy news, but a little sad too."

Ethan and Livvy gazed back, intent.

"This morning, very early, God took your mommy to live in heaven."

Ethan cocked his head. "Heaven? Where

the angels live?"

Cruz smiled. "Where the angels live."

Kneeling beside the table, Jules reached for Ethan's hand. "It's a special honor to go to heaven. Mama is going to be very happy there. No more hospitals, or sickness or pain."

Livvy reached her hands out and wiggled her fingers. Jules rose to fix a bowl of Cheerios.

"Can Mama come home now?" Ethan asked.

"No, son. Mama has to stay in heaven now." Cruz looked away.

Livvy's smile faded. "Uncle Cruz cry?"

"He's a tiny sad this morning." She patted the child's head and spoke to Ethan's concern. "Your mother didn't want to leave you ever, but she knew that someday you'll go to her."

Ethan's brow knitted. "She isn't sick anymore?"

"No, she isn't. She's very happy."

"She won't ever come home?"

"No. She can't ever come home."

The boy appeared to digest the news. "Does she have those things in her arm in heaven?"

"Needles? No, she doesn't have anything in her arms that hurts anymore. No more medicine, no more tubes or treatments. That's why this is sad but happy news."

Cruz knelt beside the child. "It's okay to cry, buddy."

Ethan peered at him. "I don't want to cry. Mama's not sick anymore. She doesn't have all those needles in her arms, and she's really happy." He pursed his lips, as if deep in thought. "I think she wants to stay in heaven."

Hot tears rolled down Jules's cheeks. "I think so too." If only an adult had a child's innocent wisdom.

Ethan nodded. "It's like when Speck got runded over by a truck. He gets to live up in heaven now."

"That's right. Just like the time your ole dog got hit by that truck," Cruz said.

"Mama said ole Speck was in a better place and we could cry, but not for long. Old Speck wouldn't want to come back if he could."

"Your mother was right; she and Speck are in an extraordinary place now," Jules confided in a hushed whisper as she set Livvy's cereal in front of her. "She's special now; very special." Not that Jules could think of a single instance when Sophie wasn't unique.

Ethan sat for a moment, and then said,

"Did she wanna go?"

"Oh yes — she wanted to go," Jules assured him. "She didn't want to leave you and Livvy, but she knew that Aunt Jube and Uncle Cruz would take good care of you until someday we'll join her up there." She glanced at Cruz. "Someday, Uncle Cruz and I — Crystal and Adan, we'll all go to meet her, and that will be a really joyful time."

"And me too?"

She turned to touch the tip of Livvy's nose. "And you too."

The little girl with Sophie's eyes and features nearly took Jules's breath when she said, "Mommy's an angel now."

Jules knelt to kiss her chubby cheek. "She always has been, sweetie. Sent to earth to be your mommy and my best friend."

"I choose to meet her there, instead of her coming back to the hospital," the boy stated. "Can I have some bacon with my cereal?"

"You may. I'll get it for you." Jules glanced at Cruz and they exchanged a mutual relieved sigh. Why hadn't they known that a child's complete trust would recognize the glory of death when adults ran from it?

But how long could Jules run from the fact that she'd lost two of the most precious

things in her life in a brief few months? Pop
and Sophie.

CHAPTER 25

Confident that she could not make it through the memorial service two days later, Jules plowed ahead with Crystal's support. Pop's service had been different; he'd lived a long life and Jules knew that he was ready to meet the Lord. Sophie was ready to meet her Maker, but her life had been cut short and Jules couldn't shake her resentment.

Sophie, as thoughtful in death as she was in life, had arranged her own service. She requested that her ashes be scattered into the wind on Heaven's Rise.

Mellon's Mortuary overflowed with floral tributes, and some area residents had to stand outside the building to pay their respects. The Delgados were loved and respected in the community.

Before sun-up the next morning, the family met and carried Sophie's ashes to Heaven's Rise. Jules assumed that Cruz and Adan would do the honors, but as the small party gathered near the rise where Sophie had sat so many times and pondered life, Cruz stepped over and handed the vase to her. When Jules met his eyes, she saw Sophie in his depths. Sweet, sweet Sophie, who was no more. "She would want you to send her home."

Swallowing back the huge lump in her throat, Jules stepped to the edge of the rise and when the sunrise burst forth in warm, welcoming rays she opened the container and Sophie flew to eternity on a soft summer breeze. *Say hi to Pop for me. I love you.*

The family then gathered in a circle and released twenty-eight yellow balloons, in honor of each year of Sophie's life here on earth, into the sky, soaring, reaching for the peace that lay beyond. The balloons lifted and flew, catching the drafts and forming a beautiful symmetrical pattern. It was as though Sophie were offered up and caught into angels' arms.

Crystal stood nearby holding Olivia in her arms. Ethan stood by her side. Lifting his hand, he waved, "Bye-bye, Mama."

Crystal drew him close, weeping openly.

Later the mourners walked to their vehicles. Jules stood at the rim of the rise, unwilling to let Sophie go.

Cruz touched her arm. "Come on, Jules.

Sophie's not here."

"I know . . . I'll be along shortly."

Nodding, he walked to his truck, shoulders bent. Adan hadn't smiled once in the past two days. When hope was a reality, they'd accepted God's timing but now that hope was gone, the enormity of what lay ahead rested heavily on Sophie's brothers. Two small children. In a single last breath, once again Cruz's life had changed and Jules felt his grief in addition to her own.

When the dust from the vehicles disappeared, Jules sat down near the ledge where she imagined Sophie had taken her heavenly flight. There'd be no more long talks, shared giggles, or cleansing cries. She'd have no one to call in the middle of the night when fears wouldn't let her sleep. Sophie always made her feel better. No more rodeos, planning weddings or marveling over new births. That part of Jules's life was over, still faintly rising in a flawless blue sky, a yellow display celebrating Sophie's life and the ones who deeply loved her.

She sat on the outcrop talking to Sophie for a very long time. About nothing; about everything. Quietness surrounded her. Up here, life was surreal, not so frighteningly real. A soft breeze touched her cheeks. Early morning sunshine drenched her hurting soul. Up here, Sophie still sat by her side, laughing, crying, and sharing her loss.

It was past one when Jules was confident enough to face reality. On the drive home, she found the Tracker pulling into The Grille. She hadn't eaten this morning; her appetite had rejected food for days. She was now responsible for Sophie's children's future. What an awful position Sophie had thrust upon her. She loved one man, and highly trusted the second one. Either would make a good father someday, but Sophie's wishes would be carried out. Jules prayed that she would make the right choice when one became apparent.

Adan's truck sat in front of the café. Jules hoped that he wouldn't want to discuss the tense situation today. The wound was too raw. She needed time to think the situation through.

Cool air washed over her when she entered the building. A few customers sat at tables. She spotted someone at the pool table.

She gave Nick her order, and then took a seat at the counter. The thought of food turned her stomach, but she'd cave in from hunger if she didn't eat.

The crack of pool balls hitting felt ceased. A man stepped to the jukebox and plugged in four quarters. A woman's voice started . . .

Blue Bayou.

Closing her eyes, Jules sensed Cruz before he approached the counter. He must be driving Adan's truck today. She should have known that; they often switched vehicles. He extended his hand, and she blindly reached and accepted it. Wordlessly, he led her to the small wooden dance floor where he turned and took her into his arms. Their feet slowly moved in unison.

His heady presence filled her senses. Their bodies effortlessly moved to steel guitar strains, coming together like an intricate puzzle. The refrain played through her mind . . .

How she longed for happier times.

Snuggling tighter, she absorbed his strength, his scent, his familiarity. They were an intricate conundrum; so complicated, so complete when they were together. Like soda and pizza. Or ice cream and hot fudge. Why did it take grief to draw them, to make them set the past aside and rest in each other's arms? Months of tension now culminated in this obscure grill in a pool of misery, months when they could have both taken and given consolation.

The steel guitar cut in, its aching refrain touching her very core. He released her; she twirled and then returned to his arms, settling back as gently as a feather.

Sophie, are you watching? You'd like this, wouldn't you. Me and Cruz. In each other's arms, dancing as though the past didn't exist, as though he loved me as much as he did four years ago. I love him as much — no, more. If I could go back in time, I'd marry Cruz and Pop would have to find another way to grow the farm. The potato plant, if it materializes, will bring wealth and prosperity, but it can never replace what I gave up.

The steel guitar and xylophone took over, the tropical strains sweeping her to a sultry beach where water gently lapped the shores. The strength of his arms held her, holding on as though he still held a part of Sophie. Jules didn't care if she served a need. He served hers in more than a thousand unexplainable ways.

Burying her face in his neck, she drank in his essence. Aftershave. Soap. Cruz. His hold tightened and they swayed to the vocal strains . . .

Ronstadt lamented that she wanted to go back someday. So did Jules, but years of regret had taught her that you couldn't go back. You lived with your mistakes.

There hadn't been a word uttered, just a holding of each other. A cove in a storm.

He would never show his feelings toward her, but Jules sensed they weren't as dead as he hoped or as hopeless as she feared.

Twirling her again, their eyes met and held as he brought her back. Goosebumps rose on her arms as their gazes locked and the steel guitar played in the background. Deep in those dark, tortured depths she saw a raw need, a need he fought. Cruz was a strong man; strong in his belief and abnormally strong in his sense of right and wrong. For Cruz, there were no gray areas in life. Black or white.

Jules lived in life's fringes, second-guessing herself, never quite sure of her decisions but gritting through them. Sophie accused her of caring more about others' needs than her own, and perhaps she was right. Maybe it was time to think of her needs, her desires. She had only one goal, and he was holding her right now, his pain so tangible she wanted to hug him, kiss away the hurt.

The music faded. For a long moment, they stood holding each other in the middle of the dance floor. If anyone noticed, they didn't catcall or make a big deal of the improper and unlikely scene. It was the cold, "food's up" that came from Nick that broke the delicate silence.

Stepping back, Cruz looked a little

stunned by what had just taken place. "I . . . thanks . . ."

"Thank you. Today — of all days, I needed to dance."

Nodding, he stepped back to the pool table, and she slid onto the counter stool.

If she'd thought food sounded awful ten minutes ago, she realized she wouldn't be able to eat a bite now.

CHAPTER 26

Jules yanked tubers out of three tubs, and flung them into a fifty-gallon oil drum. One more attempt to recreate a flawless potato down the drain.

Leaning back on the potting table, she studied her notes. So far she had only come close to reproducing the magic plant, but close wasn't good enough. She had to have the exact combination, and she couldn't recreate it. Her phone hadn't stopped ringing since the news leaked out about her "almost" find. She'd turned down more suitors than she had bedspreads the past two weeks.

She glanced up when she heard a tap at the shed door. "Enter!"

Cruz appeared in the doorway and her heart did a cartwheel. Jeans and T-shirt hugged his stocky frame. She'd barely seen him since Sophie's service except for the occasions that he and Adan had stopped by to play with the children. "Hey."

"Hey." He stepped into the shed and eyed the tubs of dirt. "Still trying, I see."

Shrugging, she closed her notes. "I assume you have a purpose for being here so early?"

"I came for the kids."

Her brows knitted. "For the kids? This isn't your day to have them."

His features sobered. "Sophie's gone. Adan and I want the kids."

She put her hands on her hips and confronted him. "You can't have the kids. I keep them until you get the farm on an even keel." Sophie made it clear that either Adan or Cruz should be appointed the legal guardian, but only at the proper time. "That's what we agreed on."

"Oh bull. You know as well as I do that Adan and I were only appeasing Sophie. Those are our flesh and blood, and we're going to raise them."

Jules's gaze clashed with his. "I have a legal paper stating otherwise, signed by Sophie and witnessed by her attorney."

"So what? We'll take you to court and fight it."

"And how do you plan to fight it? Neither one of us has the money to hire attorneys." Her heart hammered. A judge would be more sympathetic to kin than friend, but she still had the legal document stating

Sophie's last wishes. The mother's desires would surely hold weight in a court of law.

"I *don't* have the money, but I can call in a favor."

Favor. Of course. Cruz was well respected in these parts and he had many influential friends. She stiffened. But then so did she. Her chin lifted.

"Just try it and I'll call in some favors of my own." The Delgados weren't the only people in the community with prominent friends.

"Fine."

She nodded curtly. "Fine. But you'd better save your requests for something you can win. Like a new irrigation system."

His features darkened and she realized she'd nicked his pride. "Cruz . . . I'm sorry . . ."

"You're right." He met her apologetic gaze. "My crops are dying in the field from lack of water. I'm three months behind on my bank loan, and they'll repossess my truck in a few weeks, but I *will* fight you on this, Jules. All I need is a good crop this season to get back on my feet. I can convince a judge that my sister's kids belong with family."

She retraced her misspoken tracks. "I didn't mean to imply that you couldn't care

225

for them. I know you can, but I know Sophie's concerns, and I'll fight you, Cruz." The conversation was starting to sound like war room chatter. "Ethan and Olivia will come to you or Adan the moment either one of you are able to care for two children."

He snorted. "And you are?"

"No," she admitted. "The thought scares me to death, but Crystal's here to help."

"Looks to me that Crystal is pulling the full load. You're busy all day in the fields —" his gaze swept the dirt tubs, "and butting in on God's business."

"I am not *butting* in God's business!"

"Oh no? You honestly think you're going to create a perfect anything?"

"Well, half the men in the county believe I will!" They were shouting now. Pulling herself together, she forced calm. "I do more than my share around here."

True, Crystal did soothe the kids' aches and bruises and tucked them into bed every night, but that was her job. It was all Jules could do to keep equipment running and fighting pestilence. Harvest was coming up and soon she'd be busy day and night. "You can't have the kids, Cruz, and it's crass of you to come over here two weeks after we buried your sister and demand them."

"Crass or not, those kids are mine and

Adan's." He turned on his heel to leave. Then turned back. "Adan wanted to come the night we buried her." He stalked off.

"Cruz?"

He kept walking. "What?"

"Are you really that financially broke?"

Pausing he turned, his guard momentarily gone. "I'm that bad off. The old irrigation system played out, and I can't get a loan to cover a new one. I figure I have another three days, and I lose this year's crop. When I lose this year's crop, in addition to losing a field last year, that pretty well wipes me out." He bit back a remark, and then said, "I want those kids, Jules. Regardless of what happens to the farm, Sophie's kids are flesh and blood and I want them."

The image of her meager savings f lashed through her mind and she knew the amount wouldn't cover his expenses, even if he would accept a loan. She had experienced the heartbreak of working with old equipment, the constant fear it would go out at a crucial time, the endless worry of lack of rain, harvesting the crop and getting it to the buyer. "What are you going to do?"

He shrugged. "Adan thinks he can find work in Pasco. I'll probably stick around here, find work on another farm."

"What about the house?"

He shook his head. "I don't have any answers, Jules. I can't sell the house; nobody around here wants one that large. I'll lose the house —" He glanced up and met her eyes mockingly. "Or we could get married. That was Sophie's scheme all along."

Jules couldn't deny that she had come to the same conclusion. Why else would her best friend leave such a conundrum brewing?

"We could marry, and you could find that magic potato that's going to make you rich. That would solve my problem."

She faked a condescending smile. "You devil-with-a-silver-tongue. How you do go on." Her smile faded. "Might as well join the herd. Every available man in the county thinks I'm so gullible that I don't know what they're after." Were they ever going to be surprised when she was forced to admit she couldn't re-create the plant, hard as she tried, and she'd tried plenty hard. The realization sickened her, but it was looking more and more likely that her fortune had been short-lived.

A grin spread at the corners of his mouth. "Too bad Haute and Crystal are dating. He's one fine potato farmer; got a first-rate operation himself. With a magic potato, he'd be top producer around these parts."

She threw a disdainful look. "Big deal. I only saw them go out once."

"Oh. Then he's not taken. Good for you." He was back to his old goading self.

"Why don't *you* date?" In the months she'd been back, she hadn't seen him with a single woman.

He lifted a dark brow. "Haven't you heard? I've sworn off women."

"Really. All women? Or just Jules Matias."

"All that I've met so far."

"Too bad. There are a lot of good women out there."

"Yeah, all of them looking for a flat broke potato farmer with two small kids to rear."

"You don't have those kids yet. Don't count your chickens before they hatch."

He winked. "Do me a favor, honey. Jot those particular women's names down for me, will you? I'll give them a call." He turned and proceeded to the door.

She took a deep breath, then muttered under her breath, "There's one right under your nose, Goofus, one that would be content to eat dirt in order to be with you." She rammed a trowel into a tub of dirt.

He turned. "Did you say something?"

Glancing up, she flashed a grin. "Talking to myself."

CHAPTER 27

Early the next morning Jules opened the kitchen door and a man slapped a white piece of paper in her hand. When she read the enclosed document, she felt steam boil out the top of her head. She'd just been handed a court summons. Cruz wasn't blowing smoke. He intended to fight Sophie's will.

The Delgados might be down to their last dime, but they still had plenty of sympathetic friends to fight their battles.

Jules burst into the den, waving the paper. "The nerve of him!"

Crystal glanced up, newspaper in hand. "The nerve of who?"

"Cruz and Adan filed a petition to break Sophie's will."

Her sister's eyes softened. "Oh, how sweet."

"Sweet!"

"They must love those kids very much to

assume their responsibility."

"Sweet," Jules grumbled. "You do realize they'll be taking Olivia and Ethan away from us?"

"Isn't that their right?"

"No. Sophie wanted them to stay with me awhile and then later choose which man got them."

"Personally, I think that was unfair of Sophie to ask that of you." Crystal folded the court paper and set it aside. "We're not the children's family, Jules. I know you and Sophie considered yourself to be sisters, but you weren't, and honestly, if someone took your children away from me I'd fight them to the death."

Pausing in the doorway, Jules let the declaration sink in. Crystal would fight to keep her children? The thought was totally unexpected. They barely knew one another, and other than a brief past, they were strangers. A more disturbing idea crossed her mind. Would she do the same for Crystal? She honestly couldn't say that she would — or if she did, it would be out of a sense of responsibility, not a selfless act.

Crystal got to her feet and stretched. "So, what do you intend to do?"

"Get a lawyer."

"Isn't that awfully expensive — especially

since you plan to give them to the men once they're financially able to assume responsibility? And you will make the decision. I know you." She sighed. "Sophie didn't leave an insurance policy?"

"Sophie could barely feed the children and keep a roof over their heads. I don't know what Cruz and Adan will do about the hospital bill."

"I'm sure they have ways to work around folks without hospitalization. I'd dread to think about her bill."

The amount would be stupefying, and yes, attorneys were expensive and completely unnecessary. She could wring Cruz's neck for starting this war. Neither of them had the funds to support it, and unless she missed her guess, it was going to be a long, lengthy fight, a fight their "influential friends" would tire of quickly.

"I have to do this, Crystal. I promised Sophie."

"Then perhaps Sophie was wrong to make this demand of you."

Jules whirled to face her. "How dare you criticize my friend? You didn't know her."

"I knew her enough to know that what she asked is questionable." Crystal stepped around her. "Is it possible she had an ulterior motive? That she decided that you and Cruz were meant to be together, and she used the children as pawns?"

"Pawns! Sophie would never use her children for gain, and I resent your accusation." And this was the second time Sophie's questionable intentions had been brought into the conversation. First Cruz, now Crystal. *Sophie, have you double-crossed me? Or simply tried to help me.*

Crystal shrugged. "I'm sorry if I offended you. Excuse me; I hear Livvy waking up. She'll be hungry."

"Fine — but never speak of Sophie in that tone again." Jules straightened and drew a deep breath. "I have to talk to Pop's attorney. I won't be around much today."

"That's okay. We'll make it fine."

Make it fine, Jules seethed when her sister left the room. Sophie using the children as chess pieces — Crystal had no right to suggest subterfuge though Jules wouldn't put it past Sophie. She loved her children and she loved her brothers, but she knew that a hoped-for relationship between her and Cruz was over. Final. She wouldn't marry the lout now if he begged her.

Jules left the house, slamming the kitchen door behind her.

CHAPTER 28

Pretty white lights illuminated the miniature golf course. The churning windmills, frog's mouths, kitty lips, and water holes delighted Olivia and Ethan.

Jules putted the ball and watched it roll halfway up the green carpeted ramp, then roll back. Somewhere between home and the lawyer's office, she'd cooled off and realized that Crystal had a point. Cruz and Adan had every right to fight for the children's custody, and she wouldn't put it past Sophie to try to mend her best friend's severed relationship. Other than Cruz and Adan, Sophie loved her and would do anything to secure her happiness. It hurt to think that maybe her friend was wrong in asking her to be judge and jury, and the lawyer repeated much of what Crystal had said; the Delgado brothers had a good edge up in the case. Still, Jack offered to represent her for a nominal fee.

On the way home that evening, Jules realized that she owed Crystal an apology for flying off the handle this morning, so after dinner she'd suggested a round of miniature golf in Pasco. She tapped the ball again.

Giggling, Crystal made some wisecrack about Jules being no Tiger Woods.

Olivia banged the ball seven times and finally knocked it over the wood supports. Ethan jumped up and down, waving his club. She shook her head, and aimed at a doghouse with a large opening that she was expected to knock the ball through.

When it was Crystal's turn, she carefully sat her red ball down and studied it and the target. Jules was learning so much about her sister lately. She was probably some whiz-bang miniature golf player.

Eying the target, Crystal swung and missed. Retrieving the ball, she set it back in place, glanced at Jules with a grin and straightened her stance.

Second try, she swung and barely grazed the ball.

The third try produced a whiff. Setting her jaw, she glanced at Jules. "Whew. This is a *hard* course."

Later they wandered to the concession stand and let the children knock the balls around unattended. The course was empty tonight.

They ordered a box of popcorn to share, and then took a seat on a wooden swing facing a waterfall. Tension drained from Jules. The past two weeks had been the hardest in her life. She thought losing Pop was bad, but losing Sophie was different and she knew she'd only faced the tip of her absence. The long months ahead, and every rodeo from now on would be a bittersweet reminder of her friend. And now she had the added worry of which brother would raise Sophie's children. She thought of poor Adan and his unfair disadvantage. Cruz had been closer to Sophie than Adan, though Adan loved her no less. If she and Cruz were married there'd be no contest. But she and Cruz were at sword's point, so that option was moot.

"I talked to Pop's lawyer this afternoon."

"And?"

"He said about what you said: Cruz and Adan have the advantage."

Crystal reached for a handful of popcorn. "So you're not going to fight him?"

"I'm going to fight because I promised Sophie that I would, but at best I can only delay the inevitable." The mention of Sophie left her blue. She'd been emotional all day, crying at the least likely moments. Every time her cell phone rang, she checked to see if Sophie's number appeared.

She took a bite of popcorn. "Are you and Adan seeing each other?" She should know if her sister was seeing anyone. She should at least take that much notice.

"Not socially. He's come to my rescue a couple of times."

Jules nodded, recalling the seared shed and the plumbing fiasco that Crystal had never mentioned, but Joe had let the cat out of the bag.

"The Delgados are in big financial trouble."

"I know." Crystal munched a handful of popcorn. "Can we help?"

"Their irrigation system broke down and they don't have the funds to replace it. In another day or so this year's crop will be ruined if they can't get water to it."

Gazing up, Crystal sighed. "I'd forgotten. It doesn't rain much here. In Florida, we get a shower almost every day this time of year. Thunder, lightning."

"It doesn't rain here enough to raise potatoes. I don't know why we even try. We should leave potato growing to Idaho."

"Washington has marvelous apples."

"True." Though they were talking apples

and potatoes; a vast difference in these parts.

"So, can we help Cruz and Adan?"

Jules shook her head. "I've thought about offering a small loan, but Cruz wouldn't take it and honestly, I don't have it to spare. Pop was struggling."

They ate popcorn, watching the children frolic around the miniature golf course.

"Pop's crop doing okay?" Crystal asked.

"It's good — looks to be a big one this year, and we can sure use it."

"Is our irrigation system up-to-date?" Her sister always spoke in the possessive. Jules liked that; regardless of Pop's will she thought of Blue Bayou as home and its welfare her responsibility. As far as she was concerned, Blue Bayou was as much Crystal's as it was hers. Whatever the reason Pop had chosen to leave her out of his estate, any profits would be divided equally.

"It's old and breaks down a lot, but Joe manages to keep it going. I'm planning to buy a new one next season, if this crop turns out to be profitable."

"That's good." Settling back, Crystal dropped a bomb shell. "Pop wasn't my dad. You know that, don't you?"

Jules choked on a piece of popcorn. Water filled her eyes and Crystal whacked her on the back. "Are you okay?"

"What did you just *say?*"

"Pop wasn't my real father."

"Who told you that?"

"Mom. My real father was a seasonal worker. I thought you knew."

"No — did Pop know?"

"Of course he knew; why do you think they fought all the time?"

"I . . . just thought they didn't get along."

"That too. Mom said Fred was the only man in her life that she both hated and loved at the same time."

Jules knew the feeling. She could wring Cruz's neck, but then she'd want to wrap it in kisses. "Poor Pop."

"Poor *Mom.* Pop refused to forgive her. It was a onetime indiscretion that Mom regretted the remainder of her life. She begged Pop to forgive her, but he refused. He couldn't move past her infidelity, which admittedly would be difficult. In the end she knew that she was only hurting us by keeping our lives in a state of upheaval."

"Pop never mentioned a word," Jules vowed.

"He wouldn't. Fred was a Christian man in so many ways, but he did not have the capacity to forgive. And Mom wasn't exactly a nurturer, though she loved us, Jules. I've seen her cry on your birthday."

"She hardly ever sent a card. Or called — she could have called."

"She didn't talk about you a lot. I think it was too painful for her so she drowned her pain in red wine. She loved her wine. She was drinking the day she died."

"Pop made a point of telling me that."

A smile broke across Crystal's features. "She was a great lady, not without faults, but with her own unique personality."

Events were unfolding too quickly. Pop's death. Crystal's return. Losing Sophie, finding Cruz again. Learning that Pop hadn't fathered Crystal. Jules's life spun on axis. The moment overwhelmed her. "Crystal . . . I . . ."

Crystal smiled. "I know. You want to be a sister, but you can't. I understand, truly. Maybe in time we will form the kind of relationship we seek, but sisters aren't close just because they're born of the same womb; sisters grow to love and respect each other and that takes time, time we've never had together. In time, we'll form our indelible bond." She reached out to touch her. "Don't question God's motives; use your energy to prepare for the eternal."

Jules felt like an utter fool. All this time she had worried that she didn't have sisterly feelings, when Crystal had struggled — and

240

apparently understood the situation far better than she did. Sisters weren't born with a unique tie; they were created by a lifetime of events, similarities and companionship. She and Crystal had only known each other as children, not trusted confidants.

Crystal knew Jules better than she knew herself. Those were her feelings. She couldn't help but like her sibling, but sometimes — often she resented her carefree style. Pop spoke of eternal matters often while Mom had her own system of belief. Maybe if she'd left with Mom and Crystal had stayed, she might be tiptoeing through daises instead of wading through potato fields. She changed the subject. "I've been thinking."

"About what?"

"Cruz would never accept my help, but Adan might. I'm going to tell Joe to take the center pivots from the west field and haul them over to Cruz's place. If we can save one field for him, it would keep the Delgados' head above water this year."

"Pull our irrigation? What about our crops?"

"They're fine — best looking crop in years. One field can survive a few days without water, and if we lose it, we've done so for a worthy cause." So she might forfeit a new irrigation system next year; she'd faced worse.

"That's risky, isn't it? Like you said, Pop was struggling."

"Maybe, but neighbors are supposed to help out." And one commandment stood out to her: "love thy neighbor." She didn't have an ounce of rebellion with that command. "Our irrigation system is towable. We can set a field real easy. If Cruz can't get water to his crop, he'll lose everything. If we lose a field, we have a couple of others."

"What do you want me to do?"

"Call Adan and tell him that Joe will bring the center pivots over tomorrow. They'll fit because our systems are interchangeable. Tell him to have enough men on hand to install the mechanisms and get the water flowing. We can have him back in business by tomorrow afternoon."

"And if Adan refuses?"

Jules took a bite of popcorn. "He won't. He's sensible, and though Cruz wouldn't accept my help, he's smart enough to know when he's beaten."

Crystal reached in her purse and took out her cell phone and punched a number. Jules glanced over. "You have Adan's cell number?"

She flashed a grin, color creeping up her

cheeks. "I call him occasionally when I get in one of my messes."

"Really." Crystal called Adan regularly. She noted a spurt of jealousy. She was that close to Cruz's brother, and Jules hadn't noticed? A thought struck her. What if Adan and Crystal . . . What if they were to marry and ask for the children . . . ? Panic crowded her throat. That couldn't happen. She wanted those kids!

She shook the unprecedented notion aside. No way. There was no way that those two would attract, marry . . . raise Sophie's kids.

Her gaze skimmed her sister's stunning beauty and she felt a strange tightening in the pit of her stomach.

Was there?

Cruz glanced up when Adan walked into the living room. The Delgado home was man's land. A massive fireplace, overstuffed, worn furniture. The place had a rough look; shirts draped over backs of chairs. Cans of peanuts on end tables sitting next to two leather recliners. Popcorn on the wood floor. Empty glasses. Throw rugs scattered. Boots stepped out of and left anywhere.

"Guess what?"

"Just tell me."

"The Matiases are sending their center pivots from one field over tomorrow."

Frowning, Cruz wasn't sure he'd heard right. "They're what?"

"Sending their center pivots over. We can get water to the north field by tomorrow afternoon."

"Why would they do that? They have their own fields."

Adan shrugged. "Crystal called and said to expect the equipment sometime mid-morning tomorrow. We need to get a crew to install, and we'll be back in business."

Cruz stood. "That equipment isn't Crystal's to loan. This is Jules's idea, and I won't accept her charity."

"Crystal says it is hers to loan, and I'm accepting the offer." His brother sat in his recliner and reached for the remote. "You can be pig-headed on your own resources. As for me, I'm taking the offer and thanking God that it came in time. We just might be able to salvage one field, and that field will keep us afloat another year." He flipped to the evening news.

Cruz sat back, grumbling under his breath.

"You might as well ease up. So what if Jules thought of it? It's a mighty nice offer."

"I'm not going to be indebted to Jules."

"I know. You'd rather be married to her."

Cruz got up and stalked out of the room.

An hour later, Cruz pulled into the Matias barnyard. A lone light burned in the den. Shutting off the engine, he strode to the back door and knocked. It was late, and the kids would be in bed. Car lights caught his eyes and he turned to see Jules's Tracker coming up the lane.

Crystal and the kids piled out, followed by Jules. Crystal spoke as she walked past, but he noticed she didn't linger. The back screen closed and he turned to confront Jules.

"I won't take your pity."

"Good for you. I like my men independent."

She brushed past him starting for the house. He followed. "I mean it, Jules. I don't need your center pivots."

"That's not what you said. You said you were going to lose your whole crop unless you could get water in the next few days."

"I didn't ask that you lose yours in order to save mine."

"I don't intend to lose mine. Our crops are in fine shape. We can do without water for a few days. Your fields can't." She approached the step. "Just being a good neighbor. You'd do the same."

"Good neighbor, my foot."

"Is that any way to sound grateful?" Inside, Olivia let out a squeal. She motioned toward the sound. "If you want those kids, you have to have a way to feed them. And you need to start thinking about ways to feed and clothe them. Settle down."

"I'm supposed to run out, marry the first woman who looks faintly interesting, and get married so I can get my niece and nephew, who belong to me anyway?"

"That's not what I'm asking. I'm not asking you to marry, just start . . . looking around."

"Looking around." He scratched his temple. "Okay."

"Okay?"

He shrugged. "Okay. I'll look around."

"Fine. And . . . I think I'm going to start dating more. We both work too hard. We need diversion."

Swiping his hat off, he whacked it against his thigh.

"Look." She lowered her tone. "If it helps, think of the pivots as a gift from Crystal, not me."

"They aren't Crystal's to give."

"You're wrong. Pop might not have left her half of nothing, like he left me, but I consider my nothing to be hers too."

"That's big of you." His gaze locked with hers. "When did you go all soft on Crystal?"

"I haven't, I've just started to realize that sisters should have a bond. Just like brothers." She met his steady gaze.

"A commitment. From you?"

"From me. I'm capable of making commitments — when I'm sure they're the right ones. I've made a lot of mistakes, Cruz. I admit that. Because of my commitment phobia — or maybe because I want to please everyone, I let you get away. Twice. Do you think I don't regret my decisions? Haven't you made mistakes, ones you dearly long to take back but you can't? I loved you with all my heart and soul. I hurt you badly, and I'm sorry. Now can we bury the past and deal with the present? I'm tired of ignoring the fact that we once cared very much for one another."

A muscle worked in his jaw. "How did we get on the subject of you and me?"

"Because that's what this is all about. You and me. It's not the kids. If you didn't feel so threatened by me, you would let me care for the children until you could. Or Adan could. Neither one of you are in the position to raise children."

"Because the farm is going down?"

"Among other things. You don't even date

that I can tell."

"How do you know what I do?"

"I don't, but I hear talk."

"Yeah, well I hear talk too, and every man in town thinks he's got an interest in you."

"In my magic potato! Not me."

"What's the difference?"

She snorted. "Between me and a potato? If I have to tell you that, you're hopeless." She opened her purse and rummaged until she came up with a white paper.

"Take the irrigation. Save at least one field. I loved you. I was wrong. You were right to insist that we marry years ago. I was a fool. I regret my decision to serve Pop instead of you. I'm an idiot." She paused. "Have I covered it all?"

"I'm the only man you'll ever love?" he suggested.

"You are." Her eyes softened. "You are the only man I ever have or ever will love. Poor me." She slapped the paper in his hand and walked into the house and shut the door.

He glanced down and his heart sank. The woman had just served him countersuit papers!

CHAPTER 29

Jules smelled it the moment she pulled into the farm lot. Something burnt-scorched. When she opened the kitchen door, smoke blinded her eyes. Crystal sat at the table working a puzzle with Ethan.

"The house is on fire!"

Glancing up, Crystal shook her head. "No, it isn't. I'm baking a cherry pie and the filling ran over in the oven." Smoke poured from the stove. "I was going to take it out, but I figured I might as well finish baking it since the oven's already a mess."

Jules threw open a couple of windows. "You'll have a terrible mess on your hands."

Her sister shrugged. "I'll clean it up."

Heading for the bathroom and an aspirin, Jules called, "What's the occasion?"

"Lucille Miller isn't feeling well, so I thought I'd take her a pie. Want to come with me?"

"When are you going?"

"After dinner."

After dinner. Jules dumped two aspirin in her hand, thinking about the long day in the fields she'd just put in. John Mackey had stopped by and before she knew it she'd accepted a date for Saturday night. Now second thoughts plagued her. John was okay, and she didn't feel as though he was interested in her only because of her potato experiment. He was single and loving it, so a movie wasn't threatening.

You really need to tell people the experiment isn't working out. That was pure fact. She'd yanked plants from the last tub last night. Nothing she tried worked. The first "perfect" potato was the last, and hopes for a vast fortune were evaporating as quickly as a rat down a rope.

Lucille Miller's house reminded Jules of a thrift store. Odd pieces of furniture littered the small structure, all well used. Lucille had a thirst for clothing. Racks upon racks filled the musty smelling front room, and if Jules guessed correctly, the rest of the house. There wasn't a woman on earth who could wear that many clothes, certainly not Lucille, who was well up in her eighties. Jules noticed that since her last visit, tags now appeared on every piece of furniture.

"A pie for me?" Lucille shook her snow white head, peering affectionately at Crystal over the rims of her glasses. "Well, if that isn't just the sweetest thing."

"I know you love cherry pie," Crystal said.

"Oh, I do. And cherries are so good for my gout."

Nodding, Jules smiled. "I've heard that. What are all the tags on the furniture for?"

"Those? They state who that particular piece goes to when I pass. I have everything labeled now, even my shoes and clothing."

Jules's eyes scanned the racks and racks of thrift store purchases. "You've been quite busy." She hadn't meant to bring up a sensitive subject. Lucille was getting on in years.

"Little Jules." Lucille stood back admiring her. "You've turned into such a pretty woman, honey. If you'd only let that hair grow a bit . . ."

Jules ran her hand through the close-cut mop. "It's hot and dusty in the potato fields, Lucille. I have to wash my hair a couple of times a day."

Lucille nodded as though she understood, but Jules knew the red light wasn't on.

"I'll make tea." Lucille started for the kitchen.

"I'll make it," Crystal offered. "You guys visit."

Over tea and cookies, the sisters visited with Lucille well over an hour before Olivia started rubbing her eyes, a sure sign she was fading fast. Clearing the dishes, Crystal disappeared into the kitchen and tidied up. Lucille brought out the family picture album of her two sons, their wives and her grandchildren. Jules dealt with a now fussy Olivia, who tried to physically launch herself out of Jules's arms a couple of times.

Returning from the kitchen, Crystal smiled. "All done."

"Thank you, dear. You're just the sweetest thing. Did I tell you how much I enjoyed that last casserole you sent over?"

"You did, Lucille. You sent me a nice thank you note."

"I did?" She chuckled. "Where is my mind?" She walked the women to the front door.

"I hope you're feeling much better soon." Jules paused, switching Olivia to her opposite hip.

"Been feeling a little poorly lately, but I guess a woman my age expects to have an ache or a pain every now and then." She smiled. "Oh my! Before you go, Crystal, I have something I want to give you."

"Me?"

Lucille grinned. "Come with me."

252

The sisters trailed the woman into a back, even mustier smelling, bedroom. Lucille switched on the overhead light, a single bare bulb. "I want you to have this."

Jules and Crystal peered over the woman's shoulder at a bare mattress that had seen better days. Better eons. The thing must be as old as Lucille.

"Oh . . . a mattress?" Crystal asked.

Lucille stood back, beaming. "It's been mine since I was a small child. When I married Gerald I stored the bedding in the spare bedroom. We naturally purchased our own, but this one — this is mine, and I want you to have it."

Crystal reached out to take the older woman's hand. "Oh, Lucille, shouldn't this go to your sons?"

Lucille dismissed the thought with a wave of her hand. "My boys have all they'll ever need. They're doctors and lawyers, you know. Very well off."

"But your grandchildren . . ."

"Even more wealthy. Both mothers and fathers are professionals. Very high income. No, I want you to have the mattress for the goodness you've shown me."

Jules felt a tinge of envy. She'd always been kind to Lucille, but Crystal had baked pies and casseroles, took a real interest in the older woman. She eyed the gift and her jealousy dissipated.

With a grateful smile, Crystal said, "Thank you, Lucille. That is so kind of you."

"Glad I could do it, honey. You've been a real blessing in my life. Now." The woman glanced at Olivia, who was now a twenty-pound dead weight on Jules's hip. "The tiny one needs to be in bed. Thank you so much for the pie. I'm sure I'll dearly enjoy every bite."

On the way home, Jules glanced at Crystal and grinned. "Lucky dog."

Shrugging, Crystal returned the smile. "It was a lovely thought."

"What are you going to do with that hideous thing?" Jules could picture hauling the moth-eaten bedding to UPS to ship to Crystal in Florida when Lucille passed. It wasn't worth the price of postage.

"I don't know," Crystal confessed. "I know it's Lucille's treasure, but I don't have anywhere to keep something like that."

"Well." Jules made a left turn onto the highway. "Maybe she'll change her mind and leave it to someone else. She's not that old. She could live to be a hundred."

"Let's hope," Crystal agreed.

At nine-thirty the following morning, a pick-up truck backed up to the back door and braked. Jules stepped out of the shed, shading her eyes to identify the new arrivals. Two men jumped out and released the tailgate.

Jules approached, eying Lucille's old mattress. "Can I help you?"

"Got a delivery for Crystal Matias." The man extended a clip pad.

Jules eyed the moth-eaten gift. *Oh, Lucille!* "Ye gads. I thought she meant *after* she passed."

"Beg pardon?"

"Nothing." Jules signed for delivery. "Just prop it against the living room wall until I can find a place to put it."

What was a ratty old mattress compared to a zillion Tinkertoys scattered about.

"Thank goodness I didn't bake the cherry pie," she murmured.

CHAPTER 30

The crowded movie complex provided limited parking. John and Jules walked a couple of blocks and John purchased tickets. Inside the cool lobby, the smell of popcorn tempted Jules. Though she'd just eaten a large dinner, when John asked if she wanted a drink and some popcorn, she didn't refuse.

Both agreed that Clint Eastwood had never been better when they emerged later. Overheard conversations in the teeming lobby all seemed to support the actor's performance. When they stepped outside, a light rain fell. Jules glanced up, praying for a deluge. Tomorrow, she'd be forced to switch the pivot heads back to her fields. She supposed, though it was a lot of work and manpower, they'd share the irrigation system until harvest, which was coming up.

"I never thought to bring an umbrella."

John grinned, opening his jacket to shield

her. "I'll protect you."

Ducking beneath the light wind-breaker, Jules laughed as they started off and bumped smack into another couple. When she looked up, her heart sank. Cruz and Midge Parker. She'd nearly bowled them off their feet.

"Sorry," she murmured.

"Cruz, ole man!" John slapped the neighbor on his back.

"How's it going?"

"Couldn't be better. How about you, John?"

"Could use a week of this rain."

Nodding, Cruz's dark eyes fixed on Jules. "That would be a real blessing."

"Hi, Jules."

"Hi, Midge. Have you been out of town this summer?"

"I've been back east to visit my grandmother for a few weeks. How about you? I'm so sorry to hear about Pop."

"Thanks. I'm fine. Crystal's here, helping me run the farm."

Midge's features softened. "I'm so sorry about Sophie. I know how close you two were."

"Thanks." Jules blinked back sudden tears, avoiding Cruz's eyes. Well, obviously he was dating now. Trolling for a mother for

Sophie's children — at her suggestion.

"Guess we'll forge ahead." John reached for Jules's hand, opening his jacket shield wider. "See you around!"

"Yeah." Cruz draped his arm around Midge's trim waist. "See you around."

Jules fixed on the natural gesture and struggled to keep from outright crying.

Later, she entered the kitchen door and tripped over a fire truck. Catching her fall, she picked up the toy and slammed the door shut.

Crystal bolted off the sofa. "What's wrong?"

"Nothing. I have a splitting headache."

"Another one? You should get those checked out. That's the third one this week. Maybe you need glasses." Crystal sank back to the sofa and Jules noticed Adan, eating popcorn, his stocking feet propped all comfy on the coffee table. The perfect family portrait.

"Hey, Adan."

"Hey, Jules. Good movie?"

"Terrific." Now Adan was trolling? For Crystal. Sophie, I hope you're happy! You're up there walking streets of gold, but down here you've started a stinkin' matrimonial war!

Edging past Lucille's ratty old mattress,

Jules went in search of the Bayer. Somewhere between May and now, she'd lost control of her life.

CHAPTER 31

The battle for temporary custody had only begun. Two could play this game, Jules decided, when she bumped into Cruz literally everywhere she went the following week. The brief conversations went this way:

"Hi, Carol."

"Hi, Jules. What's happening?"

"Nothing."

"We need to have lunch and catch up."

"Let's — as soon as harvest's over."

"Hey, Cruz."

"Rick. How's it going?

"Holly. You're looking great!"

"Hey, Jules. It's been ages."

Jake nodded. "Cruz."

By week two of one-up's-man, Jules was exhausted. Her body couldn't take this grueling dating regimen. She longed to stay home and curl up with a hot water bottle, but instead she was out most nights on dates she didn't want to be on. She couldn't keep teenage hours and work in the fields too. Something had to give, but it wasn't going to be her. If Cruz thought he was getting on her nerves by taking her friendly advice to date, then he was sadly mistaken. She poured a cup of stiff black coffee and mashed the lid into place. There were plenty of men in her life. True, most wanted her potato — and there was no magic plant; still, they didn't know that, and if they were dating her solely for mercenary reasons, then shame on them.

Shame on everybody.

She glanced up, thinking she heard God's booming voice chastising her for the childish game. Marriage wasn't a game; it was a serious proposition, one Jules would never take lightly and she prayed Cruz felt the same. Of course he felt the same; he was a good, decent man. She was the one turning him into a basket case.

Tilting her head to see if God had anything further to add, she was met with silence. Shaking her head, she walked out of the door.

CHAPTER 32

Blue Bayou began harvest anywhere around July fourth until late October; today was the last day of August. Ten days prior to sending the big, complicated machines to dig potatoes out of the ground and separate them from other plant material, dirt and rocks, the workers had to be gentle enough to prevent bruising. Bruised potatoes would inevitably occur, so those were left in the field to cure.

Today the killing process began. Two fields would be sprayed with special chemicals that would kill the leaves and stems, and potatoes would be left in the ground for at least twelve days before harvest, allowing time for the skins to thicken. Thicker skins help to prevent infectious diseases, which can destroy thousands of tons of stored potatoes.

Jules spent the morning in the east field spraying. The big machine sent rivets of killing spray over the mature plants. She loved this time of year, when the proof of the long summer was tangible, when she could hold a large, thick skinned Russet in her hand and see the evidence of hard work.

Thank you, God, that I could help Cruz salvage one field. The yield will keep him going another year, and I'm thankful that I had the machinery to help.

If Pop were alive, he would be grinning today. The crop looked to be the best ever. If profits were as high as she thought, she could buy a new irrigation and a laser-guided planter next year; a tractor that navigated fields using satellites, and irrigation that would deliver exactly the needed amount of water.

She stopped at noon and went to the house to refill her water thermos. Crystal was working in the garden, wearing a large brim hat, looking the picture of domesticity. The children played nearby with a batch of new kittens. It hit Jules that Crystal would make some man a very good wife. She took to motherhood and home life like a moth to a flame. When her sister saw her, she smiled and waved, propping the hoe on a tomato stake. "Hey."

"Hey. Just stopped by to refill my water jug."

"I thought about coming to the field to find you, but the kids are so content."

Jules turned on the hose, took a long drink, and then doused her head. "What's up?"

"Lucille passed away this morning."

Jules let the hose dangle. "She did?"

"They found her in her chair. She must have passed away sometime during the night."

Jules sighed. "That's the way I want to go." She thought of Sophie and the indignity and suffering she'd endured.

"Me too. It's sad. I'll miss her."

"She lived a good long life." Jules started into the house and then turned back. "I don't mean to be insensitive, but now that Lucille's gone, can you get rid of that old mattress? We honestly don't have anywhere to keep it, and it's an eyesore sitting in the living room."

"Oh." Crystal's expression drooped. "Poor Lucille. She had that mattress most all of her life."

Jules knew the selfish request came too soon, but she'd stumbled over that bedding long enough. "I know she treasured it, but she's gone now. Call the junk man and have him haul it to the dump."

264

Crystal nodded. "Of course. It is in the way."

Pausing beside the kitchen door, Jules softened. "Lucille will never know — and it's useless."

Nodding, Crystal reached for the hoe. "Often it is the least valued thing in life that brings the most happiness."

CHAPTER 33

Two days later, Jules and Crystal stepped into Mellon's Mortuary. Memories of Pop and Sophie flooded Jules as they took their seat in a near empty chapel. Lucille had outlived most of her friends, and only a stray mourner sat here and there. Cruz and Adan sat in the third row, alone. Jules recalled how the two brothers had taken care of the elderly woman's house repairs and mowed for her in the summers. When she offered to pay, they had never taken a cent.

Lucille's sons, daughters-in-law, grandchildren and great grandchildren filed into the curtained family room, and the service began.

Jules counted the floral offerings, and including theirs, Lucille had six. Very pretty, but so insignificant for the many years of service in this community. Lucille had taught Sunday school since Jules was a child. She'd been in the Women's Sewing Circle, volunteer librarian and self-appointed cookie and casserole maker for the entire community.

Burial was family only, so immediately after the service Jules and Crystal walked to the truck. A man's voice called, "Crystal Matias?"

Crystal turned. "Yes?"

Jules recognized Lucille's oldest son. The family, as Lucille suggested, was upscale. The women wore Burberry suits and large flashing diamonds. Men were dressed in Italian suits and alligator shoes. Jaguars, Mercedes and Lincolns lined the parking curb in front of the funeral home.

Walking toward them, he removed a letter from his pocket. "We found this on Mom's bedroom night stand. It's addressed to you." He handed the note to Crystal.

"Thank you. I'm very sorry about your mother. She was a lovely woman."

Without comment, he turned and strode to a Lincoln and got in.

Crystal unfolded the note. "Wonder why Lucille would leave me a note?"

"She liked you, and you were very good to her." Jules watched as her sister's eyes scanned the message.

Crystal's jaw dropped.

"What?" Jules leaned closer to read the note.

Dearest Crystal,
    Your kindness has brought me many hours of pleasure. The mattress contains my life savings, which by now, should be well over a million dollars. Please enjoy.
                        Your friend in Christ,
                            Lucille

Cruz spotted the dust trail from the field. Someone was in a big hurry. Wheeling the tractor, he drove to the edge of the fence row to identify the maniac. These young farm hands drove like the wind. Jules's mini SUV came into view and he frowned.

Killing the engine, he jumped from the tractor and headed for the fence. Jules pulled up, standing the Tracker on end. She piled out, followed by Crystal.

His heart hit his stomach. "What's wrong? One of the kids hurt?"

Gasping now, Jules said, "You have to come with us."

"What's wrong? Is Ethan hurt?"

"No!" Crystal stood beside the Tracker, wringing her hands. "Get Adan. We have to search the Pasco dump."

"What?"

"The dump!" Jules screamed. "We have to find Lucille's *mattress.*" She whirled to face Crystal. "You're sure the junk man took it to the dump?"

"He said he was on his way when he picked it up."

"Okay. Calm down." Jules drew a deep breath. "We have to stay calm. He picked it up yesterday. With any luck, we can find it."

Cruz stared at the babbling women. They didn't make a lick of sense. "Anybody care to fill me in on the crisis? Where are the kids? Are they all right?"

"They're fine. I left them with Anne. Lucille gave Crystal her prized mattress, and I told her to have it hauled to the dump."

"Why would you want Lucille's mattress?"

"I *didn't* want it! It was ugly and an eyesore, but Lucille left Crystal a note on her bedside table, saying that her life's fortune was in that mattress. Over a million dollars!"

"A million dollars!" Cruz's jaw sagged. He cleared the fence with one bound.

"You drive," Jules called. "I'm a nervous wreck!"

Wheeling the Tracker around, Cruz floored the gas pedal. A couple of miles down the road they picked up Adan, who was plowing under the water deprived crop. With little more than "get in!" Adan was drafted into the search party. Crystal filled him in on the crisis as the vehicle sped down the road.

Forty-five minutes later, the truck turned into Pasco Sanitary Landfill. Bulldozers worked to bury monstrous piles of refuse in smelly graves.

The four piled out of the truck and ran willy-nilly, trying to spot a mattress. The monumental task was like trying to find a gallstone in a hospital compactor.

"Somebody better get permission for us to be digging around out here!" Cruz called. The last thing they needed was to be thrown in jail for looting.

Jules volunteered. Cruz figured she was about to lose her lunch anyway.

Permission to dig in Pasco's ruins didn't come easy; only when Jules explained the unusual request were the machines shut down.

Since a mattress wasn't a small item to spot, trash surprisingly blended. Four hours later, dirty, hot, discouraged and tired, the four piled back in the Tracker, a million dollars short of their goal.

The stench in close quarters forced the occupants to roll down windows and air out the stink.

Jules glanced over and burst into laughter. She pointed to Cruz. "You have ketchup on your shirt."

"Oh yeah?" Cruz pointed to an imaginary spot on her shirt, and then flipped her nose when she fell for the oldest trick in the world.

Even with the stench, the four were hungry. No one had eaten since breakfast. Cruz pulled into a drive-through and ordered four burgers, four fries, and four super-sized Cokes.

Over inhaled dinner, the men questioned Crystal. "You're sure the junk man was on his way to the landfill?"

"He said he was."

"Did you call to check and see if he made it?"

Crystal shook her head. "I didn't think to do that."

Adan bit into his burger and spoke around a mouthful. "Maybe we should check."

They finished up, and Cruz pulled out of the fast food drive. Tooling down the highway, they made their plan.

"Who took the mattress?" Cruz asked.

"I don't know . . . the truck said Smart Refuse."

"Old man Smart," Adan said. "He lives

out on Road 36."

It was nearing ten o'clock when they drove into Smart's drive. Not a light shone in the house.

Cruz and Jules stepped out of the SUV and walked to the door and knocked. It took several attempts to rouse the old man. Dogs barked. When he opened the door, Jules spotted a shotgun propped by the door.

Cruz nodded. "Sorry to bother you at this hour, Mr. Smart, but we have an emergency."

The man eyed Cruz in the dim porch light. "State your business."

"I'm Cruz Delgado — I live off Road 29?"

"Buff Delgado's boy?"

"Yes sir."

He opened the screen. "What's the emergency?"

"We're looking for a mattress you hauled away yesterday."

"Yesterday?"

"From the Matiases'?"

"Sure. What about it?"

"Did you take it to the landfill?"

"No."

"Where is it?"

"In my garage. Why?"

"We need it back."

"What for? It's no good. I put it in the

272

garage for my dogs to sleep on."

Reaching for his wallet, Cruz offered, "I'll give you a hundred dollars for it."

"A hundred dollars?"

"Yeah — Crystal's decided she should keep it."

"Tell her to take it. It's hers anyway."

Cruz pushed the bill into the older man's hand. "No, you take this for your trouble. Seems Lucille Miller left some money in it intended for Crystal."

"You don't say!"

Cruz nodded. Jules knew that Smart was a fair man. He wouldn't claim ownership.

"Load 'er up. Just watch the dogs. One of 'em will bite the fire outta you." He closed the door, hundred dollar bill in hand.

Jules wondered which one. Smart forgot to say.

Fifteen minutes later, and after a minor skirmish with a tenacious mutt, Cruz pulled the vehicle onto the highway with a large ratty looking mattress tied to the top.

When the final count was tallied, Crystal Matias had a cool million, five hundred, twenty-six dollars, two quarters, three dimes and four pennies. Lucille had scrimped and saved all of her life, stuffing her fortune in her mattress.

Well, good for Crystal, Jules decided.

Blessed are the merciful, for they shall obtain mercy.

CHAPTER 34

A million dollars altered a custody battle, all parties concerned knew it. Crystal and Jules now had the funds to fight him and Adan until the kids were grown. The idea hung in Cruz's mind when Jules glanced at the clock and noted the time. The children would be asleep, but the Ramseys would be wondering what happened to Jules.

"You better give Ann a call and let her know where we are," Cruz reminded.

Jules reached for her cell phone and dialed. Crystal started to clear the table of Coke cups, seemingly unaffected by her sudden windfall. "The Tracker won't hold all four of us and the children. Why don't I take Adan home, Cruz can go with Jules to pick up the children, and then she can drop Cruz off on the way home?"

Yawning, Adan stretched. "Sounds good to me. I'm beat." Sitting back in his chair, he grinned. "How does it feel to be a millionaire?"

Crystal paused, studying the thought. "Exactly the way it felt to be dirt poor."

He glanced at Jules and winked. "You'll be like Jules and her magic potato plant. You'll have to fight the men away now."

Jules clicked off from talking to Ann Ramsey. "She says the kids are doing fine. I told her we'd be over in a few minutes to pick them up."

The four left the house together. Adan spoke up. "Hey, Crystal, can you drive me by the field on the way home? I forgot to put a lock on the tractor."

Cruz frowned.

"Hey," Adan apologized. "Everything happened so fast I didn't get a chance to lock down the equipment."

"Sure, I'll take you by the field." Crystal and Adan walked to the farm pick-up while Jules and Cruz headed for the Tracker.

Jules had purchased the vehicle her senior year so the interior was as familiar to Cruz as it was to Jules. They'd spent hours in the truck, talking, dreaming of their future.

"When we marry, I want kids right away."

"How many?"

"Two."

"What if I want three or four?"

He leaned to kiss her. "Why not make it six?

276

That's a good even number."

Familiar bitterness rose to the back of his throat. Everyone told him to get over her; well he'd tried, but everywhere he turned she was there. Lending him equipment. Raising Sophie's kids, flaunting the notion that she was about to create a potato that would stun the world.

Jules pitched the keys at him. "You drive."

He caught them, resenting the familiarity the simple act invoked. She'd never driven when they were together. She didn't like to drive. She preferred sitting next to him, her arm around his shoulder as he drove. They slid into the vehicle and he started the engine. She sat far to his right, crowding the door. Was she fighting her memories? The big scene she made the other night: "You're right, Cruz. I loved you." Was that an emotional outburst or a fact?

If it was a fact, then she'd lost the battle. He'd asked her twice to marry him and both times she had walked away. He wouldn't give her a third chance even if it meant he had to fight her for the children the rest of his life. And fight his feelings for her.

Marry and settle down, she suggested.

If that's what it took, he'd do it; Jules was not going to back him into a corner on this one, but how did he find a woman that he could love as much as he loved this one sitting beside him? The thought irked him, but it was there, bold as orange hair.

Wheeling out of the barnyard, they drove in silence to the Ramseys. The front porch light glowed as they pulled in. Cruz got out and followed Jules into the house. Minutes later they emerged, Cruz carrying a sleeping Ethan and Jules lugging a limp Olivia.

Cruz laid Ethan on the driver's seat, and then walked around and reached for Olivia. Jules got in and then took the sleeping child.

A Tracker wasn't that roomy. Two sleeping kids and two adults made for a cramped front seat. "Seat belt?" Jules frowned. "I can't get mine fastened."

Cruz reached over and drew the belt across her and Olivia. Their faces at one point were so close he could smell her shampoo. Some floral scent mixed with the Pasco landfill. Memories hit him hard. Drawing back, he reached for Ethan. "We have to put them in the backseat."

"You're right."

Together they shifted the sleeping children to the backseat and fastened the seat belt tightly around them.

"Let's hope we're not stopped on the way home. This is illegal," Cruz noted.

"I'll take it easy." The farms were a couple

of miles apart. There'd be no traffic at this hour of the night. Switching on the engine, he backed up and turned the SUV around.

Jules's closeness was like a shroud. All these weeks she'd been back and he'd successfully avoided this closeness. Now she was sitting next to him, and it felt so right it hurt.

She broke the stilted silence. "What do you think about Crystal's windfall?"

"I'm happy for her."

She smiled. "It is wonderful, isn't it? Yet Crystal is the least likely to want material things."

"Can't imagine that she wouldn't welcome a million dollars."

"Honestly? I think the fun of the mattress hunt brought her more happiness. And you and Adan have been so good to mow Lucille's lawn and care for her house. Why didn't she leave it to you?"

"Does it matter? Crystal will manage the money well. Maybe Lucille sensed that."

Cruz approached the fork in the country road. "Even if your potato experiment doesn't work out, you'll have the money to fight for these children until we're old and gray."

Jules glanced over. "That isn't our intent."

"Yeah?" He turned to look at her. "What

is your purpose, Jules?" His anger boiled over. He'd lost most of his crops, he was flat broke, and now Jules was smack back in his life, the very thing he intended to avoid. What did God want of him? He wasn't a saint. "I can't fight you forever, and I'm not about to go out and marry the first available woman in order to get Sophie's children."

Headlights appeared. An oncoming vehicle barreled over the rise as Cruz pulled onto the road.

"Cruz!"

Cruz saw the impact coming. He swerved, throwing the driver's side in position to take the full impact.

The sound of metal meeting metal. Shattering glass. Then silence.

Flashing red lights streaked through the night. Jules sat beside Cruz in the ambulance, praying. The children were in a second ambulance, unhurt. Liquid from tubes ran into Cruz's arm.

The teenager driving the second car was in a third ambulance ahead. None of the injuries were thought to be life threatening, but Cruz was still unconscious from the impact. Jules held tight to his hand, urging him to open his eyes as the paramedics worked.

The ride to Pasco encompassed an eternity, but the forthcoming wait while the doctors examined Cruz and the children was even more tortuous. Jules stepped to the waiting room and phoned Crystal.

Her sister answered as though she had been expecting the late night call. "The children are okay," Jules started. "We've had an accident and Cruz . . ." Her voice broke and she lost her earlier calm. "Cruz is hurt."

"I'll call Adan and we'll be there within the hour."

Jules returned to the emergency room. The doctors insisted that she be checked for injuries. The children were already in the process.

In time she was given a clean bill of health, and she walked back to Cruz's cubicle and found him sitting up on the side of the gurney. With a cry, she went into his arms.

Wincing, he held her, urging calm. "Careful. I have a couple of busted ribs and I can't breathe."

Holding onto his neck, she whispered, "You scared me to death."

"Oh yeah?" His hold tightened. "Consider it payback, honey."

"You saved our lives."

Color crept into his cheeks. "Did you check that guy's speed?"

"I did, and if you hadn't have turned your side into the oncoming impact, the driver would have hit us head on."

"Ethan?" Cruz pulled back. "Olivia?"

"They're going to slap a stiff fine on you because both children were sharing a seat belt, but they're not hurt. Not a single broken bone or bloody nose."

He nodded. "What about the other driver?"

"Scrapes and bruises. He was wearing a seat belt. A young kid — one of the seasonal workers."

Her gaze forced his back to meet hers. "You literally saved our lives. Thank you." Her eyes focused on the streak of blood covering his shirt. "Oh, sweetie. There's blood . . ."

He caught her hand. "Ketchup. Remember?"

She recalled the afternoon at the dump and glanced down to appraise her appearance. And stench. Pathetic.

Adan and Crystal arrived an hour later, still wearing the same clothing they'd worn all day. The Landfill Collection. Nurses and aides side-stepped the strange, reeking assemblage as they went about their work.

Crystal soothed the children in their cubicles while they waited for dismissal papers. Cruz had to spend the night for observation.

When the excitement died down, Cruz lay on the gurney in a sedated sleep. When Adan offered to spend the remainder of the night, Jules demanded that she stay.

Adan grinned. "Okay. You win. You stay. I'll help Crystal get the kids home and into bed."

"You're right in the middle of plowing," Jules reminded. "Joe will run things for me, but you'll have to pick up the slack for Cruz."

Adan saluted. "Will do. Sir!"

Watching the couple carry sleepy children to the emergency entrance, Jules closed her eyes. *Thank you, God. For being there tonight. For protecting the children, and for protecting Cruz.*

"What about the Tracker?" Adan's voice drew her back.

"It's totaled." She would miss the truck and its many memories. The vehicle was a part of her . . . and Cruz.

"You need a new car anyway," Crystal soothed. "I brought the farm pick-up in case you need it. I'll ride with Adan. Thank the good Lord that everything turned out all right. This could have been a tragedy."

The couple and children disappeared through the double emergency room doors, and Jules rested her forehead against a cool window frame. Losing the car bothered her, but not nearly as much as the man lying upstairs hurt.

Cruz, heavily medicated for pain, slept through the night. She settled beside his bed, into a leather recliner and dozed. Around 5:00 a.m her cell phone rang. It was Crystal.

"Guess what."

"I can't imagine." The past twenty-four hours had been one crisis after the other. Digging through a landfill. Finding over a million dollars stuffed in Lucille's old mattress. The accident. Cruz's injuries.

"The Delgados' tractor was stolen. Adan called a few minutes ago."

Closing her eyes, she murmured, "It doesn't surprise me." She glanced at the patient. If it weren't for bad luck, Cruz wouldn't have any luck at all.

CHAPTER 35

Light streaked the sky when Jules left the hospital. It looked to be another picturesque Washington harvest day. She had sat with Cruz, holding his hand as he slept. Once, he'd lifted his head and kissed her — he was totally out of it, and told her not to worry. He was fine. She'd shamelessly taken full advantage of his muddled state and kissed him back. Several times.

Now she left him to sleep off the numbing effects, totally drained. After a quick stop for fuel and a cup of coffee, she headed home. She'd catch a couple hours of sleep, and then return to the fields. Adan would pick Cruz up when he was dismissed.

As she approached Heaven's Rise, she automatically turned into the scenic spot. Killing the engine, she slid out of the pickup. The sun topped the rise, spreading golden rays over the grassy knoll. She paused to study the intricate way the mellow light spread like a soft blanket over the grassy knoll. Out there somewhere Sophie's ashes rested.

Dropping to her knees at the edge of the cliff, she whispered, "Hi, sweetie." Settling into an Indian position, she crossed her legs and chatted. "You know how much I miss you? Especially now?"

Chirping birds flittered from bush to bush as the new day broke through a wall of cumulus clouds. Jules fixed on the sunrise. The sobriety of the duty Sophie had entrusted her with smothered Jules.

"I can't do it, Sophie. I want to, but I can't keep your children. They belong to your brothers. Their financial situation hasn't changed, but Cruz offered to give his life for the children last night. If a man will give his life for a child, then he would make a fine dad, regardless of his bank account. Cruz has always been wiser than me. And Adan's a fine man. I want to drop these silly lawsuits. Neither Cruz nor Adan has the time or money to fight this; they're having a hard enough time trying to keep the farm alive. Something's got to give, and honestly, I'm tired of fighting. So, you have to understand that I would do anything for you, anything but keep the kids away from their flesh and blood. And if you must know, I *do* love him. Just as you accused. I'm guilty. I love your brother with all my heart and soul, and I can't keep hurting him. Not even for you."

Shifting, she tried to remember Sophie without the scarf around her hair, eyes alert and bright, not emotionless or in enormous pain. *God, it's so unfair. She had only begun to live. Why did you take her?*

Crystal's voice swam in her head. *"Don't question God's motives; use your energy preparing for the eternal."* How many times had she said that over the past few weeks? She and Crystal were as different as yarn and lace, yet they shared a true faith in the Almighty. "I'm starting to wonder if Crystal and I are as different as I think." They didn't share the warmth and giggles like she and Sophie did, but in time that might come.

She smiled, reaching out to snatch a hint of wind. "I know you're not here. I picture you in heaven, laughing, racing through fields of blooming flowers, or perhaps walking with God in a lovely garden. You've surely met Mom by now. Tell her I said hi, and I'm sorry I didn't keep in closer contact with her. I'm happy for you, truly. If only there were some way that we could communicate, and everything is as perfect as I believe it to be."

Lying down on her side, Jules closed her eyes, recalling the days when she and Sophie lived life as though death could never touch them. What she wouldn't give to live one more day with her best friend; have one last Coke, one last laugh, one last good cry. She could smell Chanel, Sophie's favorite perfume. See her puckish grin . . .

Settling deeper into the grass, she drifted off beneath a warm sun.

Jules awoke to see the sun fully risen, a bright ball in the blue sky. Getting up, she stretched, blew a kiss to the wind and left.

When she drove into the farm lot, she heard the familiar hum of potato diggers in the fields. Tons of russets piled up to twenty feet were going into storage. Joe was backing out of the equipment shed when she stopped him. Killing the engine, he smiled. "How's Cruz?"

"Two non-displaced rib fractures. He's in a lot of pain. Can you pull a couple of men out of the fields and send them over to the Delgados' place? Adan will be short of manpower for the next few weeks."

Joe tipped his hat. "Sure thing." He restarted the tractor and drove off as Jules proceeded into the house.

Crystal glanced up from the ironing

board. "How's —"

"He's doing great." Jules headed for the shower to wash off the landfill stench. "The kids okay?"

"They're playing house in the backyard. Ethan hates it." Crystal unplugged the iron and trailed after her. "I'm going to give fifteen percent of my windfall to the church."

Jules peeled out of her dirty blouse. "That's admirable of you."

"I'm going to donate a new church wing in Lucille's memory."

Jules reached to turn on the shower. "Does Reverend Williams know?"

"I spoke to him a few minutes ago. He was ecstatic."

"The church has needed more room for years." Jules turned. "That's very good of you, Crystal."

"It's isn't my money. It's the Lord's anyway, and he saw fit to use it through Lucille. I'm sure she would be very happy. Want something to eat?"

"Thanks, but I need to get to the fields."

"Okay." Crystal left, closing the bathroom door behind her. Jules climbed into the shower, letting the warm water soothe her aching bones.

■ ■ ■ ■

Cruz began the healing process. Adan drove him home from the hospital and Jules went with Crystal to deliver a chocolate cake.

"All of this for me?" Cruz asked. "You remembered that I love chocolate fudge cake?"

"I didn't." Crystal glanced at Jules. "A little bird reminded me. A very thoughtful little wren."

He turned to focus on Jules. "Well, thank the little wren for me. I'll enjoy this."

Over the next two weeks, Jules happened to remember that he favored macaroni and cheese, pork chops, fried round steak and cauliflower with cheese sauce. He accepted each offering with an easy grin, and twice she and Crystal had stayed to eat dinner with the Delgado brothers.

As yet, Jules hadn't mentioned her plans to turn the children's care completely over to Cruz and Adan. Right now, harvest occupied Adan's mind, and Cruz wasn't up to caring for two small children, but she had told Crystal about her decision, and her sister had the expected reaction.

"I think that's how it should have been all along."

Jules knew how close Crystal had grown to the children, and at times, especially lately, it seemed Crystal and Adan spent an inordinate amount of time together. Crystal was a born nurturer, and the kids and Adan deserved nurturing. A recurring thought begin to nag her: what if Crystal and Adan up and married? They could easily do so. That would solve everyone's problem and create an ideal solution. Yet in the back of her mind she had one last resort; make a complete fool of herself. And soon if she retained any hope of fulfilling Sophie's wish.

CHAPTER 36

Jules had lost complete control over her life; the recognition hit her like a prodigal homing pigeon coming home to roost this morning. Pop's death. Sophie. Cruz hurt. She was fighting emotions and Cruz at the same time. She had no control over events. She'd known that — hadn't she? She didn't control anything. She was trying to swallow the bitter reality pill. The void Pop and Sophie left was bottomless. Every day she felt their absence more — experienced numerous times throughout the day when it would hit her; she would never see Pop or Sophie again — not this side of heaven.

Frustration overtook her; a feeling she lived with daily now. How easy it was to talk of faith, hope, and a better tomorrow when you're up to your ears in life's muck. She flipped on the turn signals, intent on stopping at the small gas station for milk on the way home. The children went through gallons a week.

She spotted an old Ford pick-up, dents on both back fenders. It resembled the farm truck she was driving but it was Tom Spicer's old truck. A bunch of young guys from the area got together at Old Tom's place every week to ride some of his bulls for practice. She'd heard about the Thursday night buck-out sessions — even knew a couple of young men who participated.

A grin formed. She'd never forget the time she and Sophie decided to meet Black Devil, one of Tom's prize stock, in person. The bull was old now, but in his day he was a ringer. He'd since sired many an offspring and every one got tougher to ride. Sophie and Jules's junior year in high school, Jules had decided to check Black Devil out on his own turf. Joe and Pop would never let her go near the animal at the area rodeos, and certainly not at the annual rodeo where Black Devil was the star attraction, but she'd longed to conquer that cantankerous animal since the day he had pinned her to a fence.

She wasn't supposed to be in Tom's field where he kept the bull, but in those days boundaries were meant to be broken. One summer night prior to Sophie and Jules's junior year of high school, they climbed

Tom's fence, hopped into the pasture and taunted Black Devil until Sophie lost her nerve and ran for safety. Jules hadn't been so quick to back off. Black Devil cornered her between the fence post and the gate, head down, hoof pawing the ground. He looked mean as Lucifer and twice as big from this distance.

"Get away from me, you devil," she'd yelled, screwing her sixteen-year-old face into a no-nonsense scowl.

The bull's head dipped lower. He snorted.

"Sophie," she'd squeaked. "Help me!"

Sophie whooped and yelled, beating on the steel gate, trying to divert the beast.

"Shush!" Jules knew if Tom or Pop knew they were in the field, there'd be a stiff price to pay.

Sophie quieted. "What'll we do?"

"I don't know. We have to stay calm. Pop will ground me for weeks if he knows I've trespassed on Tom's property."

"Looks to me like Black Devil is going to skin you alive first."

"Go get Joe."

"Okay."

"No, wait. Joe will tell Pop. Get someone."

"Okay."

"No, wait! What if Black Devil charges me? I'd be here, lying hurt, nobody to help.

You better not leave."

"Okay."

"No, leave! Go get somebody!"

By this time Sophie was literally ringing her hands. Jules eased a step sideways and the bull snorted, pawing his hoof.

The stand-off continued for three hours; three long, excruciating hours. The sun sank, darkness covered the field. The stars came out. A light breeze blew Sophie's blouse as she clung to the outside of the fence, keeping watch. Neither girl could think of a way out of the predicament without alerting their parents or nosy neighbors on what they had done.

They decided to pray. They'd taken shifts. Sophie first and then Jules. Jules had gone through every plea she could think of and still Black Devil's hostile eyes pinned her, kept her imprisoned. The pleas momentarily ceased while they shared a Snicker's bar Sophie found in her purse. And then the prayers resumed. Sophie was now reciting the Lord's Prayer over and over. That day was the first time Jules truly became sold on prayer. For no reason at all, Black Devil finally tired of the game and wandered off.

Faint with relief, Jules climbed over the fence and dropped to safety. Sophie slumped to the grassy knoll beside her and the girls lay prone, arms outstretched, sucking in deep drafts of air.

"Do you think it was prayer that did it?"

"Had to be," Sophie decided. "We'll have to do that more often."

Jules caught back a laugh as memories swept her. Sophie was always quick to pray after that; sometimes the prayers weren't appropriate requests but God must have known the hearts of two young girls were pure with naiveté.

She pulled into the convenience store, changed her mind about the milk, and then wheeled back out on the highway. *Okay, God. You've taken Sophie — now take me.* Jules had never once dared God to do anything, but the dismal, cloudy day made her long for happier times. She might not be able to control her life, but she could fulfill a dream. And if God saw fit, he'd ease her ache.

Tom was prone to linger, talk with the regulars at the gas stop. He wouldn't be home for awhile. The truck headed to Spicer's place, about a mile down the road. He had two hundred acres he worked but not that often. Old Tom was a bit on the lazy side, but he didn't have an enemy in the world, and he owned some of the best bull stock in the community.

Ten minutes later she pulled in beside a fenced corral where the bull riders were already gathered. Killing the engine, she stepped out of the truck, greeting a couple of guys by name. Patrick Whitson walked over to the truck, grinning. "Hey, Jules."

"Hey, Patrick."

The young, stocky built twenty-two-year-old with blond hair and nut brown skin grinned. "What brings you to these parts?"

"Thought I might try my hand at bull riding."

Patrick's grin folded. "Not a chance."

"Yep." She straightened, feeling at the moment invincible. If God wanted to take her, he would. "Always wanted to try my luck at bull riding, and I figure tonight's the perfect time." Her gaze focused on the corral and one particular bull. Black Devil, large as life. He was dark and rangy, not as muscled as he used to be. She nearly felt sorry for the old guy. But his eyes were still wild and he still snorted like he could rip her apart. Her gaze shifted to the animal beside him. "That's one of Black Devil's offspring, isn't it?"

Patrick turned to trace her gaze. He focused on a young bull, sleek, heavily muscled. Mean. "Yeah. That's one of his boys."

"Can I ride him?"

Patrick laughed. "I don't think so. Least-ways, none of us has been able to."

"I want to ride him."

He let out a hoot. "Hey, guys! Jules wants to ride The Terminator!"

Several laughs broke out, but a couple of the men sobered. One spoke up. "She can't ride that animal. He'd tear her apart."

"Come on, Jules. Cruz would shoot me point blank if I let you ride that animal." Patrick shifted his stance. Jules knew she was putting him in a bind. Patrick and Cruz were buddies, but Cruz didn't run her life, and she'd known Patrick about the same length of time that Cruz had, so in her eyes that made them even up on loyalty.

"Then we won't mention this to Cruz. Okay?" Her expression softened. "Come on, guys." She confronted the men's somber faces. "Haven't you ever had a dream you wanted to live? Mine has been to ride Black Devil once, and now he's too old. Let me have a go at The Terminator. I'll take full responsibility for my actions."

Activity had ceased. Men stood around watching the exchange. Jules knew she had Patrick between a rock and a hard place. Cruz would be furious if Patrick let her ride the bull and he found out.

298

Scratching the back of his neck, Patrick appeared to mull the thought over. "I don't know — what do you think, guys?"

"I say The Terminator will eat her for lunch."

Several agreed with a decisive nod. Protests broke out, then naysayers.

A young man Jules didn't know spoke up. "I say she can take him."

Stunned expressions sought to identify the voice.

The kid grinned. "I have twenty bucks that says she can ride him."

Bills started appearing. "I got twenty-five that says she won't last three seconds."

"Thirty over here! I'll give her three and a half seconds."

And the ride was on. Jules called above the fray, "I don't want this to turn into a gambling frenzy! I just want to ride The Terminator!"

A couple of men broke and walked out to the field to get the animal. Before Jules could lose her nerve, they had the bull in the chute and a bull rope around his belly. Pulling on her gloves, Jules approached the corral, her stomach churning. The Terminator looked bigger and meaner than Black Devil had ever appeared. Perspiration dampened the back of her neck as the animal lunged, trying to go over the chute.

The young kid climbed the stall and faced her. "You sure you want to do this?"

Nodding, Jules focused on the heaving, agitated ton of flesh. She swallowed against a dry throat, jumping back when the animal lunged, trying to take out the stall, going crazy. She'd known men who met their death on the back of less bull. Would she meet hers? *Hold on, Sophie. I may be coming to join you.* "I'm sure." Grasping the wall of the chute, she climbed up.

The kid reached and lifted her weight and settled her on the bull's back. The animal was wide as a four-lane highway.

Patrick's face swam before her. "It's not too late to back out."

"I'm not backing out — but I want everyone's solemn oath that what happens here stays here." All she needed was for Cruz to get wind of this. If the bull threw her, which undoubtedly it would, he would have a good laugh on her — if she survived, but if per chance she'd beat some of these guys' records, then she'd have a good laugh on them.

Patrick shook his head and pulled the bull rope up for her. "You can bet I won't mention it. Cruz isn't going to like this."

The bull was restless, heaving sides bumping against the stall. Jules glanced at anxious faces. "Gentlemen? Do I have your word that you won't mention this to anyone?"

Several men nodded, and then the hold-outs agreed.

Jules tightened her grip on the cinch. "If you do, I'll tell the sheriff that you're gambling out here, not bull riding."

Grumbles broke out.

"This is nuts. Get off that bull's back. You're going to get yourself killed." A man spat a wad of tobacco.

"You guys just keep silent about this and we'll all be fine." Taking a deep breath, she nodded. "Open the gate."

The gate swung wide and The Terminator shot out like a speeding freight. Jules's teeth chattered and crumbled into tiny pieces. A bomb went off in her head. The taste of salty blood filled her mouth.

The bull bucked, gyrated and twisted. She held tight, feeling her insides jar loose. A kidney dropped. Then her spleen hit her throat. She tried to let go of the rope but her hand was wound so tightly she was momentarily caught. She fought the animal and the cinch, trying to get loose. Up and down, back and forth, sideways. Finally the rope loosed and she jumped. When she hit the ground she landed on her right arm.

She thought she heard the bone crack.

She lay staring at the swirling clouds both in her head and in the sky. Men ran out and diverted the bull away from her prone body. Laughter broke out.

"That's right. Gloat," she muttered, wondering how in the world she was going to explain broken front teeth and a shattered right arm to any sane person. *Why couldn't you have just played along?*

Patrick loomed above her, checking her for injuries. "Are you okay?"

"Do I look okay?"

"No, you look like —" He caught back salty language. "I better drive you over to the clinic."

Jules struggled to sit up. "I'm fine. Other than my arm, I don't think I've broken anything but some teeth."

He shook his head. "I warned you."

"How long?"

"Three seconds."

"Three!" She laid back, head reeling. "Man, it felt like hours."

Crawling out of the truck, Jules limped to the back door. Crystal turned when she entered the kitchen. Her expression fell when she noted Jules's posture. "Holy cow."

"No. Bull, The Terminator to be exact."

She limped to a chair and eased into it. "You have to get me to the clinic. I think I broke my right arm, shattered two front teeth —" She paused, jutting two front teeth out like Shrek — "Are they broken or cracked?"

Crystal moved closer to examine the injuries. "No — they all look intact."

"Oh, thank goodness." Jules laid her head on the kitchen table. "I must have just broken my arm — and I jarred a kidney loose — and I think my spleen's in my throat."

"What have you done?" Crystal wet a cloth and moved to help her.

"I rode The Terminator."

"You *didn't!*"

"Not really. It rode me, but I was on top three seconds."

Her sister dabbed at bleeding spots on her face. "Why would you do anything so insane?"

Jules only had the strength to lift one shoulder. "Right now, I'm asking myself the same thing. I realized that I had no control over my life and I thought — never mind." She glanced up. "I don't want Cruz to know anything about this."

"Why not?"

"Because, Crystal. He thinks I'm ditsy

enough. Please don't tell him, and warn Adan not to mention a word of this."

"How will we explain your injuries?" Crystal gently eased her out of the chair. "And what about Patrick and the other men? They'll tell."

"No they won't, or I'll tell on them."

"Tell what?"

"I can't tell."

Standing back, Crystal shook her head. "Your eye is turning black, you have cuts and bruises, your arm looks — sort of — limp. Everyone will know something happened."

"We'll just say I took a fall." And that was the honest truth. The Terminator was still King of the Hill; she'd grant him that title.

"A fall."

"I took a hard fall. That's our story, and we're sticking to it."

The two sisters dropped the curious children by the Ramseys on the way to the clinic. It was after hours, but the doctor was working late.

Jules's right arm was severely sprained but not broken. She had no idea what she'd heard snap, but it wasn't her bone. All of Jules's teeth were intact, and the doctor assured her that the spleen and kidneys didn't shift positions easily. In a day or two, other than being sore as an infected boil, she'd be back to normal.

On the way back to the farm, Jules dozed through the mercy of pain pills. Every bone in her body screamed. How could she have been so naïve to think that she could ride that bull? Why was she so stubborn?

And far more worrisome, why had she dared God to take her.

It seemed that she was learning a lot of unflattering things about herself these days, knowledge that she didn't necessarily want or like.

CHAPTER 37

The church hall glowed Sunday evening for an informal reception honoring Crystal's magnanimous gift, which she insisted came directly from Lucille. The new Lucille Miller Recreation Hall and church kitchen would begin construction sometime late fall. Reverend Williams hosted the cake and punch affair after Sunday evening services.

Jules spotted Cruz in the crowd. He had a date tonight, a girl she didn't recognize. She looked young — years younger than Cruz, but she was about as pretty as they come. Pretty. Perky. Blonde. Clingy.

Frowning, she dabbed a couple of spoonfuls of guacamole dip on her paper plate with her left hand. "Who's the babe?"

Adan slapped cheese and ham in a dish. "What babe?"

"The girl Cruz is with."

"Oh, Melody." He speared a tomato slice. "Eye candy, huh. She models for some magazine." He focused on her shiner. And arm sling. "Who won?"

"I took a hard fall." Apparently the bull riders had kept their silence, not out of loyalty but fear that she'd rat them out to the sheriff.

"Out of what? A plane?"

"Something like that. Where's the babe from?"

"New York." He stabbed a pickle with his fork. "She's visiting her grandma in Pasco."

"How does Cruz know her?"

"Hey, you'd have to ask him. I'm not my brother's keeper — at least not his social life keeper." With a wink, he wandered off.

She was making small talk with one of the ladies in the congregation when Cruz approached the punch bowl.

Jules stepped away from her conversation when she spotted Cruz. She'd been toying with a nutty plan all day — even nuttier than riding The Terminator. Did she dare make the overt move? Right now they were on pretty solid ground, no fights lately. If she followed her heart instead of common sense she'd turn the children over to Cruz and Adan tonight and be done with it, but nobody had ever accused her of being an Einstein. She knew Cruz would attend the church reception in honor of Crystal. The idea she'd toyed around with all week festered. True, the scheme had been used more than once in crucial situations, and failed, but if it bore fruit, she'd be way ahead of her feelings and his obstinacy. She casually joined him at the refreshment line. He still favored his ribs, but he was getting out more these days.

Glancing up, he spotted her. He lifted an empty cup. "Want some punch?"

"Yes. Thank you."

He focused on her injuries. "What hit you?"

Her hand came up to touch the black and blue eye. "I took a fall."

"Parachute didn't open? What about the arm?"

She gave him an exaggerated grin. "Funny. I sprained my arm during the fall."

He dipped a couple of cups out of the bowl and handed her one. His gaze skimmed the large gathering. "The town's real appreciative of Crystal and your gift."

"The money isn't mine to give, but Crystal insists on putting the tithe in my name too."

"That's a nice, sisterly thing to do."

It was very nice, and Jules didn't know how to repay the generous and thoughtful gesture.

Drawing a deep breath, she asked what

she'd come to ask. "I . . . was wondering if you were free tomorrow night."

A dark brow lifted. "I guess so. Why?"

"I'd like to talk to you in private. Would you have dinner with me?"

Before he could deny the request, she added, "Nothing formal, just grab a sandwich at The Grille and discuss . . . the topic."

"What topic?"

"What I want to discuss."

He considered the offer, and then said quietly, "What time?"

"Around seven?"

Lifting the cup, he took a swallow and then set the drink down. "Okay. Seven."

"Okay."

"Jules."

"Yes?"

"I don't know if I've thanked you properly for saving that field. You kept me from bankruptcy."

Color tinged her cheeks. "We'll call it even, okay? You saved my life in the accident, I helped save a field. Doesn't seem like a fair exchange, but I'm happy if you are."

He nodded. "Did you break anything?"

"Break anything?"

His gaze focused on the arm sling. "Dur-

309

ing the fall. You should be more careful. We've had about all the loss this community can stand."

She nodded. Did he know about the bull ride?

"Look at me, Jules."

She raised her eyes. "I'm not kidding. No more crazy chances. We'll get through Sophie and Pop's death. Understand?"

"Understood."

His tone softened. "You've hit a streak of bad luck. The truck accident and now a fall. You must not be living right."

She smiled. "Must not."

"Well — my date will think I deserted her. Tomorrow night?"

"I'll be there."

Releasing her breath, she melted into the crowd. Tomorrow night. Seven.

She had an official date with Cruz.

And whether he knew or simply guessed the nature of her injuries, he cared. That was enough to make her vow to be more careful.

CHAPTER 38

Nervous as a setting hen with a fox in the hen house. Tense as a ball of wire.

Edgy as a cat watching a rat hole. Every simile Jules had ever heard raced through her mind as she dressed Monday night. She discarded a third blouse; neckline too low. She couldn't dress provocatively. Cruz would hate that. She picked up a pink blouse, held it to her chest and studied the mirror. He liked her in pink.

She tossed it aside and reached for the black one. Black. Classy. Made a statement without being overt. She studied her jeans. Should she wear a skirt? Something loose and feminine. She tossed it aside. He rarely saw her in a dress or skirt. Her intent would be too obvious. Casual. She had to keep this meeting casual and informative only.

Crystal carried a sleeping Olivia to her bed, glancing in Jules's room as she passed. Jules smiled.

"Are you going out tonight?"

"For a while. I'll be back in an hour or so."

Grinning, Crystal paused. "Big date?"

"Not really." Jules picked up a new pair of silver loop earrings and inserted them in her lobes. "I'm meeting Cruz at The Grille."

"Cruz." Crystal's grin deepened into outright teasing.

"Purely business." Crystal might not view her objective as professional, but in truth it was.

"Jules."

Jules turned to look at her. "Yes?"

"Have a great time."

Her cheeks turned hot when she heard complete sincerity in her sister's voice. "Thanks. When I'm with Cruz . . ."

"You feel complete."

Nodding, Jules felt tears surface. She felt complete. How did Crystal know?

Crystal continued down the hallway, and Jules finished dressing, wondering how all of a sudden Crystal had turned into a confidant.

Few pickups sat around The Grille this evening. In this community, folks ate early and then went home to watch television. She spotted Cruz near the pool table talking to a friend. When the bell over the door tinkled he glanced up.

Why hadn't she worn the pink blouse? Black made her look staid — incapable of compromise.

Finishing his conversation, Cruz walked to meet her. "What happened to the arm sling?"

"I don't need it. It was just a small sprain." And she couldn't try on clothes with her arm fastened to her side. She indicated the closest booth. "Want to sit here?"

"Sure." He hung his hat on the peg beside the booth, and then slid in the worn leather. She sat across from him.

"Are you hungry?"

"No." She couldn't force a bite down her throat. "Just coffee."

He motioned for two coffees and Nick nodded. Cruz's gaze shifted back to hers. "What's up?"

She'd hoped to chat a bit, loosen the apprehension. It wasn't every day she attempted something this . . . stupid? She brushed the worry aside and dove in.

"Have you noticed how close Adan and Crystal have become lately?"

He appeared to consider the question. "No. Why?"

"Well, they are. They're together a lot and at least two or three times a week he comes over to watch a movie with her and the kids."

"He likes movies."

"I'm thinking the relationship is more than one based on a mutual passion for movies."

"Adan and Crystal?" Cruz laughed.

"Laugh if you want, but I think the relationship is getting serious." If she blatantly pointed out the developing relationship he'd see the risk. Cruz loved those children and he wouldn't hand them over easily, even though Adan was his brother.

Leaning back in the booth, Cruz fixed on her. His irrepressibly good looks unnerved her. He was dressed in jeans and a white T-shirt, his hair still damp from a shower. He didn't go near a gym, but his forearms were as large and powerful as any weight lifter. The light scent of cologne — or deodorant — filled her senses and strengthened her. When he sobered, she figured he'd caught her point.

"What happens if Crystal and Adan get married and take the children?" she baited.

"What happens? Our problems are solved. Sophie would like that. The kids would have a good home, and Adan would make a great father. You've seen how Crystal takes to Olivia and Ethan."

"And you'd want that?"

"Want my sister's kids to have a good home? Yes, I want that. Don't you?"

"I love those children too — and so do you."

"It isn't as though Adan and Crystal would take them away. This is and always will be their home."

"Here isn't Crystal's home. She lives in Florida."

"But she was raised here."

"Yes, and Pop wasn't her dad."

The bombshell momentarily halted the tense exchange.

He frowned. "Come again?"

"You heard me. Pop wasn't Crystal's father. That's why he left Blue Bayou to me. Seems Mom's fling with the seasonal worker resulted in Crystal."

"Good grief, Jules."

"I know." The coffee arrived and she reached for the sugar shaker. "I was shocked, but Crystal's okay with it. Apparently Mom told her — and it explains a lot of things. All the tension we lived under, the arguments, Pop always closer to me than Crystal."

Cruz picked up his cup and took a sip.

Fishing in her purse, she removed a small box and extended it. "It's Pop's watch."

Emotion flickered across Cruz's face. He carefully opened the box and stared at the pocket watch, tarnished with age. Silence fell between them. Finally, he cleared his throat. "Thanks. Your dad meant a lot to me. I'll pass this on to my boy someday."

"You're going to have boys?" They wouldn't be hers.

"Or my daughter." He pocketed the watch and she returned to the prior subject.

"The point I'm trying to make is, this isn't Crystal's home and she loves Florida. What if she and Adan marry and decide to give up potato farming?"

He shook his head. "Adan would be miserable in Florida. Farming's in his blood."

"Maybe, but a wife is very persuasive. Do you want Sophie's kids living thousands of miles away?"

"What can I do to prevent it? Adan's his own man, and if what you say is true, I can't stop him — wouldn't try. He's old enough to know his mind."

"There is another way."

"What? Find *him* another woman?" His teasing eyes met hers. Hers sobered.

"What's that look supposed to mean?"

"It means there's another way." She drew a deep breath. "If . . . if we were to pick up

316

where we left off years ago —"

"Hold it."

She met his gaze. "Hear me out."

"Not if it leads to where I think you're going."

"If we were to set our past aside — for the children's sake and . . ." She was actually suggesting this to him? ". . . lay aside our differences and marry, we could raise the children together."

He was silent so long she thought he might get up and walk out on her. Finally he cleared his throat and said, "What about love? Don't you think Olivia and Ethan deserve to have parents that love each other?"

"I have no problem with loving you." There. The admission wasn't new to him. She'd said it once in anger, and now she'd stated it in truth. She swallowed. "Do you?"

"Are you asking me if I love you?"

"Yes."

He stared at his cup, muscles working in his jaw. "I never stopped."

Her heart took wing. "Nor did I. Not for a moment."

Finally he lifted his eyes. "You have a strange way of loving."

The second parting flashed before her eyes. He'd said that when she was ready to settle down to let him know. Well. She was ready. She cleared her throat. "I didn't back out because I didn't love and adore you. You know why I walked away the last time."

"You chose your father over me."

"Technically, that's true. I saw us as responsible adults who loved each other so deeply we could endure a small delay. I chose responsibility over my desires. I loved you so much that I thought you would always wait for me."

"Honestly, Jules? I don't know where you got that notion. I'm a man. A man who loved you so much it hurt. I would have worked with you any way I could to help Pop, but not to the point of sticking around indefinitely, waiting for you to decide where your loyalty laid. The second time you walked, I saw where that loyalty was and it wasn't with me."

"It's always black or white with you, Cruz. Life does have gray areas."

"Mine doesn't."

She sighed. "I've made a lot of mistakes in my life. Leaving you twice are the biggest ones. Crystal's the third. I've never tried to form a relationship with her — not really. I resented her for going with Mom; I resented that she got to lie on the beach while I worked my hands raw in the potato field.

The way you resent me for staying with Pop." She tentatively reached out to touch his hand and he drew back.

"Will you marry me?" she asked.

"You're proposing?" He shifted, clearly unsettled by the turn in conversation.

"I'm asking you to marry me. Tonight. We can fly to Vegas and —"

"Vegas!" His features darkened.

"It's not the ideal . . . setting, but we could marry quickly. Sophie's kids would be ours, and everyone could get back to living normal lives."

Sitting back in the booth, he studied her. "Vegas. When I marry, the ceremony is not going to be by an Elvis lookalike in Vegas. It's going to be right here where I've been born and raised, by Reverend Williams, probably in the fancy new addition provided by you and your sister."

"Lucille Miller. It's *Lucille's* mattress money."

"Whatever."

"Okay. We could apply for a marriage license here. It doesn't have to be a big wedding, something small."

He caught her wrist, holding it gently. "Look. When I get married I'll do the proposing." His features softened. "I can't marry you, Jules. We've been down that road twice."

Her pleading eyes met his. "Are you ever going to forgive me, Cruz? The Bible speaks of forgiving seventy times seven."

"I forgive you, Jules. I had to or lose my mind, but my problem is I can't forget. We've tried this Jules and Cruz thing all of our lives —"

"Almost all of our lives," she corrected.

"Okay, I'll concede that I've loved you from the minute I saw you in the church-yard, nine years old, wearing a pink dress and pink ribbon in your hair."

Pink. She knew she should have worn pink.

"Love can overcome a lot of things, but it's hard to conquer memory. I can't trust you, Jules. And marriage is based on trust and mutual respect."

She pulled back. A tight lump formed in her throat. He was saying that she wasn't trustworthy. "You know how hard it is for me to make a decision and stick with it."

"And I'm bullheaded, and refuse to fall into the same trap twice — no, three times." His eyes softened. "But I have a bigger problem. I was going to take care of this myself, but since you'll find out anyway, you might as well hear it from me."

"What?" Her heart throbbed. Had he

320

found a woman he wanted to marry this soon?

"I got a call from Matt Parker's mother a couple of days ago."

"Livvy's paternal grandmother?" The very thing Sophie feared would happen. Somehow Sophie's ex had heard about her death.

"Matt's mother," Cruz confirmed.

"What does she want? Matt's given up his paternal rights."

"I'm not sure. I fly to Waco day after tomorrow to talk to her."

"Matt wants Olivia — he can't have her. Sophie made me promise —"

"I don't know what his mother wants; she wouldn't say. She wants to talk in person."

That sounded serious. "I'll go with you."

"You're not invited."

"Please let me go." She met his steady gaze. "You're still recuperating. You can't carry luggage —"

"It's an overnight trip. I can handle a backpack and you have a sprained arm."

"Cruz —" Leaning closer, she pressed. "I promised Sophie I wouldn't let Jake or Matt take either of the children. You know both men are worthless excuses for men, not to mention fathers."

"I don't know that Matt is claiming his rights."

"Let me go with you."

"Last minute airfare will cost you a fortune."

"I have a fortune — or my sister does."

He looked away. His expression clearly said he didn't want her company, but he also knew Sophie would want her input. He turned back. "I leave on a 6:00 a.m. flight."

"I'll be ready. Do you want me to meet you at the airport?"

He shook his head. "I'll pick you up."

Smiling, she slid out of the booth. "I'll be ready."

CHAPTER 39

Stars hung overhead when they entered the Tri-Cities terminal. Jules checked the departure board to see if the Delta flight was on time. It was.

Carrying overnight bags and electronic boarding passes in hand, they went through security with ease and walked to the gate. Matt's parents lived in Waco, Texas. Jules had slept maybe an hour last night, her mind going over every possible scenario. Matt wanted his little daughter back, and his mother was the emissary. Jules wasn't sure how favorably a judge would view his case. He'd been in jail on drug charges more often than not, and was now serving time on murder charges yet he was blood kin.

The commuter was boarding by the time they cleared security. The plane was full. Jules's seat was in the very back of the plane. Cruz sat several aisles up. She stored her bag in the overhead bin, with the assistance of her seatmate, and sat down, fumbling for her seat belt. She hated to fly. No matter how often she did, she mentally kissed the ground when the plane landed.

A change of planes an hour and ten minutes later, and they were on an MD80 winging their way to Waco. This time Cruz sat in the back of the plane, and she was relegated to a cramped middle seat with a crying infant on the right and a snoring businessman on her left. Jules dozed most of the flight, exhausted from her night of subjective questions. Sophie had spoken little of Matt's parents, saying she'd only met them once.

The flight touched down on time, and she vacated the plane. She waited for Cruz, reaching for his backpack as he exited.

"I can carry my luggage."

"I know. You're strong and brave, but I'll carry it." She draped the backpack over her arm and then reached for her light bag. Pain seared her right arm.

"You're making me look like a sissy."

"Sorry. I'll try to conceal my helpfulness."

Outside the terminal, they rented a car. "Want a convertible?" Cruz asked.

Waco was hot and dripping humidity. She hated the thought of blistering sun bearing down on them during the long ride, but once they had both thought a convertible was ideal. She didn't want to spoil his fun. "Sure, why not."

Thirty minutes later they were on the highway heading for the address Cruz had entered into the GPS. Even with the air blaring, the convertible's interior was suffocating. She glanced at Cruz, smiling her enjoyment. An hour later, he pulled into a drive-through. "I'm hungry."

She was famished, but she hadn't mentioned her hunger. She determined to be silent support, but the thought of a fish sandwich almost overrode her resolute. He pulled to a speaker and cut the engine. The canopy mercifully provided shade. She tried to rearrange her snarled hair, waiting for him to ask what she wanted, but he pushed the call button and ordered the usual.

"A fish sandwich, hold the tartar sauce, double cheeseburger, two fries, one small, one large, small vanilla diet Coke and a large Dr Pepper." He rattled off the order as he had done a million times in their lives. Happiness rattled her. He remembered; even the fact that tartar sauce upset her stomach.

Removing his Stetson, he mopped sweat from his brow.

What she feared would be strained silence

during the trip never materialized. During lunch they chatted about ordinary things, safe things. The past wasn't mentioned, or as far as she could tell, even thought about.

Later they pulled out of the drive-through and resumed the trip. Twenty miles down the road they got behind a diesel shooting out obnoxious fumes. Jules brought a tissue to her nose and held it until the vehicle mercifully pulled off the road fifteen miles later. Jules was faint with heat. Did she dare ask Cruz to put the top up on the way back to the airport? She didn't want to rain on his parade, but mercy, she was dehydrated and anticipating a heat stroke. How could they have ever thought a convertible was the ultimate vehicle?

It was close to two o'clock when they pulled into a gated community. The car idled as they studied the swank addition. Matt obviously came from money. "What do we do now?" she asked.

"The lady said to push the button, and she'd open the gate." He studied the panel, pushed a button and momentarily a woman's voice answered. Cruz announced their arrival.

Seconds later the double gates swung open, and they entered the tree-lined street.

"4762 Shadowbox." Cruz noted the address.

The house shouted wealth: three-story brick, four-car garage. Porch boxes with overhanging foliage, striped green and white awnings. They got out of the convertible and walked up the groomed walkway and onto the porch. A gardener trimmed shrubs in front of the house.

Cruz removed his hat and pushed the door chime, and a maid dressed in a gray and white uniform opened the door.

"Cruz Delgado and Ms. Jules Matias."

Nodding, the woman admitted them to a marble foyer where overhead bamboo fans gently stirred cooled air. "I'll announce you to the Judge and Mrs. Parker."

Cruz turned to Jules and they simultaneously mouthed, "Judge?"

Within minutes they were escorted to a glassed sun porch where lovely white wicker furniture with blue and lavender floral cushions accented the outdoor setting. A man and woman rose as they approached. The man spoke first. "Mr. Delgado?"

"Yes." The two shook hands.

"This is Matthew's mother, Jillian."

Cruz nodded and introduced Jules.

"You were Sophie's best friend," Jillian noted.

"Yes. We were childhood friends." Matt must have spoken of his wife's life.

The maid appeared with tall glasses of ice tea containing mint sprigs. The room was a heavenly 70 degrees. The four took a seat.

Jillian appeared to be appointed spokesperson. "I'm very grateful that you accepted our invitation, Mr. Delgado. We didn't know your sister as we would have liked; Matthew has always kept his personal life private."

Jules's eyes scanned the swank surroundings, wondering how a child of this home had taken the wrong path so many times.

"I fear we don't know our only grandchild at all. That is a pity."

"Yes, ma'am," Cruz said. "But if Matt wants to claim Olivia, if this is what this meeting is about, I have to warn you that we will fight for custody."

Jules's heart sank. How long could they fight these means? But then Crystal loved those children, and she would do everything within her means to see them raised in a caring home.

The judge spoke. "My son is serving a life sentence, Mr. Delgado. He has no means or intentions of claiming little Olivia." Jules noted the pain in the father's voice.

"Matthew will never know his child," Jillian admitted. "But we would like to ask

328

that we be considered to raise the little girl."

Silence filled the sudden void.

Jules cleared her throat. "Livvy doesn't know you."

"No, and it breaks our hearts. We haven't interfered or asked for grandparents' rights until now, but with Sophie's death . . ." She bit her carefully lined lower lip. "We can provide everything the child would ever need: education, love. We invited you here today to discuss the possibility."

Clearing his throat, Cruz met the woman's pleading gaze. "My sister requested that the children be raised by either me or my brother."

"We understand that both you and your brother are single. Is that correct?"

"Yes, ma'am. For the time being."

Her gaze focused on Jules.

Jules cleared her throat. "I'm a close family friend. My sister and I help with the children's care."

"Are you or your sister married?"

"Not yet."

The woman nodded and focused on Cruz. "Then surely you would welcome our help. We could arrange shared parental rights. The child could be here during school months and with you and your brother in the summer. We understand that you're a farmer?"

"I raise potatoes in Washington."

"Really?" The judge's brow lifted. "I didn't realize Washington was known for potatoes?"

"It isn't, but we raise a lot of them up in the Tri-Cities area."

Jules ventured a remark. "Olivia has a brother. Ethan."

"Yes, we're aware of that. We'd make certain the two did not lose contact."

Cruz glanced at Jules and she read his thoughts. He didn't want them separated for any length of time.

"It would be difficult on both children to separate them," she said.

"The brother is young, he will adjust."

"He's five," Jules reminded. "And he's very close to his uncles."

Jillian's warm smile tried to calm her fear. "I'm sure that we — together — could assure that the children would retain a close relationship." She glanced at the judge. "Jim and I aren't so old that we can't give the little girl a good life."

Cruz turned his hat brim in his hands. "I need time to think about this."

"Of course. We understand. Take all the time needed, but since the child is undergoing change with the loss of her mother, we

330

feel the sooner the better."

Jules swallowed back anger. Cruz had no right to raise their hopes. Sophie had left their guardianship up to her. Had he forgotten that? Her eyes roamed the swank room. Yet Olivia's grandparents could give her everything. Everything and more. Regardless of Sophie's wishes, blood kin would have the upper edge in a court of law. And Judge Parker undoubtedly would have influential friends . . .

They chatted another fifteen minutes before Cruz rose and ended the meeting. "I'll give this some thought, Judge and Mrs. Parker. You'll hear from me within the month."

The older couple rose to shake his hand. "Thank you for your consideration." Jillian's eyes filled with tears. "We will do a better job with this child than we did our own." She touched a tissue to the corners of her eyes. "We have learned much since Matthew was born."

"Yes, ma'am. How do you stand with God?"

"If it were not for our Creator, we would not be before you today. The years . . . have been difficult."

Cruz nodded and motioned for Jules to lead the way out of the sun porch. Outside the mansion, they paused to catch their breaths. Why had he failed to mention that Jules was legally responsible for the children? Would that only complicate the matter?

Jules ventured, "What do you think?" He couldn't buy into this shared custody. He just couldn't.

Cruz shook his head, and slipped his hat on. "I think if you have no objections, we're putting the top up on that stupid convertible."

CHAPTER 40

On the way to the Marriott, Cruz suddenly took the airport exit. Jules glanced over. "This is the wrong cut off."

"I think we'll take the red-eye back tonight."

"Why?" She had been looking forward to a nice dinner, maybe some time to have a rational conversation about the day and its unlikely turn of events. The Parkers put the custody of Sophie's children into a whole different light.

"I want to go home, Jules. Okay?"

"Okay."

She remained silent as they returned the car rental, arranged for the last two seats on the midnight flight, cleared security, and then waited the four hours until they boarded. He wanted to go home; he didn't want to be pressed on marrying her or giving up his sister's children. Home was a haven. Her heart went out to him; he was in pain with the ribs and emotionally torn, but he refused to mention the discomfort.

Jules couldn't remember ever being so drained, both physically and mentally. Her head spun with thoughts of the day's newest crisis, the Parkers. She could only guess how confused Cruz must be. Separate Ethan from Livvy? Sophie wouldn't want that — she'd abhor the idea, but Jules knew her meager little temporary custody paper would never hold up in a court of law.

Around eight, she got up and disappeared for a while, leaving Cruz to his thoughts. When she returned, she carried two hot dogs and two coffees. Cruz glanced up when she handed him one. "Just like you like it. Ketchup, relish and those little green peppers you like." She had her own memories of what he liked and didn't.

"Thanks." He accepted the offering.

"When was your last pain pill?"

"I don't know — early this morning before I picked you up."

"It's time for another one."

He didn't argue, just took a bottle out of his shirt pocket, dumped a couple in his mouth and swallowed. "These things affect me — if I pass out cold you'll have to get me on the plane."

She grinned. "I promise I will not leave

you passed out cold in an airport waiting room." She met his gaze. "I promise."

He could have easily reminded her that her promises tended to go by the wayside, but he didn't. And she was thankful.

After their meal, they drifted off. Once she woke to find her head on his shoulder as he dozed. Straightening, she cleared her throat and tried to position her head in the opposite direction. Twice more she woke with her head on his shoulder.

The intercom woke them as the flight started to board. She was in the middle of the plane, he was in the back.

She glanced up when she was settled to see the flight attendant. "Your traveling companion has an empty seat next to him. Would you like to move?"

When she eased to look at Cruz, he motioned her back.

The hostess smiled and leaned closer. "He says you don't like to fly, and you'd feel better sitting next to him."

"Thank you." The back was bumpier during flight, but she didn't care. She gathered her overnight bag out of the bin and then proceeded to the back of the plane. Dropping into the empty seat, she said softly, "Thanks."

He wadded a pillow under his head. "I

know flying makes you nervous." Closing his eyes, he noted, "How are you going to play nurse if you're seven aisles away?"

Not exactly giddy, romantic banter, but good enough for now. She snapped her seat belt into place, and prepared for the flight home. As the MD80 wheels left the ground, Jules felt the familiar lifting sensation. Her hand gripped the arm of the seat. Cruz reached over, loosened her hold, and held her hand as the plane banked, gaining altitude. It was the best take-off Jules had ever experienced.

A little before seven the next morning, the commuter plane from Seattle touched down in Pasco. The sun was up; it was a magnificent morning. Ethan and Livvy would be eating breakfast, scrambled eggs and orange juice, unaware that their futures rested in the hands of two people who couldn't agree on the temperature, let alone who would raise them; although, for the past twenty-four hours she and Cruz had not exchanged a harsh word.

She prayed that the tentative truce would hold.

Cruz wheeled into the farm lot towing the center pivots that afternoon. Jules stepped away from the kitchen counter, to the mirror to check her appearance. Jeans, T-shirt, ball cap. She sighed. He'd seen her like this practically all of her life. Did he often compare her boyish appearance to The Babe's and other women he'd dated lately? If so, she'd come up short. Opening the kitchen door, she stepped outside on the porch. "I didn't expect to see you so soon."

He lifted the tailgate; sunlight caught his hair and deepened the black shine. He'd always been good-looking, even during awkward teen years, but today, in the looks department, he could easily take home a blue ribbon from the county fair. The years only enhanced his dark, Hispanic features.

"Got a busy afternoon," he called. "Joe around?"

"In the fields." She stepped off the porch to meet him, eyes on the irrigation pivots. "I heard the field yielded a good crop."

"Thanks to you." He approached her and she took a deep breath. How hard it was to love someone who didn't love you back. He paused, and his eyes met hers. "I've said it once, but I'll say it again. You know that you saved my chops."

Shrugging, she smiled. "We'll call it even since I've bruised a few of those chops too."

He gave her one of those men looks that said "let's not go there." Clearing her throat, she glanced at the equipment. "Joe will help you to unload."

Leaning against the truck, Cruz crossed his arms, eyes fixed on her. "I don't get it, Jules. You jilt me twice, I do my best to avoid the subject, but you bring it up every chance you get. What's the deal?"

She mentally sighed. "I want to be friends, Cruz." She wanted more than friendship, but why ride a dead horse?

His expression sobered. "I don't want to be friends with you."

She struggled to maintain a neutral expression but his admission, stated in stark language, stung. Tears smarted to her eyes and she ineffectually swiped them away.

Both demeanor and tone softened. "I can't be friends, Jules. I loved you most of my life, and being 'just friends,' regardless of forgiveness, isn't possible for me."

She wiped her eyes on her shirt sleeve. "I know it's not the ideal solution, but we live in the same community, go to the same church, share custody of the kids, almost every friend we have is a mutual one. If we're going to live here, can't we make an effort at friendship?"

She could not go on fighting him the rest of her life. She refused the notion, and she wasn't going to leave the community. Her roots here went too deep. It was a big world, and somehow they must learn to co-exist in harmony regardless of the past.

He shook his head. "Can't do it. If I'm around you, I want you. If I want you, you don't want me."

"I have not ever not wanted you." Deplorable grammar, but the only way she could think to say it.

A smile crossed his features. "I have an engagement ring in my top drawer that says 'you have so ever said you didn't want me.' "

"And I have a broken heart, a guilt complex that I'll never overcome, and years of wishing away the past in my memory box." She straightened, taking a final swipe at the telling moisture in her eyes. "I'll trade my remorse for your ring. At least your hurt has value."

Joe's pick-up drove up and halted the conversation. Turning on her heel, Jules walked into the house.

CHAPTER 41

Buttering a piece of toast, Jules fixed her gaze on Crystal's elaborate gift that had been delivered just after Cruz left. There it sat in the barn lot, a big, shiny candy-apple red Ford truck. Double cab, four-wheel drive, fully loaded with enough gadgets to keep Jules occupied for a month. Apparently Adan and her sister had been busy while she and Cruz were visiting the Parkers. When she protested that Crystal had spent too much, the sparkle in her sister's eyes diminished her complaint. How did one grouse about a new truck?

"I have all of this money! What else can I do with it other than buy gifts for those I love?"

The vehicle wasn't Jules's Geo Tracker. This was a bunch of elaborate steel and fancy wheels. The Tracker held her memories, but like her life, her Tracker was twisted steel.

"How did the trip to Waco go?"

"Fine. The Parkers would like shared custody of Livvy."

Crystal's features paled. "That won't happen, will it?"

"I pray not. Cruz wanted time to think about it."

The men handled the children well, but it was time to make the change. A week or two of sole "fatherhood" for either man would reinforce her case. Cruz might reconsider her proposal and view Sophie's children having both a mom and dad in a different light. Neither brother had the slightest idea of exactly how much grit it took to care for two small children on a daily basis. Millions of single men and women did, Jules knew that, but it wasn't easy.

Obviously, Cruz wasn't inclined to marry her. Her cheeks burned at her humiliation when he'd . . . well, he'd never exactly *said* he wouldn't marry her during the conversation, just strongly hinted that he wouldn't. How could she have lowered her defenses that small?

Half an hour later, she set Olivia's car seat in the backseat of the new truck and tightened the strap. The interior smelled of leather and rubber floor mats. Crystal came out of the house lugging a huge bag of toys. The sisters had spent over an hour gathering the kids' clothing.

Crystal stored the sacks in the lined truck bed. "Should I leave a few things over here? They'll let us keep the children occasionally, won't they?"

"Oh, I'm sure they will." Jules smothered a smug grin. Given a week or two of full-time fatherhood, they'd be begging for mercy.

Pausing beside the truck, Crystal focused on the toys and luggage. "I'm going to miss them dreadfully."

"Yeah." Jules closed the door. "I'm going to miss them too." Somehow she'd adjusted to sticky fingers and toy fire trucks, and dolls scattered about the house. Childish giggles, waking in the middle of the night to get Ethan a glass of water, chasing Olivia around the den to change her soiled dress.

Her eyes met Crystal's and both broke into tears. Hanging onto each other, they sank to the dusty ground and shared a good cry. "What are we going to do without them?" Crystal whispered. "I never realized how very special a child could be; little arms around my neck, sloppy kisses, sticky jelly fingers."

Jules patted her arm. "We'll have our own

children someday."

"But they won't be Ethan or Olivia. I've grown to love them so much, Jules."

"Me too. A part of Sophie is still with me when I look at Olivia. The same eyes, the same cocky grin. The house will be like a tomb without them."

Pulling back, Crystal wiped her eyes. "I guess I don't understand. Why now? Why decide to hand them over so soon? You can't be sure of how this will turn out. The Parkers might very well be granted custody. The judge will have highly influential friends . . ." She paused, thoughtful. "Why don't you and Cruz marry? That would solve everything — and you know that's what Sophie was hoping for."

"I would marry him. There's only one technicality. Cruz doesn't want to marry me."

"How do you know? Have the two of you even tried to sit down and talk this feud out rationally?"

Jules nodded, wiping her nose on a tissue. "I asked him to marry me."

Crystal's jaw dropped. "You did? When?"

"The night before we left for Waco. He refused. Sort of."

Crystal's lips firmed. "How could he refuse? Except for Sophie, you're the best mother the kids could ever have. Is he blind?"

"No, just hurt."

"He needs to get over it. Life's tough; besides, anyone who knows you, knows how hard it is for you to commit to dinner, let alone a marriage. Cruz has to know that you love him desperately. You always have."

"He doesn't have to — and he won't accept that I'm not perfect." Jules took out a clean tissue and wiped her eyes. "What about you and Adan? You two are close. Why don't you marry?"

Sighing, Crystal sat back. "He hasn't asked. Hasn't even thought about it if my instinct is correct."

"Would you?"

"Marry Adan?" Her features turned pensive. "For the children's sake, I believe that I would."

"You're in love with him?"

"Not yet — but I could be. Eventually."

"That isn't good enough. Both you and Adan deserve more." The idea was tantamount to her suggestion that Cruz marry her because it was the *noble* thing to do. "Maybe that's why Adan hasn't asked. He must sense that the timing isn't right."

"Maybe, but I know he'd do almost anything to raise the children."

"Well," Jules got up and dusted her jeans, "both Cruz and Adan are going to have them shortly."

Crystal rose. "Oh, Jules, do you think we're doing the right thing? The men make great uncles, but fathers?"

"They'll be yelling for help," Jules said. "It's what they want and we're not going to fight them anymore. We'll let nature take its course." She turned to face her sister. "I . . . I can't be around Cruz without loving him. I have to pull back. Let events fall as they will, however painful."

"But we'll see the children, won't we?"

"If they need us — and you're free to visit anytime but I'm going to stay away. Absence makes the heart grow fonder. Isn't that what they say? Perhaps if Cruz doesn't see me as often he'll realize . . ." What? That he was wise as a serpent? Or as thick-headed as a mule. "You can bring them home occasionally and we'll have a picnic, but I have to make him see that we need each other, Crystal."

Crystal fell into step as the two women walked back to the house. "Can you do that?"

"I can do it. I can't reproduce that perfect potato, but I can take control of my feelings."

"I'm disappointed in you."

Well, that seemed to be going around. Jules turned. "What's your reason?"

"You're a fighter, just like Sophie. Why are you giving up now?"

"Because Cruz as much as told me he would never marry me."

"And you believed him?"

"Do I have a choice?"

"Of course you have a choice." Crystal grinned. "Prove the man wrong."

CHAPTER 42

When Jules pulled up at the Delgado farm, Crystal asked, "What did they say when you told them we're coming?" The rambling farmhouse looked peaceful, probably for the last time in a good long time. Tractors and equipment sat silent; a couple of dogs lay on the back step.

"I didn't tell them."

"They don't *know* they're about to become full-time fathers?"

Killing the engine, Jules shrugged. "No. I figure if they're going to be fathers they need to get used to schedule upheavals." The exploding noxious fumes that rose from Olivia's diapers would be a good test of their parental dedication. No more using a straightened coat hanger to dispose of stinky diapers. They'd now be working hands-on with their charges.

She rolled her shoulders, trying to work out the stiffness. Cruz's truck was sitting

347

near the house. At least one of the Delgados was home. Climbing out of the cab, Jules said, "Hold on. I'll tell them we're here."

By now Cruz had stepped to the side door and peered out, a cup of steaming coffee in his hand. A moment later the door opened. "What's going on?" His eyes noted the new Ford.

"We brought the children over."

Frowning, his gaze traced her steps. "It's not our day to keep them."

"I know, but Crystal and I have decided that the children belong to you and Adan. The accident proved that you have their best interests at heart when you put your life on the line for them."

"You're dropping the suit?"

"I'll swing by the lawyer's office when I leave here. Where do you want their things?"

For the first time in her life she witnessed Cruz Delgado at a loss for words. He set his cup of coffee on a ledge. Speechless.

She peered around him. "Where's Adan?"

"Still asleep."

Jules checked her watch. "It's almost nine o'clock."

"Yeah — well the harvest's over and he's catching up on some shut-eye."

She turned and motioned for Crystal.

"Bring them in!"

"Hey . . . hold on —"

She pretended not to hear his protest. The convoy started. Luggage. Toys. Various tricycles and Big Wheels. Cruz's dark eyes fixed on the alarming procession.

Two children, one bearing a diaper that would rival the Pasco landfill.

Jules deposited Olivia in Cruz's arms and then bent to kiss her. "Uncle Cruz is going to take care of you for awhile, sweetie. I love you."

Olivia held out her hand and wiggled her fingers. The action broke her heart but she knew once the men settled into their roles, they could do the job or kill their pride and admit they needed help.

Stepping aside, Jules made room for Crystal to say her good-byes.

Kissing each child, Crystal then drew them to her chest and held them for an overly long time.

Cruz found his voice. "Hey, look, ladies." He held Olivia out for breathing distance. Jules had to admit that this was one foul-smelling diaper. "Shouldn't we have planned this . . . ?"

"No." Jules straightened. "Right's right. Sophie said when I felt the time was right that I should hand them over. Today, I feel it's right."

"I'm still partially broke —"

"But you're well on your way to financial stability. Crops in, life can settle down a little. By spring planting you should have this father thing down to a science. I don't want to add anything to the Parkers' case to claim them. If you and Adan have them, the courts can't deny that the kids are where Sophie wants them." Jules reached and gave his shoulder a friendly reassuring pat. "If we can help, don't hesitate to give us a call — and did I mention that Olivia is on this insane kick of waking up in the middle of the night? She won't go back to sleep until she's fed, but if you'll feed her something warm — milk, oatmeal, anything but junk, she'll eventually drop off."

She turned and nodded to Crystal. "Ready?"

With one last hug for each child, Crystal walked back to the truck.

As the two women drove out of the yard, Crystal turned to peer out the back window. Jules glanced in the rearview mirror to see Cruz holding Olivia, Ethan beside him, surrounded by luggage and Big Wheels. Tears welled to her eyes.

Crystal glanced at her. "Olivia isn't waking up in the middle of the night."

Jules wheeled out of the driveway. "I know."

"But you told Cruz . . ."

"I'm just messing with his head."

"That's a *terrible* thing to do after dropping two small children in his lap." Crystal turned back, and crossed her arms. "I don't know how the man puts up with you."

"That's the point. He doesn't."

"You're either feisty or just plain mean."

"Yeah," Jules agreed. "I fear a little of both."

On the way home, they rode in stony silence. Jules should feel a little guilty about the sudden change of heart, and she supposed that she did, a tiny bit, but not enough to change her mind.

Unfortunately, a man's heart was a bit hard to tame. And what she'd just done was downright mean but necessary. If she were to ever open Cruz's eyes to his need for her, it was now. She risked a last glance in the rearview mirror, confident the children would be back within a few days.

CHAPTER 43

Someone more profound than Jules once said: Life was like a leaf. Sometimes it was beautiful, exploding with color. Other times it was green, filled with life. Then at others the once beautiful, green thing died. And then it was barren for a season.

Jules felt as though she had entered her barren season. Without the children to care for, or potatoes to harvest, or the perfect potato experiment, her life was a brittle branch. Crystal visited the kids weekly — sometimes two or three times, but Jules steered clear of the Delgados and The Grille. Old behavior dies hard, and loving Cruz for most of her life wasn't an easy habit to break, but she was determined to break it.

She questioned Crystal daily about the Parkers' quest, but her sister said the matter was still under discussion. She couldn't imagine Cruz considering the proposal, but then she would have thought that he would have brought the children back by now, which he hadn't.

"They're thriving," Crystal told her. "Happy as I've ever seen them."

There was little Jules could do about that, but she was determined to put a stop to insincere suitors who wanted her for nothing more than her magic potato plant that would not, and never could, materialize. Like Cruz's love, the perfect potato was not destined to be.

She took out a front page ad in the *Community Gazette* stating her defeat:

Jules Matias's experimental potato research has been discontinued. Only God can create a perfect potato. Ms. Matias plans to abandon the study and turn her thoughts to new and inventive ways to fertilize tubers with less cost and manpower.

Surely the speculators would back off now.

Later that week, Crystal began preparations for returning to Florida. If Jules thought the house was quiet without the children, once Crystal left she knew that she would be living in a mausoleum.

"Why don't you come with me," her sister

invited for the third time.

"What would I do in Florida?" Jules lay on the sofa, staring at the ceiling. An odd sort of despondency settled over her.

"I don't know — lie in the sun? Swim? Shop? Enjoy the incredible sea food?"

"I can do all of that here."

Crystal turned to stare at her. "Look at you. You haven't gotten dressed in two days."

"For what? I have nowhere to go. The potato bins are full, and Joe's taking care of the farm."

"Honestly? You seem a little down."

She scratched her hair. She needed to shower and shampoo. Two days on the sofa did do a job on a person. "Down?" She rolled to her back. "I'm not down."

Packing a couple pairs of jeans, Crystal eyed her. "Why not come and help me? My assistant needs time to prepare to go back to college. Let Joe run the farm, and you come to Florida with me. You can lie in the sun while I run the shop. Get a taste of my life."

"I don't want to go to Florida. I have too much to do around here."

"Like what?"

"Like, help Joe. Invent cheap fertilizer."

"Joe doesn't need any help, and fertilizers

354

can wait. Get up, take a shower, wash that hair, pack your bag and come with me."

"Nah. Too much effort." Jules rolled to her side, staring at the television. "Are there any of those old *Beverly Hillbillies* reruns on?"

Sighing, Crystal picked up the phone. "I'm booking a ticket for you on my flight."

Jules rolled to her back. Great. A bumpy, hair-raising flight. Just what she wanted.

Friday morning Jules trailed her sister to the check-in line. In her hand she carried a coach ticket to Fort Walton, Florida. From there, they'd take a cab to Crystal's shell shop in Destin. In the end, Crystal had convinced her that she owed it to Mom to glimpse her life "after Pop." Jules, having nothing more to do than yawn, finally relented to one week. One week of sun and fun. She needed a year.

The Gulf of Mexico sparkled like a large green gem in the sunlight. Clear, tranquil: thousands of miles away from Washington State, potatoes and heartache.

The quaint shell shop with living quarters in the back perked her spirits. Like Crystal, there was placidness to the surroundings. Relaxing, tranquil. By the second morning when Jules sat outside the small residence sipping Crystal's special blend of herbal tea and watching porpoises leap and play in the water, she decided her sister had her best interest at heart when she'd bought that airline ticket. Here, her troubles felt less intrusive, if Cruz could ever be intrusive.

She sighed, amazed at how well he and Adan were handling full-time fatherhood. The big goons had taken to the position like women to chocolate.

An ache settled around her heart when she thought about Ethan and Olivia. She missed the little imps. She missed Sophie. She missed Pop. *Lord, they say that bad things come in threes. If it's possible, may I avoid a number four?*

Crystal wandered out to join her. Out here, they could listen for the bell over the door, and enjoy the lazy morning. "Enjoying the view?"

Jules closed her eyes and drank in the sea air. Gulls swooped and dipped overhead. Egrets raced across the sand on spindly legs. "You were right. This is exactly what I needed. I can see why you and Mom love it here."

"Yes." She took a chaise next to Jules. "The sea brings me closer to God."

"How so?"

"Maybe its power? I'm reminded how big

and wondrous this world is."

Yes, God was large and powerful. The thought had been with her since she arrived. The sea, the waters. At night she watched the stars come out — so many thousands. A falling star reminded her of how Sophie used to say that it was a soul on its way to heaven.

They sat in silence, listening to a buoy bell tinkle in the distance. Soft breezes touched their face. This was the closest Jules had ever come to a real family. Sharing a moment with a sister, a moment when nothing needed to be said. By now Crystal knew all her faults and shortcomings and still wanted to be with her. If only Cruz had such unconditional love. Relationships were a lot like potatoes: unless cared for properly they could develop a lot of dark spots, bruise, and sprout eyes. Rot.

Time stopped and Jules rested in silky breezes, waves lapping the white sand shores and the endless cries of seagulls and ocean birds flitting about their daily lives.

What was intended to be a week's sabbatical turned into two. Then three. Joe was handling the farm just fine without Jules and encouraged her to stay. Each time Crystal spoke with Adan or the children, everything was swimmingly good.

Jules discovered she actually liked selling seashells to the tourists, watching children's delighted expressions as they held the ocean's treasure up to their ears and listened for the anticipated sound.

Evenings, she and Crystal ate shrimp at places like Louisiana Lagniappe while watching the sunset on the outdoor deck. Other times they enjoyed a hamburger at Pompano Joe's overlooking the Gulf of Mexico.

One night they found themselves on the shell shop verandah eating Vienna sausages and Doritos.

"I didn't know you liked Vienna sausages," Crystal said around a mouthful of canned meat.

"Are you serious? They were Pop's staple. Don't you remember how he used to feed us cans of these things when Mom wasn't looking?"

"That must be why I crave them." Crystal popped another in her mouth, and then lay back in her lounge, wiggling her toes in her flip-flops. "Have you tried the barbecue flavor?"

"Yeah, but I like the original ones best." She glanced over. "You're vegetarian? What's the deal?"

"I am — except for the occasional Vienna

sausage pig-out." Her grin was pure mischief. "And a hamburger or burrito thrown in occasionally."

"How often does that happen?"

"When I can't live another moment without the addicting things."

"I know what you mean."

"Did Pop still eat canned chili?"

"Only when he wasn't eating Vienna sausages." The sisters giggled, heady on canned meat.

"What about Mom? Did she still spend hours in the bathroom doing who knows what?"

Crystal nodded to the shell shop entrance. "I used the public bathroom every morning before we opened shop."

Reclining, Jules popped another fat sausage in her mouth. "I climb out of bed, wash my face, brush my teeth and stick a hat on before I go to the fields — which reminds me, I'm out of toothpaste."

Crystal shrugged and reached for the sack of Doritos. "I have plenty. Help yourself."

"Thanks." Jules snuggled deeper into her chair. That's something Sophie would have said. Lying back, she smiled, wondering what catastrophe awaited the two new "fathers" today, for surely there had been those. She glanced at Crystal. "What did

Adan have to say last night?"

Shaking her head, she perused a magazine. "Not much."

"I say pride won't let them ask for help." Cruz would never ask for her help, or even hint that he wasn't up to the job. She dropped a Dorito in her mouth. He had to be up to his hips in fatherhood.

CHAPTER 44

"Adan!"

He stuck his head around the doorsill, holding Olivia in his arms. "You bellowed?"

Cruz studied the sheet of paper his brother handed him at breakfast. "What is this?"

"We have to potty train Livvy."

Cruz's gaze shifted to the little girl. "We have to what?"

"Potty train. Livvy. She's two, and I've been reading this article on potty training. It says she's ready."

"I don't know how to potty train a girl."

"Neither do I, but the article says it's time we trained her, and you have to admit, those diapers are murder."

Cruz nodded. Those daily stink bombs were killers, but potty training? He glanced at the paper heading: "Three days? It takes that long?"

"That's what it says."

Olivia presented a cheeky grin.

Cruz shook his head. "You have to do it, Adan. I've got a weak stomach."

"Who doesn't? You're not pawning this off on me."

"It isn't my idea."

"Get used to it. We can't have her wearing diapers until she's four."

"What do I have to do?" The bitter irony of Jules's sneaky trick struck home. She had been right. Two was better than one when it came to caring for children. He could do it, but he couldn't count the times he'd wished that Jules was here to help.

"Nothing except take care of Ethan for the next three days."

"That's all?"

Adan motioned to the article he'd downloaded off the internet. "The article says to stick to the kid you're training like glue. Every hour or so, I tell her to tell me when she needs to go potty."

"You don't ask her if she needs to go?"

Adan took the paper and studied it. "No. It says I tell her to tell me."

"That ought to work like a charm," Cruz groused. "She doesn't understand the meaning of 'potty'."

"All I know to do is follow instructions." Adan winked at Livvy. "Right, little girl? We'll show 'em, won't we?"

Livvy giggled.

Cruz got up from the table. "And *she's* going to tell you."

"I don't know exactly how it works, but I'll give it a shot. What's your schedule the next three days?"

"I don't know — routine, I guess."

"Then you can assume Ethan's full care?"

"I guess."

Adan squeezed Olivia. "Okay, Cricket, we're going to potty train you."

The child stared back, wide-eyed. "Potty."

Nodding, Adan grinned. "Potty."

Cruz closed his eyes, admitting the obvious. Sophie was right. He wasn't ready to be a full-time father without Jules. *Without a wife,* he mentally corrected.

Later he went downstairs to the waiting mountain of laundry. Either the Delgados were the dirtiest or cleanest folk in town. The laundry had doubled — tripled since the kids had been here. Stuffing towels, jeans and whites into the washer, he dumped a capful of liquid detergent in the dispenser and pushed the hot water button. He couldn't keep up with the laundry. He washed day and night but there was always another load waiting.

Turning to last night's dryer load, he started to fold towels. There were a hundred. Overhead he heard Adan's boots thumping against the kitchen floor. The day Jules brought the children on a permanent basis was the last day the men had been on schedule. They'd divided the work. Adan cleaned, Cruz did the washing and cooking. They'd hired a neighbor to watch the kids while they did outside work. Next year Ethan would start kindergarten, but Olivia would need daycare. Daycare in these parts was no small feat, but they had the winter to look for a responsible housekeeper and nanny.

He tossed the empty basket aside and picked up another one. Where was Jules? She hadn't called; he hadn't spotted her new truck around town for the past few weeks. Nobody seemed to know where she'd gone including Joe. He had a hunch she'd taken off for Florida with Crystal. *Fine. You lay in the sun and surf. I'll potty train Livvy.* The Parkers were on his back; they were nice but they wanted an answer. There was no way they were going to get full custody or even shared custody of Livvy. He'd see that she visited often, but that was as far as he'd yield.

"Hey, Adan!"

Adan's voice returned from upstairs. "Yo!"

"Did Jules go to Florida with Crystal?" It

was the first time he'd inquired of Jules's whereabouts and he didn't want Adan getting any crazy notion in his head.

"Three weeks ago!"

Cruz folded tiny dresses. *Three weeks. Florida.* Well how nice for them. Anger mixed with an odd miss. He missed her. *Come on, Cruz.* When had she turned into a miss and not an irritant? This father thing was good, but it would be better with her by his side.

Adan came down the stairs carrying a full basket of dirty clothes. Cruz glanced up. "Come on. Are you standing out on the road asking for this stuff?"

"Hey, I don't create laundry, I just deliver it." He set the overflowing basket down on the dryer. "Do you want me to lay out some hamburger meat for supper?"

"We just ate breakfast."

"Yeah, and we've got lunch and supper left."

Cruz folded a tiny blouse. "What's running upstairs?" A steady hum filled the upstairs den.

"Ethan's vacuuming."

"You can't let a five-year-old vacuum! He's scratching up all the furniture."

"He does a fairly decent job. It's a lightweight machine."

"He sucked up all the Tinkertoys yesterday."

"I know. I emptied the bag and he's back in business."

Three weeks ago Cruz wouldn't have given vacuuming or supper a passing thought. He'd have stopped at The Grille, grabbed a burger and fries, shot a couple of games of billiards, maybe taken a woman to a movie. But no more. The kids didn't fare well in public. Not during meals. And the only vegetables The Grille served were French fries, fried mushrooms or onion rings. Lean meat, green and yellow vegetables and milk weren't on the menu. These days, the bright spot in his life happened after supper when the kids were in bed and he could enjoy a Coke and bowl of popcorn without wiping up spills, or whacking backs to clear a popcorn husk.

But Jules. *Jules* was in Florida. So much for her, "Oh, Cruz, I really care for the children. They need both a mother and a father." He tossed a towel on the folding table. Both a mother and a father. Right.

She is right, you fool.

Ignoring his own thought, he paused, staring at the sock in his hand. Where the heck did the extra sock come from?

366

CHAPTER 45

Sighing, Jules settled back in her lounge, staring at the stars. Millions twinkled over the glistening water. She was so relaxed she was lethargic. Her skin was now a warm creamy brown. The tropical smelling lotion she applied every night made her skin petal soft. She hadn't thought about a potato in weeks. She missed the kids dreadfully. Both she and Crystal couldn't enter a shop without each picking up something for Ethan and Olivia. The kids would have an abundance of new clothing when she got home.

Crystal came out of the living quarters carrying two large frosty glasses. "Peach tea?"

"Thanks." Jules set the sweaty glass on the table beside her. Snuggling deeper into her lounge, she sighed. "I suppose I should think about going home."

"I wish you wouldn't. I can't think of a

better time in our lives than these past few weeks."

Reaching for her sister's hand, Jules squeezed it. "Me neither." A relationship they'd both wanted and desired had formed. She felt as close to Crystal tonight as she felt to Sophie.

Thank you, God, for giving me what I didn't even know that I needed so badly.

Crystal didn't replace Sophie. Nothing or no one could ever do that, but she was starting to hold her own special place in Jules's heart. A sister's place.

Taking the lounge beside her, Crystal settled. "I think about the kids so often. And Adan."

"Me too — not Adan." Jules glanced over sheepishly.

"I'd hope not. But you miss Cruz."

"Yeah. I miss him." Funny, but a few weeks ago she'd have kept that to herself. Now, the admission came easy with Crystal. She worried that she'd put too much on him; thrust him into the role of full-time fatherhood. He could handle it; she knew that now, but she wondered if he ever wished that she was there to help, to share in the joys and pitfalls of parenting.

Crystal wrinkled her nose playfully. "We've allowed the men enough time to settle into a routine. Let's both call and see how they're doing."

Jules shook her head. "Cruz doesn't want to hear from me."

"You don't know that."

"I do know that — I told you I asked Cruz to marry me and he refused."

"Outright refused?"

"He wasn't enthusiastic about the idea."

"What man would be with you two's history? He'll eventually come around."

"I wish I could be as certain."

"Nothing's certain, Jules, but this moment." She reached for Jules's hand. "Try and trust that God's in control, and both you and Cruz are exactly where he wants you to be right now."

"I wish I had your faith."

"It's like riding a bike. You'll take a few painful spills, but if you practice enough you'll get good at it." Reaching in her pocket, Crystal removed her cell phone. "I'm calling Adan."

"Fine." Jules lay back, staring at the stars. "He's always glad to hear from you." Somewhere Cruz was under this brightly lit canopy. With Ms. Eye Candy? Trying to fall in love with her enough so that he could marry and provide both mother and father for Sophie's kids? Envy rendered her silent.

Crystal hit speed dial and in a minute she was talking to Adan. Jules only caught half of the conversation, but it sounded as though the two brothers were taking fatherhood in stride. Crystal chatted, telling about their day, the adventures they'd had, the perfect relaxation.

Before she knew what was happening, Jules found the phone in her hand. She sat up straighter when Cruz's voice came on the line.

"Hi."

"Where *are* you?"

"Fine, thank you. And you?"

"Adan says you're in Florida with Crystal."

"I am, and we're having a lovely time. How are the children?"

"They're good. When are you coming home?"

"Oh . . ." She leaned back, balancing one flip-flop on the end of her toe. "I haven't decided. Joe says everything is going well with Blue Bayou, and it couldn't be a more lovely time to be down here. The beach is great, the crowds have thinned."

"Sounds nice. When are you coming home?"

"Do I have a deadline?"

"No . . . but the kids keep asking where

you are. You can't just up and disappear." A thin vein of neediness filtered through his tone.

"The kids miss me?" She brightened. "Are they okay?"

"They're fine. They just want their Aunt Jube."

"Ah, that's sweet. Can I talk to Ethan?"

"He's in bed."

"Can you wake him —"

"Good grief, no! That would wake Livvy. Adan's potty training her. It's been a day I wouldn't relive. I've been sidestepping crackers, chips, salty stuff to make her go — it's been a nightmare, and we're out of juice and milk again. She won't go if we can't get a lot of liquid in her."

"Potty training?" The picture of Adan and Cruz potty training flashed before her eyes. They wouldn't know where to start! She sobered. She'd planned on training Livvy. Envy spilled over more. She glanced at her watch. "It's pretty early for them to be in bed, isn't it?"

"Same time they go to bed every night."

"Okay — maybe I'll call later in the week and talk to them."

"How long do you plan to be gone?"

"I haven't decided. Do I need to come home?"

"No . . . unless you want to."

"Then I don't know how long I'll stay."

"Jules . . ." She recognized that tone. He wanted to say something but didn't know how to phrase it. Did he miss her? Could he form the words to tell her so? If he couldn't, she might as well stay here forever.

"Yes?"

"Nothing. It wasn't important."

"I'll call later in the week."

"Have a nice time."

"Thanks. I will."

She clicked off. The prior peace that filled her now bubbled like a cauldron. Why did she let this man upset her? Obviously he wanted her to come home, but why? Because he loved her, that he couldn't live without her?

Please, God, let that be the cause of his silent reserve.

CHAPTER 46

"Okay." Adan appeared after breakfast holding a sheaf of papers. "I've downloaded this off the web, so we'll have a better grasp of the situation."

Cruz glanced up from the newspaper he was reading. "What is it?"

"It's that article on potty training. There's all sorts of approaches on the Web."

Cruz's attention pivoted back to the paper. Adan's efforts to train Livvy were tantamount to bulls ramming heads. Useless. Livvy was more stubborn than any bull Adan had met. "I thought you could do it in three days."

"I can — I was going about it the wrong way. Hank Sites — you know him. Lives over near the Brown place? He and his wife had a baby a couple of years back, Hank says he trained his girl in nothing flat. I've downloaded the instructions, and it seems Hank left out a few steps. Starting today, we'll see some progress."

"Fine." Cruz perused the sports section. They'd gotten nowhere so far. The familiar diaper stench permeated the hallway.

That day, Adan stuck with Livvy like glue. Every so often, Cruz heard the now familiar phrase, "Livvy, you tell me when you have to go potty."

All morning Livvy pretty much ignored the issue. The words "cookie," "dolly," and "go way!" came through clear enough. Adan didn't press the issue, but said every half hour or so, "Livvy. Tell me when you have to go potty."

By noon, Livvy shoved the Tinkertoys aside and said, "Potty."

Cruz stuck his head around the kitchen doorway. "What'd she say?"

"She said she has to go potty." Adan beamed.

That night, Livvy wet her diaper, soaked her bed, and everything including her blankie had to be washed.

Day two, the accidents were less frequent. Cruz assumed full care of Ethan and Adan stuck to Livvy like honey to skin. The two sat in the middle of the living room floor, building Tinkertoys, playing dolls, reading books until it was time for the child to go to bed.

"Livvy, tell me when you have to go potty."
The occasional nod sufficed.

Cruz said a prayer of gratitude for Adan's patience. The method was boring and taxing, but Livvy was starting to respond. *Jules, I don't think you'd be as patient as Adan.* He grinned at the thought.

By the third day, the child was not only telling Adan when she needed to go, but she was completing the process herself.

Adan and Cruz bought a T-bone steak and grilled out in celebration.

Twice during the meal, Livvy interrupted with, "I hafta go."

Moonlight glistened off the ocean water. Jules closed her eyes, picturing Cruz and Adan at home, with the children. She'd bet the two men were tearing their hair out with the new responsibilities. Potty train Livvy, indeed. They'd never have the patience. She'd helped Sophie train Ethan and it had taken months, months of frustration and wet clothing. By the time Jules returned home, Cruz would be only too happy to hand the child's bathroom training over to her.

Crystal slipped into the house, leaving Jules to stare at the ocean. The past few weeks had brought about an incredible change, one that she warmly welcomed. Jules was relaxed now, non-combative. Sophie's untimely death had settled her down, made her look at life with a new perspective. Was that Sophie's intent? Or was her request to bring Cruz and Jules together, to make them realize they were paired for life? She had no doubt that it was the latter. Was Cruz learning the same lesson? With Sophie's passing, no one would ever know her full intent, but Crystal was grateful of the small role she now played in Jules's life. For the first time ever, she had a sister.

She reached for the cell phone and hit Adan's button. His voice came on the line after the third ring.

"Hi — I thought I'd get your voice mail."

His tone brightened. "I'm at The Grille. It took a minute to recognize your ring."

"I have a special ring?" She never bothered assigning fog horns, pin ball machines, old cars, or cyber beeps to friends. A simple ring found her.

"Yeah, you're the song that made Sonny and Cher a hit: 'I Got You Babe.' "

Laughing, Crystal walked into the privacy of her bedroom. She never knew when Jules would come in and find her talking to Adan. There had been numerous hushed talks over the past weeks and she was fortunate Jules hadn't caught her in the act yet.

"Hey, I think Jules is weakening."

"Yeah? So is Cruz. He's a basket case. I don't know if he's angry with Jules for staying in Florida so long, or scared that she might not come back, or that she refuses to tell him when she's coming home."

"She doesn't know when she's coming home." She sat down on the side of her mattress. "One moment she talks about selling Blue Bayou and moving here, and the next she's crying, wishing she was home with the children. If she thought for one moment that Cruz wanted her there, she would be on the next plane out."

"I can't read him," Adan confessed. "But he's got a burr under his saddle about something."

"What we're doing is best, isn't it?"

"It's right." Background music faded as he stepped to a quieter location. "I know how you're feeling because I'm feeling the same way. I love the kids, but like we discussed, Jules and Cruz are the logical parents. Just let nature takes its course."

"I agree, but it's hard." Crystal missed the little imps, the board games, messy hands and peanut butter and jelly smiles.

"Come-on, Cris." He used her pet name.

"We're young; we can have all the children we want."

"So are Cruz and Jules. They're not ancient."

"They're not, but you don't think for a minute that Sophie had anything other than Cruz and Jules in mind when she hatched up her plot. That's Sophie, always thinking ahead."

"But she didn't know how critical her situation was; how could she?"

"She knew. From the moment she got the diagnosis she knew. And she turned a tragedy into a blessing." Pride filled his voice. "That's my big sis."

Crystal sighed. "Of course you're right. Not for a moment did I believe that Sophie's request wasn't carefully planned, but suddenly there are logical options other than Jules and Cruz. The children might be better off with me, or the Parkers. Either of us could easily give them a life of luxury, while Cruz and Jules can only offer potatoes."

"And love. Don't forget the main ingredient."

"You don't think the Parkers or I would love them?"

"Sure you would; and grandparents adore their grandchildren, but nature has a way of slowing us down. The Parkers would need a heap of energy, energy they don't have in order to raise two small children, participate in school activities, gymnastics, dance, church activities. Then there's the teen years, cars, dating —"

Crystal closed her eyes, exhausted thinking about the hectic schedules. "Agreed; we'd all make good parents."

"Hey."

"Yes?"

"Are you still okay with this? I thought we'd agreed a long time ago our part in this was to get Cruz and Jules back on track."

She touched a tissue to her eyes. "It's just harder than I'd imagined."

"Yeah, when the heart's involved, it is usually tough, but we're doing the right thing. Cruz needed time to get over his hurt; the past few months have weakened his resistance toward Jules, and anyone can see that Jules is still in love with the guy."

"You think that Cruz is now able to move on?"

"Getting close. Real close. Give him another week or two without her around and he'll see the wisdom of swallowing his pride and facing the inevitable —"

"I wish she would stay here — for purely selfish reasons." Crystal had gotten used to waking up to the smell of Jules's fresh brewed coffee, though she'd never drink a cup. She loved to hear her puttering around the house, in the bathroom, watching the early morning news, reading the newspaper. Their long walks on the beach, gathering shells. Loneliness settled around her, and the small living quarters suddenly felt very large and empty. Would she ever be as content here when Jules left?

"Yeah? You two have gotten pretty close lately."

"We have, and that's an added blessing that Sophie never thought about."

"I wouldn't bet on it."

She frowned. "You don't think —"

"That Sophie knew how much Jules would need a sister once she passed on? I'd think that — in a New York minute."

Crystal shook her head, stunned by the woman's perception.

"Face it, Cris. There's a mate for every one of us, and —"

"Cruz and Jules are one whether they like it or not," Crystal finished the thought.

"He doesn't like it," Adan chuckled. "But he's stuck with it."

Crystal smiled. "Ever thought about vacationing in Destin?"

His tone sobered. "Every day. I miss you."

"I miss you too. So are you going to come

and visit?"

"You never know; one night you could look up and I'll be standing on your doorstep. You can show me the sights."

"I'd love that, Adan."

"Then count on it," he said. "You are coming home for the holidays?"

Home. Crystal never thought of Washington State as home, but the past few months had altered her perception on a lot of things. She had a home, Blue Bayou. There were pleasant memories there as well as unpleasant ones. "I wouldn't miss it."

"I'll have the tree, presents and turkey. You bring dessert."

"Make sure it's a live tree." She missed the fragrance of a freshly cut tree, a fire burning in the fireplace. "What's your favorite pie? Pecan? Pumpkin?"

"I was thinking of you."

"Oh." His implication registered: she was dessert.

She giggled. Now that had to be the sweetest thing a man had ever said to her. "Jules wonders why Cruz doesn't call."

"Cruz is wondering why she hasn't called. He's a coward; I don't know about her. If he hears her voice, he worries that he'll be on a plane to Florida to bring her home. Why don't you call us in a few minutes?"

"Better yet, give me half an hour and you phone us. Jules would like that."

"What are you doing in the meantime?"

"Me? I'm about to advance to stage two of the plan."

Jules was still staring at the sky when Crystal returned. "Just look at this night."

Crystal paused in the doorway and closed her eyes. "Ah . . . salty air. Don't you love it?" After a moment, she opened her eyes. "Have you ever made a sand angel?"

"A what?"

"Sand angel." She reached for Jules's hand. "Come on. The tide receded hours ago, and the sand is the perfect texture."

"Crystal! It's —" Jules held her wrist to the doorway light checking the time. "It's eleven o'clock."

"So what? We can catch the late church service in the morning and sleep in. Come on. It'll be fun."

Fun. Until this trip, Jules had never particularly associated the word with Crystal. Fun was Sophie. Girl talks, shopping, movies. She and Crystal had done all that and more lately, and the emptiness she'd felt since Sophie's death was starting to lift. Ever so slightly, but getting more comfortable with the idea that her best friend was gone. Was it possible that God would provide her a Sophie for every season of her life?

Jules slowly crawled from the comfortable reclining chair. *Sand angels.* She could just imagine the grit they'd track in the house.

Halfway down the beach, Crystal broke into a trot. The choppy waves were thigh to waist deep. Wind whipped her hair and she sang out with the joy of life. "Isn't God's handiwork divine?"

Trudging through the sand, Jules focused on the night. Stars hung suspended overhead. A full moon bathed the swirling foam. Salty air incited her senses. It was the most beautiful sight she'd ever witnessed and she wished with all of her heart that Cruz was there, walking beside her. Indeed, God's handiwork should be admired.

She paused, tilting her face up to catch the soft breeze blowing off the waters. Fish and algae. Tide pools rushing in, and then out. The world was at peace with itself here, relishing its creation, the earth praising its Creator in the gentle white foam riding the crest of tranquil waves. Blue Bayou and all she held dear were thousands of miles away from Destin, and yet she relished these gifts, longing for the lives she loved so far away. Cruz. Ethan. Olivia.

Casting her sandals aside, she broke into a run and tried to catch Crystal. Wind caught her hair as her bare feet flew over the damp sand. Maybe she could outrun her emotions, run so long and so hard that she would forget that Cruz ever existed.

Ahead, Crystal dropped to the moist sand and began to move her arms, up and down, making a sand angel in the receding waves. When Jules approached, she dropped to her knees, then rolled to her back and engaged in the childhood antic. Above, a sky more beautiful than jewels twinkled.

"Isn't this the most peaceful experience?" Crystal reached out to take hold of Jules's hand. Though Cruz was thousands of miles away, he was here, beneath this breathtaking canopy of stars. "If it's meant to be, he'll come around."

Only Sophie had known the true depths of Jules's love, yet tonight Crystal unaccountably felt it. "I've lost him forever," Jules whispered — or whimpered. She did that a lot lately.

"Perhaps, but there is the matter of forgiveness."

Yes, there was that matter. Pop couldn't forgive Mom and it led to a life of misery. Would the same happen to Cruz?

"How many times can a man forgive a

woman for walking away from him?"

"Seven times seven?"

"Your faith never falters."

"Didn't Pop teach you the value of trust?"

"I don't think he knew it himself, but regardless, I don't see that either one of us had much to trust in when we were children. I don't know about you, but I lived in a world where I was certain that one or the other would leave us one day, and they did."

Crystal rolled to face her in the moonlight. "We can't choose our parents. Or our childhoods, but we can choose our adult lives. We can't let Mom and Pop's shortcomings determine ours."

"So what are you saying? That I should keep trying with Cruz, even when I've made a fool of myself endless times?"

"You love him, don't you? He's the only man in the world that you feel this ravenous tie to?"

"I suppose there is this indelible bond between us. Maybe more a gut feeling that he's the one — always will be."

"Then you should go back and work out the problem. Obviously he hasn't found anyone to take your place. It will take him time to forgive and regain trust, but you're up to the wait."

Squeezing Crystal's hand, Jules relented.

It could possibly take the rest of her life, but the goal was worth it. Beginning now, she chose to no longer fear. It wouldn't be easy, but if she were willing to fail, there would be no need to fear — especially if Cruz were the goal. If she had created the problem, there was still hope that she could undo it. He was speaking to her. They had a bond through the children.

Later the sisters walked hand in hand back to the shell shop. Jules turned on the hose and rinsed the sand off her, and then turned the hose on Crystal. The cold water brought a shrill and a retaliatory water fight. Crystal armed with buckets from the water barrel, Jules wielding the hose. Both were laughing so hard they almost missed the ringing phone.

Dropping her bucket, Crystal mopped water out of her eyes. "I'll get it."

Toweling dry, Jules trailed her into the house in time to catch the first part of the conversation. Adan was on the other end of the line

"I'm back. What's plan two?"

"No kidding!" Crystal squealed. "That's wonderful! She played her part. "In how long?"

"Amazing."

"What?" Jules mouthed. "Is something

wrong with one of the kids?"

Shaking her hand, Crystal listened. "Truly fantastic. I'll bet Cruz is happy."

Jules tugged on Crystal's blouse. *"What?"*

Her sister shrugged her hand aside. "Oh, swimming. And making sand angels.

"Yeah, hard life." She flashed a grin. "Hey, Adan — hold on. Jules is going ballistic." She covered the mouthpiece with her hand. "Adan potty-trained Livvy in three days."

"He what?"

"Potty-trained Livvy." Another grin. "And you thought they couldn't do it."

"You read my thoughts." Jealousy coursed through Jules. She wanted to train Livvy. Show Cruz what a capable mother and potty-trainer she could be. A second even more agonizing reaction hit her. Adan would make a tremendous father. No matter who he married.

Sophie's children aren't crackerjack prizes! She caught her faulty reasoning process. They were precious little souls who deserved all that either Cruz or Adan could give them. Crystal's voice penetrated her brain. "She's right here. Does he want to talk to her?"

Waving the suggestion aside, Jules walked out of the room. She didn't need Adan or Crystal's pity. If Cruz wanted to talk to her, he would have made the call. Right now, she could barely absorb the fact that he could, and quite nicely, carry on his life without her.

A hot shower and clean pajamas failed to erase the deepening ache in her heart. She longed for home — but what awaited her wasn't the ideal. An independent Cruz. Conflict. He didn't need her — he didn't need anyone.

She glanced at the bedside clock. 1:00 a.m. Ten at home. The phone shrilled.

Starting, she reached for the cell and her heart leaped when she saw the number. Adan was calling back.

Only Cruz's voice met her greeting. "How come you didn't want to talk to me?" The question was more inquisitive than demanding.

"I had sand all over me."

A smile appeared in his voice. "Have you been out rolling in it?"

"Actually, I have." Sitting up straighter, she ran her hand through her damp hair. What did he want at this time of night?

"I guess Adan told you the news?"

"You guys potty-trained Livvy. Congratulations."

"I didn't have anything to do with it. It was Adan's deal."

"Still, it's quite an accomplishment. And in only three days."

"Yeah, Adan got the how-to information off the internet."

Jules picked at a loose thread on the sheet. You could find anything on the internet these days.

Cruz tone lowered. "So. When are you coming home?"

"Soon. Maybe next week. Why?"

"Why so long?"

"It's very restful here." She noted his gradual change of tone. Gentle. Almost coaxing now. His question was more than polite inquiry, but how much more?

"Is . . . there a reason I should come home?" She closed her eyes, praying. *Please, please . . .*

"No reason — the kids miss you. They ask about Aunt Jube every day."

"I miss them too."

Silence.

"Next week?"

Well, it wasn't exactly like Romeo and Juliet — or even romantic, but it was something. "I'll check the airline schedule. I should be home by Monday evening."

"Okay. Want to call me back on the time? The kids and I can pick you up."

She glanced at the clock. "Check tonight?"

"Sure. I'm awake."

But there was a three-hour time distance between them. Still she was never one to look a gift horse in the mouth.

"Okay. I'll call the airlines." Her heart hammered in her throat. *He's asking you to come home* . . . No. He was asking for the children's sake. No, he was asking for his sake. She'd known him long enough and well enough to know when he wanted something, and he wanted her to come home.

She closed her eyes. *Thank you, God. I don't deserve this, but thank you. And I won't fail you or him this time.*

Still . . . A small part of her had to be certain of what he was asking. She cleared her throat. "Cruz?"

"Yeah?"

"Are you asking me to come home for the children's benefit . . . or yours?"

Silence. Then. "Right now for the kids. But later . . ." He paused then started over. "I don't know, Jules. I —" He drew a deep breath. "I miss you."

Closing her eyes, she held the receiver closer. "I miss you too."

"Maybe . . ."

"We could start over?"

He chuckled. "No thanks. No start overs,

but we've both grown. Maybe I didn't understand your needs, and maybe you didn't understand mine. We could work on knowing each other better."

"I'd like that very much."

"Jules."

"Yeah?"

"Call the airline."

Twenty minutes later she was booked on flight 329. She'd be in Pasco at 9:14 p.m. the following Monday night.

When she called to tell Cruz, he picked up on the first ring.

"9:14 p.m., next Monday."

"I'll be there." He paused. "Will you?"

She supposed she had that coming, but he couldn't gain complete trust with one phone conversation. "I'll be there, Cruz."

"I'm dead serious, Jules. Will you be there this time? To stay?"

She despised the hurt, yet the hope she heard in his voice. She'd be there. Nothing could keep her from this date.

"It's a promise. An adult-we've-both-grown, promise. I will be there." Never again would she allow anyone but the Almighty to come between them. That was a pledge she'd have no troubling keeping.

"Then I'll be at the gate waiting for you. 9:14 p.m. Monday evening."

CHAPTER 47

Jules cringed when a sharp bolt of lightning lit the bedroom. She was packed, ready to leave for the airport, anticipating a bumpy flight, but she'd face anything to get back home and into Cruz's arms. Sitting down on the bed, she repeated the thought out loud, loving the sound. Cruz and her. With work, they could regain what she'd neglected twice; she had no doubt that their love could overcome this last dreadful obstacle — regaining his trust. She'd loved Pop, respected his wishes, but it was now her time to fully love the one man she'd never stopped loving.

Crystal called from the kitchen, "We'd better go or you're going to be late for your flight!"

Jules chuckled, laying her cell phone on the bed. Only an act of God could make her late for this flight. Slipping off the mattress, she closed and locked the suitcase and then set it on the floor. Outside, rain and thunder lashed the windows. Shuddering, she imagined a turbulent flight with this kind of weather, but right now she'd fly a Canada goose back to Cruz.

"I'm getting in the car!" Crystal called. "Traffic will be horrible this time of day."

Reaching for her purse, Jules grabbed the luggage handle and rolled her case to the garage where Crystal's old Fiat sat covered with a blue tarp. Her sister rarely drove, preferring to ride her bike or walk. The tarp came off, and the luggage was stored in the backseat. The two women climbed in and buckled up. The old engine cranked refusing to turn over. Jules checked her watch. "Will it start?" They'd gone for dinners and ice cream a few times since she'd been here, and once the old motor refused to cooperate. They had walked home and sent a mechanic back for the Fiat the next morning. She checked her watch. She still had plenty of time to call a cab.

"It'll start. It's just fussy." Her sister turned the key, coaxing the motor to life. Eventually the engine caught and sputtered. Black smoke poured from the tailpipe as Crystal slowly backed out of the shed.

Rain pelted the canvas roof during the drive to the airport. Severe lightning moved on, but a steady downpour flooded the streets. Halfway there, Crystal glanced at the wavering gas needle. "I need gas. I'm running on fumes."

Jules checked her watch. "Can't we make it to the airport and then you can get fuel?"

"No." She checked the rearview mirror. "We won't make it to the airport. There's a truck stop up ahead. Hold on."

Anxiety building, Jules grasped her seat buckle as Crystal crossed three lanes and exited. Thunder boomed.

Climbing out of the car, Crystal raked her credit card through the pump station, and then started fuel flowing. Checking the time, Jules ticked off the minutes.

"Aunt Jube's coming home!"

"Aunt Jube!" Olivia mimicked Ethan's antics, racing around the living room floor with Cruz chasing behind him holding his coat.

"Come on, Ethan. You've got to put your coat on. We're going to be late." He glanced at the wall clock. Six-thirty. They still had plenty of time before Jules's plane landed, but while he was in Pasco he wanted to shop — buy Jules a little something to say welcome home. The last thing he'd bought her was an engagement ring. He still had it in his top drawer: only been worn twice. *Are you setting yourself up for another fall? Would she show up this time?*

He hoped so; with everything in him, he hoped so. Without her, his life was empty and meaningless. He'd thought for a long time he would find someone, some other woman that ignited his passion, but he hadn't. Nobody could replace her. He didn't like the idea, but he was stuck with it. And he was weary of fighting his feelings. Maybe God created Jules for him, and if he missed the opportunity, he would go through life wondering where he'd taken the last wrong turn.

Cruz knew his road map. And he wasn't taking any more wrong turns.

Once he was through shopping, he'd feed the kids and drive to the airport. He checked the clock again. Doubt nagged him but he shoved it aside. Trust had to start somewhere, and the past few weeks had proven that he still needed her. Oddly enough, he liked the idea. The only person he'd been kidding the past few years was himself. He couldn't get her off his mind or out of his heart. The years had made a difference in both their lives. She'd matured and so had he. Neither one was perfect, but they could work on their differences. They were no longer starry-eyed teenagers; they knew if a goal was worth working on, it meant trust and sacrifice. With God's help, they would defeat their obstacles. He wasn't willing to go through life like Pop, miss out on the best life had to offer, family, love, because he was incapable of forgiving. It was time to bury the past and acknowledge that in time mistakes could be overcome. He and Jules wouldn't straighten everything out at once, right every wrong or correct every mistake, but he was betting they could, given time. And they both had lots of time.

"Ethan! Slow down and put your coat on."

The boy slowed and Cruz slipped the child's arms through the heavy fabric. Temperatures were in the low twenties at night. He thought about Jules coming out of balmy Florida and how she'd resent the climate change. Washington wasn't Florida, but it was home, and he knew home took precedent over environment in her heart.

God, don't let her back-out on me again.

He shook his head, refusing to consider that she'd give her word and not show up. She loved the kids too much, loved him too much. He could see it in her eyes when she looked at him. She wouldn't stay in Florida when he was offering her a chance to start over. Would she? He reached for one of his heavy jackets, knowing she wouldn't be wearing one when she got off the plane.

Adan appeared in the doorway, capturing Olivia. "Come on, Cricket. It's time to bundle up."

Cruz turned to look at him. "Are you going with us?"

"You want me to?"

"It's not necessary." He'd hoped to have the time at the gate alone with Jules. There was a lot to talk about, a lot of rebuilding to start.

"Then I won't go. I'm going to The Grille, eat and play a game of pool." He put Olivia's coat and mittens on her. The child was bundled tight as a tick. "Crystal's not coming, is she?"

"Jules didn't mention her. I assume she'll stay in Florida, run the shell shop."

Adan sobered. "I hope not."

"You want her to come back here?"

Shrugging, Adan tied on Livvy's hat. "Can't say that I'd mind. She's a lot of fun, great to watch movies with, and she loves these kids."

Grinning, Cruz wondered who would beat whom to the altar first. He and Jules? Or Adan and Crystal. "Uncle Adan?"

Adan glanced at Livvy. "Yeah, Cricket?"

"I hafta go."

■ ■ ■ ■

The Fiat pulled back onto Interstate 10, heading eastbound. Jules glanced at the digital clock Crystal had mounted on the dash. "It's eleven o'clock! The plane leaves in an hour."

"An hour and seven minutes," Crystal corrected. "We have plenty of time."

"Drive faster."

"You're always in such a hurry." Crystal mashed on the gas pedal and the Fiat streaked down the interstate.

Or not. Jules grasped her seat. A dead Jules would be worthless. She'd like to get there alive.

"Here's where Mom had her accident."

Jules whipped her head to look as the car shot past. Poor Mom. She must have been terrified when she looked up and spotted the diesel coming toward her. Had her life flashed through her mind? Had she thought of me and Pop? Did she have regrets? *It's okay, Mom. I know mistakes are hard to correct. I forgive you.*

Fifteen minutes later, the Fiat screeched to a halt at arrivals/departures. Jules piled out, grabbed her bag from the back seat, hugged Crystal, and promised to keep in close touch. She even got a little misty during the leave taking. For the first time in her life, Jules meant it when they both said the obligatory "I love you." Sometime during the past hectic months, she'd fallen in love with her sister.

She took advantage of curbside check-in and entered the terminal through the manual door.

The airport was full. Chairs were filled, walls lined with sleeping flyers. Jules sensed a hitch when she approached security. She eyed the long line and her stomach fluttered. "Is there a problem?" she asked a woman standing in front of her.

"The storm knocked out power. The tower is down."

Jules's stomach tightened. "Flights are delayed?"

"Afraid so." The woman sighed. "This could be a long day."

Jules reached for her cell phone and then realized that she'd left it on the bed. She'd have to find a public phone, call Cruz and tell him the plane would be late. Did they even have public phones anymore? Lights flickered. A murmur went up. Then they came back on.

Then everything went dark. A murky gray consumed Jules and she swallowed back rising hysteria. Voices floated around her. Disgruntled. Frantic. She was standing in the security line but she couldn't move an inch. She'd always had a good sense of direction but at the moment she couldn't make out right from left. She had never once thought of being in a strange airport with no lighting and a black storm overhead.

Voices filtered through the abyss. "Where's the back-up power?"

"What's going on?"

She turned, completely at a loss of direction. The largeness of the airport engulfed her. Until the lights came on, she was imprisoned. Five, then ten minutes passed. An eerie calm now swallowed the terminal. No one could move with any certainty. Occasionally a small flashlight beam swept the packed area. Jules was still in the security line. Standing. Finally she thought of the woman in front of her and she bent and spoke into the void. "Do you have a cell phone?"

"Why . . . yes. My daughter gave me one last Christmas. It's disposable, but I have seventeen minutes left. I carry it for emergencies — do you know how to use it?"

"I can try." Jules knew Crystal's cell number by heart. If she could get a signal, she'd have Crystal turn around and come back for her. They could call Cruz and inform him of the delay . . . She couldn't let him go to the airport and not find her on the flight — but then the flight wouldn't be going out. Elation filled her. He'd know the flight was delayed.

"May I try and use the phone?"

The reply came swiftly. "Yes." A phone landed in her hand. Turning it on, she carefully counted off the buttons and punched in Crystal's number. The phone rang four times.

"Come on . . . Crystal. Pick up."

Five more unanswered rings.

Jules closed her eyes and was about to click off when Crystal answered. "Oh thank goodness. Turn around and come back. The storm knocked the power out in the airport."

"How bizarre. Don't they have generators?"

"I don't know — if they do they're not running. Come back and get me. And call Cruz immediately and tell him my plane's been delayed."

"Okay. I'll turn around and come back. Do you want a burrito? I was just about to pull through a drive-in."

"I don't want a burrito! Call Cruz and I'll feel my way back to the front entrance and meet you there." Even she knew the idea was ludicrous, but she'd do it. Somehow, she'd find that manual door she'd walked through fifteen minutes earlier.

"Are you serious? That's a big airport, and you're not familiar with it."

"I'll do it. Just turn around and come back." She'd crawl to that door if she must. She reached out to return the phone. A hand took it.

"Thanks."

"You're welcome."

Mentally she retraced her steps with the help of stranded passengers to the arrival entrance. Easing through the darkness, she gently parted bodies with no faces or shapes; stepping on toes, making apologies when someone said something not so encouraging. Only the feel of fabric and audible grunts met her efforts. She had a strong sense of direction in her favor. One or two flashlight beams focused, momentarily blinding her, but she kept her pace.

She had to find that entrance door.

Crystal punched the Delgados' home phone number as she wheeled off the exit ramp eating a drippy burrito. The phone rang five times before the answering machine picked up.

"Hey, Cruz. This is Crystal. Jules's flight is delayed. She won't be in on time. There was an earlier electrical storm, and it's knocked out power to the airport. She wanted me to call. So don't go to the airport. She'll let you know when air traffic resumes." She clicked off and turned around, taking the nearest exit back to Fort Walton.

When she pulled into the terminal, the place was dark. She sat with the engine idling, spooked. Nothing was stirring. It was like one of those horror movies when some alien force had struck and left only a few survivors.

She was one of them.

Creeping the Fiat to the airline arrival gate, she wondered how Jules could possibly escape the dark cavern. Her headlights beamed on the airline employees standing around, some smoking cigarettes, others sitting on pieces of luggage. She pulled up and leaned over to crank down the window. "I'm looking for my . . ."

Jules shot by the attendant and got into the car. "Step on it. If we hurry, I might be able to catch a flight out of Panama City yet today."

Crystal swallowed a yelp. *Alien* was her first thought. "What about your luggage?"

"It'll catch up with me. Just get going."

Crystal gunned the motor and the Fiat surged ahead.

As the car pulled onto the interstate, lights in the terminal flickered, and then came on.

CHAPTER 48

Armed with a gold bracelet, wrapped with a large yellow bow, Cruz came out of the jeweler's and headed for the mall patio. He checked his watch. Eight p.m. Still plenty of time before Jules's flight landed.

"What do you kids want to eat?"

"Chicken!" they chorused.

"You're both going to turn into a chicken," he teased, tickling Livvy under her chin. "Chicken nuggets, chicken strips, cashew chicken — no nuts or green onions, chicken drumsticks." Olivia held out her hand and wiggled her fingers.

"Okay. Chicken it is." His eyes scanned the patio, and then focused on the teenage server. "A round of chicken strips, my good man, and make those extra crispy." He was feeling generous tonight.

"This weather is murder!" Crystal scooted closer to the steering wheel and tried to clear the fog off the windshield. The wipers could barely keep up with the now falling rain. "I'm dying of thirst, Jules. Can't we take a moment to hit a drive-through and get something to drink? I was in such a hurry to get you I forgot to order a soda."

Jules was caving in, herself. It had been hours since breakfast, and then she had only eaten a protein bar. But if they hurried, she could still make it home tonight.

"There's a truck stop up-ahead. Pull in there."

"I'll take anything." The Fiat rolled off the exit ramp and pulled into the big lot where rigs were nearly stacked on top of each other. "It's the rain," Crystal explained. "When it comes down like this, the truckers stop and eat."

When the women entered the building Jules spotted a case with hot food. Corn dogs, chicken strips, tater tots, some dried-up macaroni and cheese, baked beans. She glanced at the restaurant door situated between the men's bathroom and showers. A hamburger wouldn't take that long, and she was most likely going to fly stand-by on a red-eye flight.

Minutes later Jules slid on a stool next to a burly looking driver. He glanced over, smiling.

Nodding, she ordered a burger and two large drinks to go while Crystal visited the ladies' room. When she returned, she had to sit on the driver's opposite side. Jules peered around him. "Did you call Cruz?"

"I did, but nobody was home. I left a message."

Jules frowned. "But what if nobody goes home before it's time to meet my flight? I'll be very late getting in . . . he has to know."

"I don't know, Jules. I called, and nobody was home. He'll find out when he gets to the airport."

"Did you try his cell phone?"

"No . . ."

She reached over the driver. "Give me your phone."

Crystal handed it over and she punched in Cruz's number.

"Come on, Livvy. Give back my phone, and eat your dinner." Cruz reached for the cell, Olivia's favorite toy. She fiddled with the ringer off and on and babbled to her imaginary friend. She was telling "Tote" everything that happened in the last five minutes. Cruz forbid her from touching the keypad and the child was content with Tote's end of the conversation. The imaginary friend knew they were now sitting at the mall, eating chicken at the Dairy Queen before they picked up Aunt Jube at the airport.

Olivia covered the mouthpiece. "Can Tote get Aunt Jube with us?"

"Sure." Cruz took a bite of fry, used to deciphering her kid talk. "Tell her we'll swing by and pick her up at the gas station."

"Kay." She relayed the message. "You can come, Tote." She crossed her leg. "But you hafta tell Cruz when you have to go potty." She pretended to hang up. "Drink?"

"If I get you a drink, you'll have to go potty again."

Ethan nodded. "Just eat your fries."

"Drink."

Mentally groaning, Cruz got up and ordered a milk. When he set it on the table, the child's face wrinkled. "Orange."

"Drink your milk." Maybe if she didn't fill up on caffeine, it would cut down on the potty stops.

Livvy crossed her arms. "Orange."

"No can do. They don't have orange," he fibbed.

She pointed to a child at a nearby table. The clear plastic cup clearly indicated that somewhere nearby had orange soda.

Livvy met his eyes and he saw Sophie's determination. He glanced at his watch.

Then shoved back from the table. "A small one."

The little girl grinned and wiggled her fingers. "Orange."

Jules clicked off with disgust. "He doesn't answer."

"But you left a message?"

"I left a message." Jules handed the phone back to her. "I'd feel more comfortable if I could reach him."

"I tried Adan earlier. He doesn't answer either."

The trucker beside her turned to address her. "Got problems, lady?"

Jules briefly relayed her dilemma.

"You gotta get to Washington tonight?"

"It isn't a matter of life and death, it's a matter of keeping my word. I promised the man I love I'd be back tonight, and I've let him down too many times in my life. I am going to be there if I die trying."

A grin broke across the trucker's face. "Ah . . . a lady in love. I can't get you there by truck, but I got a friend who flies for Wings Express. I might be able to get you a hitch on his plane tonight."

Jules sat up straighter. "Does he fly to Pasco?"

"Pasco? Nah, he goes into Salt Lake City

409

but you could hop a commuter from there and be in Pasco probably not much later than your original flight."

She'd be late — and technically not there on the dot, but she'd be there.

Her sister gave her a warning look. "That seems a little drastic, Jules. Cruz will get your message and understand, and even if he doesn't get the voicemail, the airport will inform him of the delayed flight."

"Crystal, for once in my life I intend to keep my word to that man. I know he'll understand when I tell him what's happened, but if I *prove* that I can keep my promise regardless of circumstances, that will go a long way in winning him back."

The trucker snorted. "Why can't I meet a female like you?"

"I know it's insane, but I'm going to do it." Jules turned to the man. "Can you set it up?"

"I can try. It's against all regulations, but my buddy owes me one." He flipped his cell phone open. "Can you be at Bay County International by three o'clock?"

"That's where we're headed. I can be there."

He punched in a cell number. Shortly he said, "Hey, buddy. Remember the time when I told your new girlfriend that your old girlfriend — the one you were still dating — had left you for another man? Do you recall how I told that blonde how heartbroken you were, and how hard it was to find a good woman?"

CHAPTER 49

Cruz walked into Tri-Cities Airport thirty minutes before Jules's flight was due to land. The kids were tired and fussy, but insistent they see Jules tonight. The closer to the hour of her arrival, the more anxious Cruz felt. A long time had passed when he'd felt good around Jules. He'd never stopped loving her, but fighting those feelings all these years had become a habit. A hard one to break. She would be here this time; he didn't have a doubt in his mind, yet maybe he did. Once she walked off that plane, into his arms, he could rest. He could start to plan for the future, a future he wanted with this woman. He wondered what would have happened if Jules had raised the perfect potato. Would she have married one of those jerks chasing after her? Over his dead body. He didn't want her perfect potato, he wanted her. Just her. He checked his watch. And he'd have her in twenty-eight minutes.

Back in his arms where she belonged.

He located three vacant chairs and set the kids in two. Ethan was already asleep.

Curling up beside him, Olivia rested her head on his chest. Her upper lip was rimmed in orange soda. They'd stopped twice on the way here. "Aunt Jube? Home."

"She'll be here soon." He patted the little girl's head. "When she gets here we're never going to let her go again."

Minutes ticked by. Cruz watched the clock. Five minutes before arrival time, Jules's flight landed. The PA system said the plane was on the ground. Taking a deep breath, Cruz straightened his collar, brushed back his hair, and waited.

Jules grabbed the ballpoint from the monkey's finger and held on. "Let go, you pesky little thing!"

The tenacious monkey held tight.

She jerked, wrestling the pen away from the animal as the overnight express plane bounced through turbulent skies. She was strapped in a funky looking seat, beside a cage of monkeys. She bent, trying to read the shipping label. They were going to a zoo. The plane dropped and took her stomach with it.

Clamping her eyes shut, she took deep

413

breaths. She was going to be sick. Her eyes scanned the cargo bay. Everywhere she looked she saw eyes peering back at her. The plane was carrying nothing but animals. Stinky, noisy animals. She now smelled worse than the afternoon she'd spent in the Pasco landfill looking for Lucille's ratty old mattress. She stared at a cage of hybrid roosters.

Cruz, I hope you know what I'm doing for you . . .

She glanced at her watch, heartsick. Ten p.m. Had he gotten her message? Of course he had. If he were out earlier, he'd have gotten it when he came home. If by chance he hadn't gone home, he would have checked his cell messages and found hers waiting. Still, she had so wanted to be home on time. She gasped as the plane hit another air pocket and lurched.

A furry hand snaked out to reclaim the ballpoint.

She snatched it back, and the thing reached around and threw a handful of excrement.

Dodging the missile, she shrugged out of her jacket and draped it over the cage.

Thieving monkey.

CHAPTER 50

The wall clock hands jerked to 10:30 p.m. Cruz sat in the airport waiting area, lost in thought. A large screen television broadcast an old movie. She hadn't shown. Her plane had landed. And Jules wasn't on it. So he'd stayed for the last incoming flight. He been so certain that she'd come back to him — as sure as the first time he'd asked her to marry him. As confident and full of hope as the second time, but the last flight landed twenty minutes ago, and she wasn't on it. What was it with her and promises? Was she like Pop? So wrapped up in her problems she couldn't distinguish daylight from dusk? She loved the kids. He had no doubt about that. It was him she couldn't love, him she couldn't commit to.

He glanced at the sleeping children. *Sophie, I tried. I love her with all my heart, but it's not in the books for us.* A man couldn't love a woman who couldn't or wouldn't love him back.

It was late. He needed to get the kids home and in bed. He glanced at the empty gate. The vacant reservation desk. Nobody manned the station. No more incoming flights tonight.

Running his hand through his hair, he tried to swallow his frustration. A man didn't get depressed. He got fed up. Straightening, he reached for his hat. A moment later, he'd gathered the two sleeping kids in his arms and started out of the terminal.

"Where do you think you're going?"

At the sound of Jules's voice, he whirled to see her standing in the terminal, chicken feathers wedged in her hair. She had — what on the front of her blouse? And she looked mad enough to eat a rhino.

"Jules?"

"Obviously you didn't get my messages."

"What messages?" He lowered the sleeping children into a couple of empty chairs. She was here. How, he wasn't certain. She wasn't on any flight that had come in since eight-forty. But she was here. For him.

"Crystal left one at your house, and I left one on your cell phone." She picked up her purse and started walking toward him. The stench of monkey washed over him.

416

"I gather you didn't check your phone messages tonight."

"No — I went shopping, took the kids to eat, and then here, to the airport —" He paused, his eyes scanning her appearance. "Where have you been?"

"In a plane trapped with animals, then on a packed commuter from Salt Lake City. I got the last seat on the plane, and this woman in front of me got her carry-on stuck in the overhead bin — oh, never mind. You wouldn't believe the story if I told you."

"Oh." He nodded as if the explanation made perfect sense. He opened his arms. "Welcome home."

She stepped into them, holding on to him as if he were a life vest in a stormy sea. "Oh, Cruz."

Holding her tightly, he closed his eyes as her essence washed over him. It didn't matter why she was late; she was here this time. She'd found her trust. "I thought you weren't coming."

"Never," she vowed. "I'm sorry I'm a little late. It's a long story, but I'll tell you all about it after I've kissed you senseless."

"Yeah, I was thinking I'd ask — after I kissed you senseless."

"You're not mad that I'm late?"

"No — you're here."

"You never doubted that I would be?"

"No — yes." He held her tighter. "Yes. I thought you wouldn't come, and I didn't see how I was going to live the rest of my life without you."

"You couldn't," she murmured. "I wouldn't let you."

He held her so tightly he was afraid he would break her.

"I'm sorry, Cruz. I know that I've broken your heart twice, but never again."

"I'll hold you to that."

"You won't have to." She pulled back to gaze into his eyes. "I'll hold myself to it."

The hue of his eyes deepened. "Let's go home."

"I'm more than ready."

Jules scooped up Livvy, and Cruz carried Ethan on the way out of the airport. The children stirred momentarily, long enough to say hi and pat Aunt Jube's cheek before they dropped off again. It was difficult to hold Livvy and cling to Cruz, but Jules managed to voice what had been weighing on her mind during the bumpy flight. "What about the Parkers? If they file suit to claim the children —"

"They won't," Cruz said. "The judge and his wife are reasonable people. When they think about it, they'll come to the same conclusion that any court would: the children will be better off with younger parents, parents who can keep up with all the activities a child involves."

"Then there's Adan and Crystal," she reminded. "They love these two little imps as much as we do."

He glanced over with a youthful grin. "What's wrong with a child having four parents? One of us will have primary care, but Crystal and Adan will always be a part of these children's lives."

She noticed that he seemed to take for granted that they would be the custodial pair.

They walked through the empty airport carrying the sleeping children — children Jules prayed would be hers soon. For the first time in many years, life felt so right. Absolutely perfect. "Do you think Sophie is looking down on us right now?"

Cruz grinned. "No, I think my sister is most likely sitting in the middle of a Krispy Kreme conveyor belt, eating to her heart's content — if heaven has a Krispy Kreme."

Jules chuckled. Heaven must undoubtedly have a Krispy Kreme. "She was a sweet freak." She sobered. "This is what she wanted, you know. She set this whole thing up, praying that we would fall for her scheme."

"I think we both came to that conclusion a long time ago." He turned and stole a kiss. "Good for her."

They paused, his eyes twinkling with mischief. For the briefest of moments, Jules recognized Sophie lurking in that rascally grin. "Got something for you." He fished in his pocket and took out a small wrapped box. Jules's heart thumped so loudly she thought he might hear her reaction. "For me?"

A ring? She assumed it would be months before he fully trusted her enough to propose marriage a third time. She untied the ribbon and opened the box to find a gold bracelet. Disappointment flooded her but she kept a brave face. "It's lovely — thank you."

Tipping her face to meet his, he said softly, "One day at a time?"

Nodding, she slipped the token of his love on her wrist. "One day at a time."

Rome wasn't built in a day, and neither was confidence. The only thing that mattered was that his love and trust was under construction.

She leaned to kiss him as they walked through the automatic double terminal doors, each balancing a sleeping child on their hip. "Wise woman, your sister."

"Sophie was the best," he agreed.

The best friend a woman ever had, she silently agreed. Sometimes the greatest tragedy brought unspeakable joy.

Funny how God works.